TRAGEDY AT PIDDLETON HOTEL

A Churchill & Pemberley Mystery Book 1

EMILY ORGAN

Shortlisted for the
Amazon UK Kindle Storyteller Award 2019

Runaway Girl Series:
Runaway Girl
Forgotten Child
Sins of the Father

First published in 2019 by Emily Organ

emilyorgan.com

Edited by Joy Tibbs

ISBN 978-1-9993433-4-7

MRS ANNABEL CHURCHILL stood in the cobbled high street and surveyed her new business premises in the pretty village of Compton Poppleford. One of her chubby hands clutched her handbag and the other held a bunch of pink carnations which her maid, Flossie, had tearfully presented her with at Waterloo Station. The view before her now was an enticing window display of crusty loaves and plump fruit buns which made her stomach rumble. All she had eaten that day was a soggy wedge of bread and cheese - ambitiously described as a sandwich - in the dining room at Dorchester train station.

Churchill tore her eyes away from the baked temptations of Bodkin's Bakery and instead turned her attention to the drab door just left of the bakery window. It bore a dull bronze sign that read: 'Atkins's Detective Agency'.

"The sign will have to go," she said to herself. "I shall replace it with a bright, shiny one bearing the name *Churchill's Detective Agency*."

A loud honk made her startle and drop the flowers. She

bent down to pick them up and turned to see the shiny fender of a red motor car a few feet from her nose.

"What the dickens are you doing standing about in the road?" cried out the young, floppy-haired man behind the wheel.

"I could ask the same of you!" retorted Churchill, who never liked to admit she was in the wrong.

"But it's a road," shouted the driver. "For cars!"

"And noisy, irksome things they are, too!" Churchill shook her fist at him and walked toward the drab door by the bakery window.

She retrieved a bunch of keys from her handbag and spent some time twisting each one in the lock before realising the door wasn't locked after all.

"Typical estate agents," she muttered. "Half the population of Compton Poppleford has probably been inside my office now and stripped it bare."

Beyond the door was a narrow wooden staircase which just about accommodated Churchill's generously proportioned frame. She felt quite out of breath by the time she reached the glass door to the right of the small landing at the top. Stuck to the glass in tall black letters were the words, 'Atkins's Detective Agency'.

"Not any more," she said as she set about peeling away the letter A of 'Atkins'. It was stuck fast to the glass and she only managed to chip away a small part before realising the damage she was causing her nail. Giving up on the lettering, she pushed open the door and walked briskly into the office.

It was a capacious room which smelt pleasantly of baked bread from the bakery below. A desk stood by the window just as Mr Atkins had left it with a leather chair pulled up in front of a typewriter. A row of filing cabinets ran along one wall and a portrait of King George V hung above the fireplace.

Churchill strode over to the desk, lay the carnations on it and tried out the leather chair for size. It was rather comfortable, and from the window she had a commanding view of the high street. She decided she liked the desk and its position, but before she could make herself too comfortable she would need a vase for her flowers.

She got up again and began to scour the room, but there was no sign of a suitable receptacle. In the far corner of the room was a locked door, but after trying the handle Churchill decided to unlock it later with one of the numerous keys she had been given. Meanwhile, her carnations were in a critical condition after their long journey from London to Dorset.

"I must have a vase!" she declared.

She recalled seeing a bric-a-brac shop on the other side of the high street and figured it would only take a moment or two to purchase a vase from the establishment.

"Are you the lady what's bought the detective agency?" asked the man standing behind the counter. The shop smelled of beeswax polish mingled with over-boiled vegetables. Its proprietor had a large, grey moustache. He wore a tweed waistcoat with missing buttons, and his rolled-up sleeves revealed heavily tattooed arms.

"I am indeed."

"I've 'eard as you's come down from London."

"Yes, I've moved down here from the big smoke."

Compton Poppleford was clearly the sort of place where news travelled fast.

"Why've you came down 'ere, then?"

"I saw the detective agency for sale in *The Times* and decided the purchase of it would make for a charming little project."

"But why down 'ere?"

"Well, aside from the fact that *down here* is where the detective agency is located, I rather fancied a change of scene, if truth be told. London is such a busy place and it begins to sap one's energy as one nears a certain age."

"So you's a detective, is you?"

Churchill tried not to wince at the rustic accent and forced a smile instead. "I am the widow of Detective Chief Inspector Churchill of Scotland Yard. I was married to him for forty years, so there's very little I don't know about investigating crimes." She glanced at the clutter around her, feeling overwhelmed by the sheer volume of it. "Do you have a vase here in your bric-a-brac shop?"

"It's an *antiques* shop," he corrected, his moustache twitching irritably.

"Really?" Churchill surveyed the clutter a second time. "What's antique in here?"

"Everythin's antique in 'ere."

"I see. Would you happen to have an antique vase?"

"Yes, there's one of 'em in the windah."

Churchill stepped over to the window display and saw a blue china vase standing on top of a dusty top hat. "How much?" she asked.

"Fifteen shillin's."

"*Fifteen?*"

"It's an antique vase."

"Is it indeed? I see what you're doing here, Mr…?"

"Smallbone."

"I see what you're doing here, Mr Smallbone. You think that because I've travelled down from London I'll be prepared to pay London prices. That simply won't do, Mr Smallbone. That won't do at all."

"Fourteen shillin's."

"What nonsense, Mr Smallbone."

"I beg your pardon!"

"Nonsense, I say. That vase is worth ten shillings at the very most. Look, it has a chip."

"That ain't a chip; it's a feature."

After beating Mr Smallbone down to seven shillings, Churchill returned to her office with the vase. She marched through the glass door to rescue the limp carnations and was astounded to discover that they were already in a vase. She was even more surprised to see a thin, bespectacled woman with scruffy grey hair sitting behind the desk. Her cardigan looked as though it had once been a shade of lilac or pink.

Uncharacteristically for Churchill, she was momentarily unable to speak. She managed to cling on to her vase, but her mouth hung open in an unseemly manner.

"Good heavens! Who are you and where did you get that?" she said, pointing at the vase.

"You must be the lady who bought the detective agency," said the woman with a smile.

"Yes, I am," replied Churchill, plonking her vase down on the desk.

"I'm Miss Pemberley," replied the woman.

"Jolly good. Can I ask what you're doing in my chair?"

Pemberley raised her eyebrows. "But this is *my* chair."

"What nonsense. Of course it isn't." Churchill puffed out her cheeks, snorted and steeled herself to drag the woman out of the chair by one of her spindly arms.

"Perhaps Mr Atkins' solicitor didn't explain?" Pemberley said.

Churchill snorted again, louder this time. "Atkins' solicitor explained nothing whatsoever. He was the most useless solicitor I have ever had the misfortune to come across. And I've come across a fair few, I can tell you."

"I'm part of the detective agency. One of the fixtures and fittings, so to speak."

"Which are you?"

"Sorry, I don't follow."

"Are you a fixture or a fitting?"

Pemberley gave this some thought. "I don't really know. A fixture, I suppose. I hadn't really considered it until now. Thank you for the flowers, though. They're quite delightful."

"They're *my* flowers! A gift from my former maid. How could I possibly have bought them for you? I didn't even know you were here! I looked everywhere for a vase but couldn't find one."

"It was on the windowsill in the water closet."

"Water closet?"

Churchill glanced around the room and noticed that the door which had previously been locked now stood ajar. She strode over to the door and saw a lavatory beyond it.

"That's where you were when I arrived?" she asked. "In the water closet with the vase?"

"Yes, that's right."

"Didn't you notice me trying the handle of the door? You should have shouted out to let me know you were in there!"

"I didn't want to alarm you."

"It was far more alarming to return to my office and find you sitting at my desk!"

"*My* desk."

Churchill marched toward Pemberley, removed the flowers from the vase and placed them in the one she had just bought. Then she poured in the water.

"There. I prefer them in the blue china vase," she said. "It's an antique, you know."

"Is that what Mr Smallbone told you?"

"How do you know Mr Smallbone?"

"I've worked in this office opposite his shop for fifteen years."

"Have you? *Have you indeed?* Good!"

Churchill stood by the desk with her hands on her hips and considered how to manage this unforeseen pickle. Although Miss Pemberley seemed a little wet behind the ears, there was no doubt that her local knowledge would be a useful asset to Churchill's Detective Agency. Besides, she had been planning to hire a secretary anyway.

"Were you a secretary of some sort to the late Mr Atkins?"

"Yes. That's exactly what I was."

"I see. And as you're a fixture of the detective agency you could continue to be a secretary of some sort, I suppose?"

"Yes. That's my understanding of the matter."

"Jolly good." Churchill looked around for another chair to sit on, but there was none. "Did Mr Atkins have a desk?"

"Yes, but his widow requested that it be returned to the family estate." Pemberley's voice trembled, and her eyes grew damp. She retrieved a balled-up handkerchief from the sleeve of her cardigan and squashed it into each eye.

"Did she now? I see. A slight inconvenience, but never mind." Churchill gave an awkward cough and looked up at the ceiling. She felt uneasy when people displayed emotion. "I imagine Mr Smallbone will have an antique desk and an antique chair for sale. Are there any means of boiling water here? I haven't had a cup of tea since Dorchester and the branch line from there is dreadfully slow. It would have been quicker to walk."

"Tea?" replied Pemberley, her face lighting up. "Yes, there's a kettle and gas ring in the water closet."

Chapter 2

AFTER A RESTORATIVE CUP OF TEA, Churchill bought a desk and chair at a knockdown price from Mr Smallbone's shop. She paid two boys found loitering on the high street sixpence apiece to carry the furniture up the stairs to her new office.

Her desk was placed between the door and the fireplace, which Pemberley assured her was where Atkins' desk had stood. When Churchill sat at her desk and glanced around the room she felt that it occupied an inferior position to Pemberley's. She made a note to herself to broach the subject of swapping locations at a later date.

Churchill opened her handbag and had no sooner placed her notebook and pen on the desk when a broad, bald man in white, floury overalls sauntered into the office holding a tray of baked indulgences. He had thick grey eyebrows and Churchill wondered why his hair had so readily left his head yet clung so resolutely above his eyes.

"I'm Mr Bodkin," he stated. "You must be Mrs Churchill."

"Indeed I am, Mr Bodkin. You are the proprietor of the fine establishment downstairs, I do believe."

"The very same," he replied, placing the tray on her desk.

Churchill's mouth watered at the sight of the chocolate eclairs and custard tarts.

"How very thoughtful of you!" she said, clapping her hands in glee.

"You look like a lady who enjoys a cake or two," he replied, eying her ample figure. "And these will only be thrown out otherwise. They're too stale to sell. I often give the stale ones to the tramp who lives in the old police box by the duck pond, but I haven't seen him for a few days. So I thought I would gift them to my new neighbour instead."

"Are we neighbours?" asked Churchill. "I'm on top of you. I thought neighbours were more of a side by side affair."

"Neighbours can be top and bottom as well," said Pemberley as she walked over to Churchill's desk and selected a custard tart.

"I suppose they could be," conceded Churchill, biting the end off an eclair. "Have you been running your bakery for long, Mr Bodkin?"

"About thirty-seven years," he replied. "Flour and dough are in the blood."

"Are they indeed? Without any adverse medical effects, I hope?"

"Any what?"

"I was just having a little joke with you, Mr Bodkin."

"Joke?"

Churchill pushed more of the eclair into her mouth, deciding that Bodkin probably wasn't the sort of man who laughed very often.

· · ·

"What's going on up there?" a voice called up the stairs.

"Oh no," groaned Bodkin.

"What's the matter?" asked Churchill.

"It's *her*," he said, his face turning pale.

"Who's *her*?"

"I must be off," said Bodkin, dashing into the water closet.

"Why? Whatever's the matter?" asked Churchill.

"It's Mrs Furzgate," said Pemberley. "She's a frightful woman; a meddler and a snoop."

"That's the water closet, Mr Bodkin," Churchill called out. "You need to take the stairs!"

"I know where I'm going all right," the baker called back. "There's a fire escape leading down from the window."

"A fire escape? In the water closet?" asked Churchill.

"Just outside it," said Pemberley. "Mr Atkins had it put there in case of emergencies."

"What sort of emergencies?"

"Unwanted visitors, for one."

Churchill might have continued her line of questioning had she not been distracted by the short, myopic woman who had appeared in the office.

"Hello, who are you?" asked Mrs Furzgate. She wore a brown tweed coat and a floppy velvet hat.

"I'm Miss Pemberley," Pemberley replied.

"I know who *you* are. I meant *her*," said Mrs Furzgate, pointing at Churchill.

"I'm Mrs Annabel Churchill, and I'm a private detective," she announced proudly. "And who are *you*?"

"If you were a proper detective you wouldn't need to ask!" laughed Mrs Furzgate.

Churchill bristled. "I find your manner impertinent. Are you a client?"

"No, I just came up to see what was going on."

"Then you may leave the way you came."

"What qualifications do you have?" Mrs Furzgate's thick spectacle lenses magnified her beady eyes.

"Pardon me?"

"To be a detective. Do you have a detective qualification?"

Churchill curled her lip. "There's no such thing. Now don't let me detain you. You should be on your way."

"Then how can you be a detective?"

"Quite easily. Now shoo."

"You can't just buy a detective agency and call yourself a detective, you know. It takes a special set of skills."

"I said *shoo*."

"Do you have a special set of skills?"

"I do indeed. I was married for many years to Detective Chief Inspector Churchill of Scotland Yard."

"Were you indeed? Are you a widow or did he divorce you?"

"I'm a widow."

"Any children?"

"I'm sorry, but who did you say you are?"

The woman laughed. "I didn't, but everyone knows me, don't they Miss Pemberley? I'm Mrs Furzgate. I'm the self-proclaimed village gossip!"

"And I'm a self-proclaimed private detective." Churchill strode over to Mrs Furzgate, spun her round by the shoulders and guided her toward the glass door that led to the staircase.

"I knew it! You don't have any qualifications after all!" Mrs Furzgate cried. "Are you the woman who's renting the cottage by Fernworthy Farm? I heard a Londoner was moving in there."

"I am not a Londoner. I'll have you know that I hail

from the Home Counties. Goodbye, Mrs Furzgate. So lovely to meet you."

Mrs Furzgate stumbled down the first few steps but managed to regain her balance about halfway down.

"You pushed me!" she called back up the stairs.

"I won't hear a word of it. Goodbye, Mrs Furzgate!" Churchill grinned widely and waved.

"I could have broken my neck!"

"Shame she didn't, isn't it?" said Churchill to Pemberley, closing the glass door firmly behind her. "Do people often just walk in from the street?"

"Yes, I suppose they do. Mr Atkins used to call it walk-in business."

"In other words, just about anyone can walk in."

"Yes. Some of the best work comes in that way."

"Does it indeed?" Churchill sat herself behind her desk and picked up a custard tart. "So I suppose we just sit here and wait for the work to walk in. Did Atkins do that?"

"Mr Atkins didn't have to wait for work; he was always busy. He had an extensive client base."

"Did he now? Where did he get that from?"

"He built it up over many, many years."

"I suppose he must have. Never mind, we all have to start somewhere. I'm sure his early days were quiet."

"Actually, they weren't."

Churchill polished off her tart. "Perhaps if you have some time before the end of the day, Miss Pemberley, you could peel Atkins' name off the glass door."

Chapter 3

"HOW DO you find the cottage you're renting?" Pemberley asked Churchill soon after she arrived at the office the following morning.

"Rather rustic. And terribly draughty. It's quite an exposed location up on the hill by the farm, isn't it?" Churchill placed her hat on the hat stand and smoothed her silver, lacquered hair.

"It is quite exposed, but old Mrs Drumhead, the farmer's mother, loved it there. She was born and died in that cottage."

"Died in it? Recently?"

"About two months ago. Probably in the very bed you slept in last night. There's only one bed, isn't there?"

"I believe so." Churchill shuddered and marched over to the filing cabinet. "What's in here?" she asked, pulling open a drawer.

"All of Mr Atkins' cases."

"Is that so? They should make for an interesting peruse then. I shall begin with A," she said, pulling out the first paper file. "'The case of Mr Aardvark'. Is there really someone called Mr Aardvark, Pemberley?"

"There *was*."

"Oh, I see. He is with us no longer, then?"

"That's why Mr Atkins worked on the case."

"A serious one, was it? Murder?"

"I think it was a little more complicated than that."

"How so?"

"The file will explain everything. Mr Atkins kept exceptionally detailed records."

"Well, he would have. It's the first rule we private detectives must follow. Always keep detailed records."

Churchill read the file while Pemberley made a pot of tea. She soon found herself gripped by a story of love, betrayal and shadowy underworld figures.

"Goodness," she said as Pemberley placed a cup of tea on her desk. "Old Aardvark diced with death, didn't he?"

"Yes, and he ended up dead."

"Are you familiar with all the cases in these filing cabinets, Pemberley?"

"Most of them, I think."

"You must have an encyclopic brain."

"Encyclopaedic."

"That's what I meant to say, only my tongue was on the wrong side of my teeth."

She sipped at her tea and decided that beneath the bird's nest hair of her new secretary lay a half-decent brain.

"Where do you live, Pemberley?" she asked.

"Froxfield Row."

"Where's that, then?"

"At the end of Muckleford Lane."

"Which is where?"

"Do you know St Gabriel's?"

"No."

"Well it's just past there, second on the left. It's what we locals call 'The Mulberrys'."

"What we need in here, Pemberley, is a map. We could put it up on the wall, and then I could use it to acquaint myself with the area. I'm surprised Atkins didn't have one."

"He did."

"Really?"

"Yes, he had it on the wall right there." Pemberley pointed to a large rectangle where the wallpaper was slightly darker. "He used to put pins in it and attach them to pieces of string that connected up photographs, notes and other useful pieces of information."

"So where is it now?"

"His widow requested it."

"Another thing that went to the widow, eh? I think the map should have counted as one of the fixtures and fittings." Churchill sipped at her tea. "This drink demands some sort of accompaniment. I wonder if Bodkin has something tasty downstairs for elevenses."

Churchill's stomach grumbled as she walked into the bakery, the broad variety of delicious-smelling buns and cakes left her quite spoilt for choice. She was surprised to see a cricket bat hanging on the wall behind the counter, and as she glanced around she noticed several other cricketing items on display: bails, stumps, balls and various bats.

"I see you're a cricketing fan, Mr Bodkin."

"Not me."

"So why all the cricket paraphernalia?"

"I was joking. Yes, I used to be a bit of a cricketer."

"How amusing. Bowler or batsman?"

"Batsman, of course. See this bat on the wall behind me? It belonged to none other than Freddie Carnegie-Bannerman. He used it during our tour of Australia in 1907 and 1908. Unfortunately, we lost the Ashes four to one."

Churchill tutted. 'Typical."

"But the bat's worth a fair few bob. He signed his name on the back."

"Good old Freddie whatshisname. Please may I purchase six currant buns?"

"Of course. That comes to sixpence." He placed the buns into a paper bag and handed it to her.

Churchill laughed awkwardly. "But I'm your new neighbour, Mr Bodkin. Remember?"

"Of course I remember."

"Must neighbours pay for your goods?"

"I'm afraid so, Mrs Churchill."

"Can we negotiate?"

Back in the office, Churchill held the bag of currant buns under Pemberley's nose. "Have a bun and get some meat on those bones."

"Thank you, I will." Pemberley helped herself from the bag. "I can eat all I want, and for some reason I never put on weight."

Churchill flinched at this comment. "Well, what seems a blessing when you're young can become a shortcoming as you grow older," she retorted. "I think a bit of extra padding gives an older woman gravitas. Never underestimate the power of an imposing bosom." She sat back behind her desk and took a currant bun from the bag. "I've got us a reduced rate with Bodkin. Next time you're in his bakery, Pemberley, quote him the acronym CDA and he'll give you a fifth off the price."

"What does CDA stand for?"

"Churchill's Detective Agency!"

"Of course, silly me. That reminds me that you asked me to remove Atkins' name from the glass door. I shall do that after my bun."

Churchill opened the next file; the case of Mr and Mrs Abrahams.

"Compton Poppleford must be very different from London," said Pemberley. "Do you miss it?"

"In some respects. But I was growing rather tired of the London lifestyle; all those bridge parties, the opera, the theatre, restaurants, dinner parties and the suchlike. There's only so much one can do before one finds oneself yearning for something rather different."

And what a difference it was too, Churchill thought to herself. She had spent the previous evening making a draught-excluding sausage out of a pair of old stockings. There wasn't a door or window in the entire cottage that fitted properly.

Pemberley used a scissor blade to chip away at Atkins' name on the glass door, while Churchill read his case files, which allowed the next few hours to slip by agreeably. The more she read the more she realised what a place of scandal and depravity Compton Poppleford was.

"There's no need for me to join the local library here, Pemberley. Instead of borrowing books from the mystery section I can simply read Atkins' cases. There's one here where ten strangers were summoned to an island and then summarily bumped off one by one!"

"I remember it well," said Pemberley, nursing a cut on her finger. "It was a tricky one for Mr Atkins to solve."

"He must have been quite the sleuth."

"He was."

Churchill noticed, with alarm, that Pemberley's lower lip was beginning to wobble. She had seen this occur before when Atkins' name had been mentioned. "Shall we have another cup of tea?" she suggested brightly.

Then she heard the downstairs door creak open, followed by footsteps on the stairs.

"Wait a moment, Pemberley, I think we have a client! Do you hear that?"

The footsteps neared the top of the staircase.

"Excellent," said Churchill, rubbing the palms of her hands together. Having read through a number of Atkins' cases she felt well prepared for a sordid case that had left the police baffled. "Quick, close the door so our visitor can knock on it!"

Pemberley did as Churchill asked, and the visitor almost immediately knocked at the door.

"Come in!" said Churchill in a sing-song voice.

The door swung open and a bewildered-looking man wearing a brown woollen suit shuffled into the room with his hat in his hand.

"Good afternoon, sir!" sang Churchill. The man gave her a nod before walking over to Pemberley's desk.

"Is this the detective agency?" he asked. "I need some help."

"Yes, it is," said Pemberley. "How can I help you?"

"Well, you see it's about—"

"Excuse me!" called out Churchill. "Over here. Hello!" She waved at the mystified man. "I'm the detective!"

"Oh, I thought you were the secretary," he replied, shuffling over to her desk.

Churchill forced a smile. "Sit down, then. What can I do for you?"

The man took a seat. "Well, you see, it's about—"

"Excuse me just a moment while I prepare a file." Churchill gathered some papers into a pile and clipped them together. "A detective must keep exceptionally detailed records, you understand. Your name please?"

"Mr Albert Greenstone."

"And before we start, can I ask how you heard about my detective agency?"

"It's yours, is it? What happened to Atkins?"

"He passed away, Mr Greenstone."

"Did he? How?"

"He was eaten by a crocodile on the Zambezi River."

"That's in Africa, isn't it? What was he doing there?"

"I don't know the full details, but I believe he was holidaying in the region at the time." Churchill heard a stifled sob from Pemberley. "I'd rather not talk about it," she whispered to Mr Greenstone. "Miss Pemberley is still terribly upset about the whole affair."

"I see. Well, I suppose it is rather upsetting. No one wants to be eaten by a crocodile, do they?"

"Quite."

"Or any other reptile for that matter."

"Or indeed eaten at all. It can't be a nice way to go. How can I help you, Mr Greenstone?"

"I've come to see a detective about a spot of trouble I'm having."

"With what?"

"My cat."

Churchill felt her heart sink.

"Is it lost?"

"No, not lost. But I think someone else is feeding him. He goes out, you see, and he seems to be gone a long time, and then when he eventually comes back he just goes straight to sleep."

"Reminds me of my late husband!" laughed Churchill.

Mr Greenstone looked even more baffled. "He's not a human being, though. He's a cat. And when he comes home and goes straight to sleep he sleeps for a number of hours, and when he wakes up he only eats about half his food. And then he goes out again."

"What is your cat's name, Mr Greenstone?"

"Zeppelin."

Churchill wrote this down. "Quite Teutonic."

"A what now?"

"It doesn't matter. May I suggest, Mr Greenstone, that Zeppelin is displaying what I'd describe as normal cat behaviour? They're not particularly affectionate creatures, are they? In fact, they're often quite selfish and ungrateful, and treat your house as if it were some sort of cat hotel."

"But he hasn't always been like this. He used to hang around with me a lot more and eat all his food. And he looks at me differently these days, as if something's changed between us. I can't put my finger on when exactly it happened. Perhaps it was the middle of last year, or perhaps it was before then, but——"

"It doesn't really matter when. What exactly would you like me to do about it, Mr Greenstone?"

"I want you to find out who's feeding him."

Churchill sighed. *Was this really to be Churchill Detective Agency's first case?*

She grew significantly more interested when Mr Greenstone pulled his wallet out of his pocket.

"I don't know what your fee is, but if I give you ten pounds now will that cover it?"

"Well, thank you, Mr Greenstone. That will indeed cover a few personal expenses."

Chapter 4

CHURCHILL'S INVESTIGATION into Zeppelin's alleged infidelity began in earnest the following day. She stood beneath her umbrella and watched the cat staring back at her from under a large hydrangea in Mr Greenstone's front garden. Zeppelin was large and grey with blue sombre eyes.

"Show me where you go, kitty cat," she said for the fourth time. "Come on, I don't have all day."

The dispiriting reality was that Churchill did have all day. As she listened to the raindrops drumming down on her umbrella she wondered what she would have been doing at this moment had she continued her life in London. She would probably have taken in a little exhibition at the Royal Academy followed by a spot of lunch at a favourite French eatery of hers in Old Bond Street.

Churchill refused to allow the word 'regret' to enter her mind. *Regret is for the feeble-minded*, she told herself. *Besides, mundane tasks such as watching a cat shelter from the rain under a bush are character-building. They are a test of the human spirit.* Weaker individuals would have given up on Zeppelin after an hour or two, but she was nowhere near to giving up: she had only just started. Few people could have matched her determination.

She wondered whether Atkins had been expected to follow cats about. She hadn't come across any similar cases in his files. Perhaps he had only documented the more exciting cases: the blackmail, kidnappings and murder. She had all that to look forward to, of course; Zeppelin was merely her apprenticeship. He was breaking her into the work of a detective gently. In fact, she was grateful to him for this simple induction.

But where on earth had the feline gone?

He was no longer beneath the hydrangea.

"Pussy cat?" she called out. There was no reply.

"Zeppelin!"

He had slipped away. Stealthy and unseen.

"Silly puss," she muttered to herself as she marched across Mr Greenstone's lawn. Her heels sunk into the grass and she wished she'd had the sense to put on her stout walking shoes.

"Kitty?"

She rummaged about in the hydrangea and then in the neighbouring laurel. Nearby was a flattened patch of dahlias, which she deduced was almost certainly Zeppelin's favourite sleeping spot on a sunny day.

Only it wasn't a sunny day. Churchill's stockings were soaking up water in the flowerbed and then her umbrella got caught up in a climbing rose. She wrenched it free, showering herself with confetti-like rose petals. The effect might have been quite pleasing had she not been in a frightful temper.

"Zeppelin!" she barked.

Now her first case wasn't going to plan at all. She could see the trap she had allowed herself to fall into: the supposed simplicity of the case had caused her to become complacent. She had underestimated her target and was paying the price.

She stomped into the middle of the lawn, realising that Zeppelin might have travelled off in just about any direction he fancied from here. It was futile trying to second-guess him.

It was then that she noticed a pair of eyes staring out at her from the window. Two blue, sombre eyes set in a grey, fluffy face.

Zeppelin was sitting on the windowsill inside his house.

"How did you get in there?" she shouted at the animal. She shook her fist at him, but he appeared unperturbed.

Churchill marched up to Mr Greenstone's door and hammered the knocker up and down until he answered.

"Goodness, it's you," he said, trembling slightly. "I thought you were going to break my door down."

"What's the cat doing on your windowsill?"

"I'm not sure. He's probably just looking out of the window. They can do that for quite some time, can't they? It's a wonder they don't get bored."

"I was supposed to be following him. He was out in the front garden just now."

"Was he? Well, he's come in now. He doesn't like the rain much."

"Neither do I," snapped Churchill.

She assumed the next step in the conversation would be an invitation from Mr Greenstone to join him for afternoon tea. But instead he gave her a blank stare and her empty stomach rumbled.

"Oh, never mind, Mr Greenstone. I'll try another day. Perhaps when it's sunny and Zeppelin is feeling a little more adventurous."

.   .   .

Churchill arrived back at the office damp and hungry to find Pemberley wringing her hands and weeping.

"Good heavens, woman!" said Churchill as she hung up her wet coat. "You must try to get over Atkins' demise! He wouldn't have wanted you sobbing about him every day. I understand it must be difficult, but you need to move on with your life. Just think how proud he would be of the way you have continued his work. The man himself may have gone, but his work lives on!" She gestured at the filing cabinets, then around the office, but noticed that Pemberley's histrionics showed no sign of subsiding.

"I'm not crying about Atkins," Pemberley stuttered between sobs. "Look at this!"

With trembling hands she held up a copy of the *Compton Poppleford Gazette*. The headline read: 'TRAGEDY AT PIDDLETON HOTEL'.

"Oh dear," said Churchill. "What happened?"

"It's Mrs Furzgate," sniffed Pemberley. "She fell down the hotel staircase and died!"

"Cripes. The woman never was very good on staircases, was she? You saw how she almost fell down our own stairs the other day. I cannot understand why you're so upset, Pemberley."

"Because she is dead!" Pemberley wiped her eyes with her saturated handkerchief.

"But you didn't like the woman! Don't you remember what you said about her? Something about her being frightful, and a meddler and a snoop."

"Yes, but I didn't know she was going to die, did I?"

"Would you have been more polite about her if you'd known that her demise was imminent?"

"Yes, I think so. Sometimes you can find someone quite annoying when they're alive, but then they die and you realise that perhaps you were being oversensitive about their personality and maybe they weren't so bad after all. And you feel rather guilty for having been rude about them."

Churchill sat behind her desk with a sigh. "Grief can be a complicated emotion, Pemberley, but I wouldn't waste your tears on that woman. Bodkin so despised her that he had to climb out of the water closet window to escape her."

Pemberley quietened a little. "I don't like it when people die."

"Nobody does, Pembers. How about you go downstairs and fetch us a little pick-me-up from Bodkin's shop? Perhaps he has some of that nice coffee and walnut cake in again. And don't forget to quote our special discount."

Chapter 5

TRAGEDY AT PIDDLETON HOTEL

By Smithy Miggins

A popular local lady has tragically died after falling down the stairs at Piddleton Hotel. Mrs Thora Furzgate, 59, had been taking afternoon tea with friends. After commenting that she needed to pay a trip to "the little girls' room", Mrs Furzgate lost her footing at the top of the staircase and tumbled down twenty-four steps, knocking into a valuable floor vase housing an aspidistra as she went.

The Manager of Piddleton Hotel, Mr Bernard Crumble, said: "The vase can be mended, but tragically Mrs Furzgate cannot. The Piddleton Hotel's thoughts and prayers are with her family and friends."

Local physician, Dr Sporrin, said: "I was called to Piddleton Hotel earlier this afternoon to attend to a lady who had suffered a fall down the staircase. I made every attempt to revive her but was sadly unsuccessful. It appears that she tripped over a discarded teacake, which would have resulted in little more than a few bumps and bruises when walking on the level; but when such an occurrence takes place at the top of a flight of stairs the results can be fatal, as we have seen today."

Mr Crumble would not be drawn on claims that a squashed teacake was seen lying near the top of the staircase shortly before and after Mrs Furzgate's fatal fall.

As of this morning (Thursday), friends of Mrs Furzgate remained too distressed to speak to the Gazette.

"I suppose it is rather sad," concluded Churchill, folding up the newspaper and placing it back on Pemberley's desk. "But we all have to go at some time, don't we Pemberley?" She peered out of the window. "Ah, it's looking rather brighter out there now. I wonder if Zeppelin plans to go exploring. I should get out there and see if I can find out who's feeding him. I'll stop off at mine on the way to pick up my walking shoes. Will you be all right here manning the fort?"

Pemberley nodded sadly. She seemed to Churchill a rather pathetic figure with her long, pale face, unruly hair and thin cardigan the colour of pea soup hanging from her slumped shoulders. The poor woman needed cheering up.

"How about you come and join me in my investigation?" said Churchill brightly. "A bit of fresh air would do you the world of good."

"No, thank you. I'll stay here and woman the fort."

"Woman?"

"Because I am one. If I stay here then I can ensure we don't miss any new clients who come calling."

"True. We need all the clients we can get, as we don't have many at the moment. In actual fact, we have just the one. Good idea, Pembers. I'll be back before you know it. Toodle pip!"

As Churchill arrived at Mr Greenstone's cottage she was pleased to see the mid-afternoon sunshine had coaxed Zeppelin outdoors again. He strode confidently down a narrow track proudly signposted Muckleford Lane.

"Ah ha, puss. I've got you now!"

Churchill followed him down the lane, which wound past another cottage, an old well and then beneath a clothes line, where a woman was pegging out her laundry.

"Good afternoon!" Churchill said to the woman breezily.

The cat jumped over some box hedging and strode across the front lawn of a pretty, timbered house with sweet-scented honeysuckle growing around its door.

"This looks as though it might be the place where the mysterious cat feeder lives," Churchill said to herself.

She lifted her tweed skirt, stepped over the low hedge and pursued the cat. She was grateful for her stout shoes, which she had last worn on a walking holiday in the Lake District with her late husband two years prior. She rubbed a gloved hand over her eyes, which had misted for a moment, and continued on her mission.

Zeppelin paused beneath a bird bath to lick his back foot.

"I see what you're up to, puss," she said. "You're lying in wait for a feathered friend, aren't you? They're not completely bird-brained, you know. They'll keep their distance until you move on."

At that moment, one of the pretty house's little mullioned windows flung open, and the angry face of a middle-aged woman appeared.

"What d'you think you're doing?" she shouted.

"Sorry to intrude!" Churchill gave a conciliatory wave. "I'm carrying out an investigation."

"What sort of investigation?" barked the woman.

"A private one. Mrs Churchill's the name. I'm a private detective. I would give you a carte de visite but they're still at the printers. I won't keep you long."

"You won't keep me at all. Get out of our garden. You've trampled on my geraniums!"

"Have I? Oh, I'm sorry. Can you tell me if you've been feeding this cat?" She pointed at Zeppelin, who was cleaning his back with a repetitive motion that looked as though it might strain his neck.

"No. Why would I feed that mangy animal? He's fat enough already!"

"There's nothing wrong with a little extra padding!" retorted Churchill.

"It's not padding. He's *fat*. Now, are you going to get out of my garden or will I have to summon my husband, who just happens to be the local police inspector?"

"Oh, there's no need to call him. I was married to a police officer once myself. He was a detective chief inspector. Is your husband only an inspector? Not a *chief* inspector?"

"You can ask him yourself when you're locked up in a cell for trespassing."

Churchill laughed. "I hardly think it's an imprisonable offence."

"Get away! Now!" The woman's face was as red as the tomatoes in her perfectly maintained vegetable patch.

Churchill glanced about and could see the woman who had been pegging out laundry quickly approaching. An embarrassing scene appeared inevitable.

"There's no need to raise your voice quite so much, madam. I was just going. Lovely to meet you. Goodbye!"

She avoided the damaged geraniums and stepped carefully back over the hedge.

"Cheerio!" she said to the other woman. "I was just leaving." She marched as quickly as she could back to the office.

Pemberley was fixing something to the wall when Churchill returned.

"You got us a map, Pembers! How wonderful!"

"I hope the scale is large enough," said Pemberley, standing back to admire it. The map took up most of the wall next to King George V.

"It's perfect. Thank you," said Churchill.

"I got us some pins and some string so we can create a detailed incident map with all the bells and whistles. And I've just made a pot of tea."

"Pembers, I could kiss you."

"How was Zeppelin?"

"I've managed to rule out one suspect: the wife of the local police inspector. He's just an inspector, is he? Not a *chief* inspector?"

"I don't know. I've always known him as Inspector Mappin."

"Hmm, probably not chief then, otherwise you would have heard him described as such. Mrs Mappin is rather rude, isn't she?"

"Is she? I've always found her quite pleasant."

"Perhaps it seemed that way because I met her under rather awkward circumstances. Anyway, we can now update our incident map to reflect the progress of our investigation.

The map needs a pin to mark Zeppelin's home. We don't have a picture of Zeppelin to put up there yet, but I can draw a picture of a generic cat to represent him for now."

Churchill sat down at her desk, found a pencil and paper in the drawer to her right and began to sketch.

"Why are you drawing a hippo?" asked Pemberley from her position beside the map.

"It's not a hippo. It's a cat."

"Why's it got such an enormous nose?"

"Those are its ears!"

"May I draw the cat?"

"Please do." Churchill flung the pencil and paper across her desk in the direction of Pemberley. "I've had a difficult day. Did Atkins have difficult days?"

"Regularly."

"Oh dear. I suppose it comes with the territory. People can be terribly defensive about their gardens, can't they? You'd think that as the wife of a police inspector, Mrs Mappin would have been understanding about the work that needs to be carried out in the course of an investigation, but she was only worried about the state of her geraniums."

"Did you stand on them?"

"Only in the course of my investigation. I didn't do it deliberately. Pembers, that's a most astonishing cat you've drawn there. It looks almost lifelike!"

Pemberley shrugged. "I like to practise a little sketching now and again."

"And so you should; you're quite the artist. Pin Zeppelin up on the board and let's have a cup of tea."

Chapter 6

A POLICE OFFICER with brown mutton-chop whiskers and steel-grey eyes visited Churchill's Detective Agency the following day.

"You must be Inspector Mappin," said Churchill warmly. "Do come and join Miss Pemberley and me for a cup of tea and some lemon cake."

"That's a kind offer, Mrs Churchill, but no thank you. I'm on duty." He removed his hat.

"Of course. I understand the duties of a police officer; my late husband was a detective chief inspector, you know."

"So my wife informs me."

"Please do apologise to your wife, Inspector. Our initial meeting did not take place under the circumstances I would have wished for. I was carrying out an investigation at the time, and I'm sure you're aware how complicated matters can be when you're out in the field, eh?"

"Indeed. I've come here this morning to follow up on reports of a large, elderly lady ruining my wife's geraniums while trespassing on our property yesterday."

"Large? *Elderly?*" Churchill suddenly had a score to settle with Mrs Mappin.

"Was it you, Mrs Churchill?"

"Yes, it was. I hope you will accept the apology I have so readily given, Inspector. Are you sure you won't have a slice of cake? I'm certain it would be sufficient recompense for the damaged geraniums."

"I'm afraid it wouldn't be, but three shillings would."

"*Three shillings?* Whatever for?"

"To replace the geraniums."

"Is that how much they cost you? Where on earth did your wife buy them? Harrods of Knightsbridge?"

"No, Mrs Churchill, merely the local plant nursery."

"Tell your wife she should grow them from seed. It's practically cost-free if you can source it from a friend or neighbour. And it's so much more rewarding when you take the time and effort to grow plants from seed; so much better than planting something that's ready-made, as it were."

"And probably even more disappointing when your efforts are trampled on by a local busybody."

"I beg your pardon, Inspector! *Busybody?* I'm a private detective!"

"Do you have three shillings to settle the score?"

Churchill sighed and pulled her purse out of her handbag. "Very well, Inspector, here's your money. I always pay my dues."

"Thank you." The inspector pocketed the coins and glanced around the office. "So you're the lady who's bought Atkins' place, eh? It currently says 'tkins Detective Agency' on the door."

"My secretary is yet to remove the remaining letters that aren't right, isn't that so Miss Pemberley?"

"They're rather tricky to scrape off," she replied.

The inspector looked up at the wall. "Nice map."

"Thank you. Do you have one like it at the station?"

"Not on that scale, no. Yours is quite impressive."

"I have Pemberley to thank for it. Do you have a Pemberley at the station?"

"No Pemberleys for me. We operate on a tight budget." Churchill felt rather smug.

"Atkins and I used to rub along rather well," continued Inspector Mappin. "It's a shame the old chap's gone."

Churchill gave Pemberley a wary glance as her secretary's lower lip began to wobble once again.

"We used to enjoy a tankard of scrumpy or two in The Wagon and Carrot," continued the inspector. "And we played tennis together. Atkins had a strong backhand."

"He was very good at tennis," sniffed Pemberley.

"I can play a bit of tennis," said Churchill. "I was a member of the Richmond-upon-Thames Ladies' Lawn Tennis Club, albeit briefly. Any time either of you fancy a knockabout just let me know." She noted a lack of enthusiasm from both parties. "Fine, suit yourselves," she continued. "I'm sure there is no shortage of tennis partners in Compton Poppleford."

"You're not one of those meddlers are you, Mrs Churchill?" asked Inspector Mappin.

"Certainly not!"

"It's just that you do hear of these older women, often widows, who reach a time in their life when they find themselves wishing to solve something more challenging than the daily crossword. They're usually rather nosy and have too much time on their hands. That's when they begin to meddle in police business."

Churchill laughed. "What odd notions you have, Inspector! I have never come across one of these meddling women you speak of. As for myself, I am far too busy running my private detective practice to meddle in any of *your* business. I'm currently building an extensive client base."

"Good. So it's safe to say I shan't be encountering you too often then?"

"Absolutely not, Inspector. You will hardly see me at all. You have your work to do and I have mine. We shall sail past each other like ships in the night."

"That's what I like to hear," said the inspector, donning his hat. "Nice to meet you, Mrs Churchill. I shall bid you and Miss Pemberley a good morning."

Churchill spent the next few hours reading more of Mr Atkins' files.

"Thank goodness Devon is a long way away, eh, Pembers?"

"It's not, though."

"*It's not?*"

"No, it's the next county along."

"Along from where?"

"Here."

"*Here?*"

"We're in Dorset and if you travel in a westerly direction from here you'll reach Devon."

"Goodness, really?" Churchill felt a shiver.

"What's the matter, Mrs Churchill?"

"Well, I shan't be travelling in a westerly direction to Devon and the hellish Dartmoor any time soon."

"Oh, I know which case you've been reading about."

"Was it actually a wolf? Or some terrifying oversized hound? I can't believe Atkins survived it!"

"He was very lucky," replied Pemberley. She glanced away, distracted by something just outside the window.

"What is it, Pembers?"

"I think we have a visitor."

"Who is it?"

Hearing the throb of a motor car's engine, Churchill got up from her chair and marched over to the window. She peered out to see a bright, red shiny automobile parking up outside Bodkin's Bakery.

"Oh no, it's that greasy oik who almost ran me over while I was standing in the road the other day."

"It's Mr Cavendish," said Pemberley. "He's quite the charmer."

"Is that so? It takes a lot to charm me, Pembers, let me tell you."

Chapter 7

"I BELIEVE I have the pleasure of addressing Mrs Annabel Churchill!" said Mr Cavendish as he breezed into the office. "I've heard all about you."

He was about thirty and wore an immaculate beige suit with well-polished brogues. He held a boater hat in one hand and an umbrella in the other. As he spoke, Mr Cavendish flicked his head to swoosh a wave of blonde hair out of his blue eyes and smiled broadly to reveal two rows of neat white teeth.

Churchill was immediately disarmed. She brushed the cake crumbs from her ample bosom and jumped to her feet. "You've heard all about *me*?"

"Of course." He winked.

"Little old me?"

"Little old you, Mrs Churchill. And less of the *old*, surely?"

"Naturally," she giggled. "Do sit down. It's Mr Cavendish, isn't it? Pemberley will fetch us some tea."

Mr Cavendish carefully placed his hat on the hatstand and tucked his umbrella into the base.

"Before we begin, Mrs Churchill, I think we need to have a little word." He hitched his trousers up at the knees as he sat down and his face grew sombre.

"Do we?"

"You were rather a naughty girl the other day, weren't you?"

"Was I?"

"You were standing in the middle of the road."

"Oh yes, well you were the rather naughty man who almost ran me over!"

"I'm afraid I was, Mrs Churchill, and you frightened me a little when you shook your fist at me like that."

"Oh, surely not?"

"Surely."

"Really?"

"Indeedy."

Pemberley placed two cups of tea on the desk and rolled her eyes.

"Is this merely a social visit?" Churchill asked Mr Cavendish. "Or do you have a secondary motive for visiting our detective agency today?"

Mr Cavendish feigned disappointment. "Is a social visit not enough for you, Mrs Churchill?"

"Well it is, but…"

"Time is money, am I right?"

"Since you put it that way, it is indeed."

"I'm joking with you, Mrs Churchill. Of course there's another reason for my visit." He grinned.

"Oh, you jester!"

"As you may have noticed, I'm rather a light-humoured individual, but there are some occasions when I must be quite serious, I'm afraid." Mr Cavendish's face grew sombre again.

"Of course." Churchill readied herself with pen and paper.

"Sad circumstances have prompted me to visit you today. The death of my dear godmother."

"Oh, Mr Cavendish, I'm so sorry." Churchill couldn't help but feel a twinge of excitement that she was about to be presented with a proper case to investigate. "When did your godmother pass?"

"Just a few days ago."

"May I ask how?"

"I should like to know how myself. It's the reason I'm here today."

"I see."

"Her ending was untimely, Mrs Churchill, and sadly rather unpleasant."

"Strewth! What happened to her?"

"She fell down the staircase at Piddleton Hotel."

Churchill and Pemberley gasped in unison.

"Mrs Furzgate?" said Churchill. "Your godmother was Mrs Furzgate?"

"Yes. I knew her as Auntie Prissy."

"I've lived in this village a long time," interjected Pemberley, "and I never knew Mrs Furzgate was your godmother, Mr Cavendish."

"Yes. She was a good friend of my mother's," he said sadly.

He looked so bereft that Churchill had to fight the urge to clutch him to her bosom.

"They went to school together," continued Mr Cavendish. "The school only had four pupils back then."

He went on to give a potted history of his mother's life and how it had entwined with the life of Mrs Furzgate. Churchill found herself becoming rather bored but allowed him to continue talking seeing as he was clearly grieving.

"That's all very interesting," she interrupted when she felt she had heard enough. "But it's not clear to me how I can help you."

"Oh, it's quite simple, my dogged lady detective," replied Mr Cavendish. "The circumstances of her death are suspicious."

"Is that what Inspector Mappin says?"

"No, it's quite the opposite of what Inspector Mappin says. That's why I'm here! Inspector Mappin says her death was unquestionably an accident."

"And how do you know that it wasn't an accident?"

"Because my godmother would never have fallen down the stairs!"

"Mr Cavendish, you may not like what I'm about to tell you, but it just so happens that your godmother visited this office on the day I moved in here. She came in to welcome me to the village, which was very thoughtful of her. But I can tell you that as she departed she actually slipped on our stairs!"

"Are you sure?"

"Yes! I witnessed it with my own eyes."

"She wasn't given a slight nudge or a push?"

"Of course not, Mr Cavendish. Why would you suggest such a thing?"

"It happened to her quite often. People were usually keen for her to leave their premises."

"Not us though, eh Pembers?" Churchill turned to her secretary for reassurance, but none came. "We were flattered that your godmother came to visit us."

"There's no need to lie, Mrs Churchill. She was a most exasperating woman."

"Well, perhaps *flattered* was a slight exaggeration."

"Pure exaggeration, Mrs Churchill. My godmother was an irritant. But she was still my godmother."

"Absolutely. She was *your* godmother."

"Few people liked her, and therein lies the first clue."

"Which is what?"

"That barely anyone liked her."

"Oh."

"Which means plenty of people would have been pleased to see the back of her."

"Oh no, Mr Cavendish. Surely not!"

"It's a motive, Mrs Churchill. Don't you see? If plenty of people disliked her, perhaps one of them was keen to cause her some mischief."

"Are you suggesting your godmother was murdered?"

"I most certainly am."

Churchill gasped again at the excitement of the suggestion. "And you'd like little old me to track down her murderer?"

"Absolutely. Little old you. Just name your price."

"Price? I hadn't given it any thought. Erm, how about twenty pounds upfront and we'll take it from there?"

"Twenty pounds upfront is perfect, Mrs Churchill." He removed the money from his wallet so quickly that she wished she had asked for more. "And another thing you need to know is that I suspect my godmother knew some things she shouldn't have."

"Really? Such as what?"

"I can only suspect, Mrs Churchill, I don't know for sure. But she was an extremely nosy person; always sticking her proboscis into places where it didn't belong. It wouldn't surprise me if she had chanced upon something extremely private."

"Goodness! The mind boggles doesn't it, Mr Cavendish?"

"Yes, it boggles all right. Would you like to look around my godmother's home? She lived at Pebblestone House in Hollyhock Lane. It's rather a humble, spartan place but an eagle-eyed lady detective such as yourself might spot a clue or two. My godmother's solicitor, Mr Verney, will be there tomorrow morning at nine o'clock. Just tell him I sent you."

"That would be most useful. Thank you, Mr Cavendish."

He checked his watch. "Goodness, is that the time? I must be on my way if I'm to make my next appointment. You have an impressive ability to cause time to fly, Mrs Churchill!" He grinned and jumped up from his seat.

Churchill laughed. "May I take that as a compliment, Mr Cavendish?"

"Of course." He winked again and placed his boater hat back on his head. "I expect you'll need to pester me with endless questions as your investigation progresses. You may telephone me whenever you wish."

He placed a neat card on her desk.

"Thank you, Mr Cavendish. My cards are still at the printers, but I shall give you a carte de visite as soon as they're ready."

"Please do. Adieu, Mrs Churchill."

"Adieu to you, Mr Cavendish!"

"Adieu, Miss Pemberley," he said, picking up his umbrella.

"Goodbye," replied Pemberley.

"Deary me," Churchill said with a chuckle as she heard Mr Cavendish descending the stairs. "That fellow, Pembers, is what my mother would have described as a bounder and a cad."

"I knew you'd be charmed by him."

"I wasn't the least bit charmed."

"What was all the *little old me* business, then?"

"Rapport, Pembers! A private detective must always establish a rapport with her clients. I merely mirrored his manner. Now, let's get started, shall we? I shall make up a file."

Churchill hummed a cheery tune as she gathered some papers together and filled her pen with ink. Then she stared down at the daunting blank page in front of her.

"I shall write down a list of reasons to support the assertion that someone might wish to murder Mrs Furzgate. First of all we have the fact that no one liked her. And second of all she may have known something she shouldn't have."

Churchill resumed her humming as she wondered what else she should write down.

"Atkins always used to start with the victim," said Pemberley. "He believed that understanding everything about a victim's life often revealed the killer's motive."

"In that case his approach was exactly like mine," replied Churchill. "A pretty standard approach all private detectives should follow."

"He also used to visit the murder scene, preferably at the same time of day or night the murder took place."

"Yes, that's another common aspect of a private detective's approach. Exactly what I would have said." Churchill glanced at Pemberley's wan features and decided she needed some air. "How about we take a little wander down to the Piddleton Hotel Pembers? You look like you could do with some colour in your cheeks."

Chapter 8

"I CAN THINK of worse murder scenes. It's actually rather pleasant here, isn't it?" Churchill and Pemberley took afternoon tea on the mezzanine floor at Piddleton Hotel. Churchill's bone china cup was so tiny she could barely fit her forefinger through its delicate handle.

A tiered cake stand laden with baked indulgences stood at the centre of the table. Gentle, orchestral music floated up from the ground floor, and a pleasing chatter hummed from the tables around them.

"Very civilised indeed. I shall be mother," said Churchill as she lifted the teapot and filled their cups. "Are you going to have the pink iced fancy, Pembers, or shall I have it?"

"I'll have it," said Pemberley, snatching it from the cake stand rather too swiftly for Churchill's liking.

Churchill consoled herself with a slice of battenberg. "Those stairs over there must be the ones our unfortunate Mrs Furzgate tumbled down," she said, nodding toward the grand staircase with its gilded balustrade. "I counted the steps when we climbed them and there are twenty-four in total, which is precisely what the news article reported, isn't it? The article also mentioned a rogue teacake. I think we should order one so we can examine a typical example of the teacakes they serve here."

She snapped her fingers at a nearby waiter and placed her order.

"Now then, Pembers. You've lived in Compton Popple-ford for some time, am I right?"

"Yes, a long time. I was born here, in fact."

"So you've lived in this village for your entire life?"

"Apart from an interlude as a companion to a lady of international travel."

"How interesting! You must tell me about that some time. In the meantime, tell me everything you know about Mrs Furzgate."

"Well now, let me see." Pemberley picked up a yellow iced fancy. "I first met her about forty years ago, back when she was delivering milk."

"She was a milkmaid?"

"Yes, she used to walk around with one of those wooden yokes across her shoulders and a bucket of milk hanging down on either side. It looked rather uncomfortable, I must say. My mother always used to complain that the milk was sour, and she would usually be ready with a rude response. She knew a lot of profanities for such a young woman."

"What was her name before she was married?"

"Miss Smallbone."

"Then she is a relation of Mr Smallbone, the bric-a-brac shop owner?"

"Probably. Most people are related to each other around here."

"I see." said Churchill. "There is a lot of intermarry-ing, then?"

"Indeed, yes. It's the reason I never married, to be honest."

"Couldn't you have travelled to another town and found a husband there?"

"I could have done, I suppose, but I was always too busy for that sort of thing."

"What of Mr Furzgate? Who was he?"

"Miss Smallbone's cousin. I think his name was Bert. He was fond of a drink and died young."

"Oh dear, what of?"

"The official reason was a weakness of the kidneys, but unofficially he was believed to have syphilis."

"Good grief! Where on earth did he get that from?"

"I prefer not to dwell on it. Anyway, the long and the short of it is that Mrs Furzgate led a life of meagre means at Pebblestone House."

"And who were her acquaintances?"

"There was Mrs Volkov. She also sadly died of syphilis. Then there was a friend from school… I suppose that would have been Mr Cavendish's mother. Her name was Iris. She became Iris Cavendish when she married; I forget her maiden name."

"But she is no longer with us?"

"No."

"More recently then, Pembers. Who were Mrs Furzgate's acquaintances?"

"I'm not really sure, though I believe she used to play bridge."

"A fellow bridge player, eh? I like a bit of bridge myself. Perhaps she frequented the local bridge club?"

"Actually, I'm not sure she was a bridge player as such, but I know she frequented the club."

"Why would you do one and not the other?"

"That's the sort of woman she was. And I think she was a member of the church choir."

"So she did have a talent after all! A voice like a song-bird, was it?"

"I don't know about that. But I do know she was asked to leave a few times but kept turning up for practice anyway. Eventually they asked her to stand at the back because she was quite diminutive, as I'm sure you remember. And at the back she was well hidden."

Churchill placed her cup down on its saucer rather mournfully. "I'm beginning to feel quite sorry for Mrs Furzgate."

"Oh, I wouldn't. She once murdered a chicken."

"You mean slaughtered?"

"No, it was murder apparently."

Pemberley took a sip of tea as the waiter placed a teacake on the table. Churchill decided to ignore the chicken incident for the time being and began to examine the teacake.

"Look, Pembers, it's well buttered. You may recall that I didn't ask for it to be buttered, which suggests to me that teacakes here are served buttered by default. You know what that means, don't you?"

"No, what does it mean?"

"Butter is a naturally slippery substance. It explains the suggestion that Mrs Furzgate may have slipped on a teacake. The butter would have lubricated the sole of Mrs Furzgate's shoe, causing her to slip more readily than if the teacake had remained unbuttered."

"Perhaps she just tripped."

"Well, that's the same thing."

"Not necessarily. She may have seen the teacake on the floor and tried to avoid it, causing her to trip."

"Good thinking, Pembers. However, the news article

states that the teacake was squashed, which suggests to me that it endured the full weight of Mrs Furzgate's shoe."

"Unless someone else had trodden on it before her."

"We can't rule that out. But had that happened I suggest the person in question might have recognised the teacake as a hazard and removed it from the floor. Or perhaps instructed a member of staff to do so."

Both women nodded as they considered this.

"You know, Pembers, I'm rather enjoying bouncing ideas off you. I think we make quite a good team."

Pemberley's face broke out into a smile. "Do you really think so, Mrs Churchill?"

"Yes, I do," she replied, suddenly embarrassed by her brief expression of mild affection. "Now drink up and let's go and investigate the staircase in more detail."

Chapter 9

CHURCHILL AND PEMBERLEY put on their overcoats, picked up their handbags and began to descend the stairs.

"Look here, Pembers. The twelfth stair is deeper than the others and acts as a sort of halfway point. It's where the floor vases are sitting. Oh dear, they haven't glued the crack in that one very well, have they?"

The two women walked over to the repaired vase and examined it.

"It's a far from perfect mend," stated Churchill. "I know a chap in Marylebone who does an excellent job with this sort of thing; I could have recommended him to them. The aspidistra is relatively unscathed, though. Just a few bent leaves really. Distinctly less damage than poor Mrs Furzgate suffered."

"Asparagaceae are fairly resilient plants."

"You should use a handkerchief when you sneeze, Pemberley."

"I didn't sneeze."

"Yes you did; just before you talked about resilient plants."

"I said 'asparagaceae'."

"Bless you!" Churchill said with a titter. "Do you mean asparagus?"

"Yes, that's another name for it. Aspidistra is part of the asparagaceae, or asparagus, family."

Churchill stared at her secretary. "Are you saying that aspidistra is asparagus?"

"They're related to one another."

Churchill frowned. "I hope that you leave enough room in your head for useful information too, Pembers. We're working on a complicated case here."

She strode down the remaining stairs with Pemberley in hot pursuit. Once they reached the bottom they turned to look back up.

"So the unfortunate Mrs Furzgate tumbled all the way down here," said Churchill.

"Knocking into the vase along the way."

"Indeed! Rather unpleasant, I must say. I estimate that she ended up in a heap around here." Churchill tapped an area of the carpet with the toe of her shoe. "I don't suppose the hotel owner will allow us to draw one of those chalk outlines of her position, which is a shame as that would have been rather useful. I'll tell you what, Pembers, how about you lie on the floor here so we can get a good idea of the final tableau? We can't be sure as to what position Mrs Furzgate ended up in, but I'm sure that if you spread-eagle yourself somewhat it'll give us a fair idea."

"I'm not lying down on the floor, Mrs Churchill."

"There's no need for any nonsense, Pembers. Recreating the scene is an essential element of the investigation."

"I don't look anything like Mrs Furzgate. She was a short, round lady, and I'm—"

"Tall and thin. Yes, I see what you're saying, Pemberley.

I bear more of a resemblance to the late Mrs Furzgate than you, don't I? Here, hold these."

Churchill thrust her hat and handbag at her secretary, then lowered herself to the floor. "The old knees tend to complain when one attempts these things. Still, it has to be done."

"Mrs Churchill, I'm sure there's no need for this," said Pemberley, glancing around in the hope that no one would catch sight of her employer splayed out on the floor.

Churchill lay on her back, her turquoise overcoat bunching uncomfortably beneath her throat.

"I can't see my legs from here," she said in a strangulated voice. "But I'll attempt to place them akimbo, and you can let me know if the effect is convincing." She puffed as she twisted her legs into an unnatural and highly unladylike position.

"I can see your petticoat, Mrs Churchill."

"That's good; we need this to be realistic. How do you suppose her arms would have ended up? I imagine one would have been twisted up like this." Churchill moved one arm above her head, but doing so pulled her coat even tighter around her throat. Her face grew hot and she felt a sharp pain in her neck.

"Good grief, Pembers! Isn't clothing restrictive? If the fall down the stairs doesn't kill you then your overcoat surely will. Now then, I can't hold this position for long. Get the camera out and take a photograph."

"What camera?"

"You didn't bring the camera with you?"

"I hadn't realised we would need one."

"It's a standard approach when carrying out investigations, Pemberley. Don't tell me I've contorted myself into this position for no reason."

A scowling, bearded face loomed above Churchill. Its owner was a large man in a loud, green plaid suit.

"Good afternoon!" she said. "I don't suppose you have a camera, do you?"

"No I don't! Do you mean to tell me that you wish this macabre spectacle to be photographed?"

"Never mind, a piece of chalk should do it. Do you have one? If so, please lend it to my secretary, Miss Pemberley, so she can draw around me."

"She will do no such thing! Get up off my floor immediately, madam!"

"I beg your pardon! May I ask who you might be?"

"Mr Crumble, the owner and manager of this hotel."

"Owner and manager, eh?"

"Get up, I say!"

"I would very much like to get up, Mr Crumble, as this is rather an uncomfortable position, but I'm afraid I can't." Churchill attempted to roll onto her side. "I appear to be stuck. Can you give me a hand?"

Churchill was righted to her feet with the help of two hotel porters.

"Goodness, what a palaver," she said, retrieving her hat and handbag from Pemberley. "One doesn't routinely have much call for getting down on the floor. I don't think I've laid down on the carpet like that since my courting days!"

"Are you aware that a lady lost her life in this very location just a few days ago?" hissed Mr Crumble. "Your tomfoolery is irreverent and disrespectful."

"Mr Crumble, I can assure you my actions are the very opposite of tomfoolery. I am Mrs Churchill of Churchill's Detective Agency. I have been tasked with investigating

Mrs Furzgate's death, and Miss Pemberley, my secretary, is assisting me."

"What? Two old ladies?"

"*Mature* ladies, Mr Crumble. My guess is that I only have ten years on you."

"More like twenty!"

"Mr Crumble, I'd like to ask you a few questions about this most unfortunate incident. Did you witness it?"

"I won't be answering any of your questions, Mrs Churchill. Please leave my hotel this minute."

"I don't think you quite understand. We have been tasked with investigating by a close acquaintance of Mrs Furzgate."

"I didn't realise she had any acquaintances. As her sad demise was an accident, no further investigation is required. Please leave my hotel now, Mrs Churchill, before I call the police."

"Inspector Mappin, you mean? He's a good friend of mine, you know."

"You have one minute to leave before I set the dogs on you."

"There's no need for threats of a canine nature, Mr Crumble."

"Mrs Churchill, I think we should leave," said Pemberley. "*Immediately*."

Churchill pursed her lips and glared at Mr Crumble. "It's a terrible shame you don't wish to cooperate with us, Mr Crumble. I had been planning a return visit to partake of your iced fancies again, but I shall take my custom elsewhere."

She turned to leave and then stopped as she thought of something else to say. "And when my London friends come to visit I shall recommend that they stay at the Marchmont Hotel and avoid this shabby establishments at all costs!"

Chapter 10

"WHAT A BADLY RUN HOTEL!" Churchill declared as they left the building and walked down the driveway. "No wonder people die in it. I don't think the *owner and manager* understood the gravity of what I meant when I told him I wouldn't be recommending the place to my London friends. That includes Lady Worthington, nonetheless. The silly man will be denied her patronage, but he only has himself to blame. And what a terribly garish suit he was wearing; no hint of class about him at all. Hello? Is that another way in?"

There was an open door leading to a side wing of the hotel.

"Please don't go back in there, Mrs Churchill," said Pemberley. "We really will be in terrible trouble."

"Don't fret, Pembers. I'm just going to have a little peek."

Churchill strode across the lawn toward the open door. She peered inside and saw a number of residents reading or snoozing in a lounge area. She turned to look at Pemberley, who was loitering nervously on the driveway, then put two fingers in her mouth and blew a sharp whistle. Mouthing "Come here!" Churchill beckoned to her with an exaggerated arm movement.

Pemberley reluctantly trudged across the lawn with a nervous expression on her face.

"Liven up, Pembers!" hissed Churchill. "This won't take a moment."

Churchill marched through the lounge, smiling politely at the residents she had startled with her whistle.

Pemberley followed. "What if we bump into that Crumble man again? He won't be happy," she whispered.

"Can you imagine that clot ever being happy about anything?" retorted Churchill.

They left the lounge and found themselves in a brightly coloured corridor.

"I couldn't bear to stay in a place with a carpet as loud as this," said Churchill. "There's something rather tawdry about it, isn't there? Very poor taste."

"What are we doing here?" whispered Pemberley.

"We need to speak to someone who was here when Mrs Furzgate fell down the stairs," said Churchill.

She spotted a young woman in uniform about to enter a room further down the corridor.

"What's she? A chambermaid? A waitress? Either way, she'll do."

Churchill dashed after the woman, who seemed startled by her speedy approach. She paused with her hand holding the half-open door.

"Mrs Annabel Churchill, private detective," Churchill said as she accosted her. "Do you work here?"

The maid nodded.

"Were you working here on the day Mrs Furzgate fell down the stairs?"

The maid shook her head.

"Darn it! Can you find someone who was here on the day for me? Anyone except the *owner and manager*, that is, because I've already spoken to him and he doesn't like me very much."

"You could talk to Peter," suggested the maid.

"Peter? Who is he exactly? Does he have a surname? Where do I find him?"

"Peter Brown."

"And who is he?"

"I think he was working here at the time."

"And where might he be found at this moment?"

"He works in the restaurant."

"I see. My good friend and I are trying to be rather secretive about our investigating, so would it be too much trouble for you to fetch this Peter fellow for us? We'll wait in this room here."

Churchill walked in at speed and knocked into a mop and bucket.

"It's a cupboard," said the maid.

"Yes, I can see that now, thank you," replied Churchill as she squeezed herself against a pile of towels. "Stop hanging about in the corridor, Pemberley. There's plenty of room for you to join me in here."

The two mature ladies crammed themselves into the cupboard as best they could. The maid stared at them, open-mouthed.

"Stop goggling at us woman and go and fetch Peter," Churchill ordered.

The maid did as she was told.

"I'll close the door," said Churchill. "We don't want to be seen. You're not afraid of the dark are you, Pembers?"

"No. I hope the maid hasn't gone to get Crumble, though," Pemberley whimpered.

"Stop worrying about Crumble! He's completely

harmless and clearly has no idea how to run a hotel. He also lacks sartorial elegance and has an appalling taste in decor. A dreadful man in every respect."

"It's very dark in here," said Pemberley. "I don't like it when it's this dark because I can't be certain that I haven't lost my sight."

"Of course you haven't lost your sight, you ninny."

"But if I wave my hand in front of my face I can't see it at all. And although rationally I know there's no source of light, there is nothing to either prove or disprove whether I have lost my sight."

"I'm beginning to see what you mean, Pembers. I'm holding my hand directly in front of my face and yet I can't see it at all! What if I've gone blind?"

"Exactly."

"Well that's soon answered by opening the door and readmitting a little light."

Churchill tried the doorknob, only to realise that it wouldn't turn.

"Oh dear, Pemberley, this isn't good." Her heart began to thud heavily.

"What?"

"I think this is one of those cupboards that can only be opened from the outside."

"No!"

"Calm yourself, dear, this is no time for histrionics."

"But I hate the dark!"

"I checked this with you before I closed the door, remember? You told me you weren't afraid of the dark."

"What if no one ever comes back for us and we're stuck in here forever?"

"What nonsense, Pemberley."

"With nothing to eat! We'd have to eat the towels!"

"I'm sure it won't come to that. Anyway, this door

seems rather thin. I think we could barge it open if we were truly desperate."

"I *am* desperate!"

"Now come on, you're a grown woman."

"I'm a grown woman who hates being in enclosed spaces! Oh, get me out! I need to get out! I need to get out!"

"Hold your breath and count to one hundred."

"*Get me out!*"

"Oh, for heaven's sake, Pemberley!"

Churchill leant back and propelled herself at the door with so much force that it flew open with a horrible splintering sound.

"There! Happy now?" cried Churchill.

Pemberley stumbled into the corridor, weeping with relief. Her spectacles fell onto the floor and she scrabbled around to find them.

A young man with a wispy moustache stood watching them.

"Please tell us you're Peter," said Churchill, dusting herself down.

"I'm Peter."

"Good."

"What have you done to the cupboard door?"

"Oh, it's nothing. I'll have a look at that in a moment," replied Churchill, smoothing her skirt and readjusting her hat. "Now then, Peter, I understand you were working here when Mrs Furzgate fell down the stairs? Did you see what happened?"

"Yes."

"Oh good! What did you see?"

"I saw her tumble down the staircase."

"And where were you when she fell? At the top or bottom of the stairs?"

"At the top."

"Good, good. And was there anyone else standing near her when she fell?"

"I can't be certain, but I don't think so."

"Anyone close enough to push her?"

"I don't think so."

"Could someone have surreptitiously poked their foot out and tripped her up?"

"I'm not sure."

"And what about the teacake on the floor? Did you see that?"

"Yes, I did. I picked it up and discarded it."

"Good, good. We have confirmation on the teacake, Pembers. It was buttered, I presume?"

"Yes."

"Excellent. And I don't suppose there is any way of finding it again and examining it?"

Peter frowned. "I put it in the kitchen waste, which goes to Farmer Farnley's pigs."

"I see. So the pigs are likely to have consumed it by now."

Peter nodded.

"Shame. Nonetheless, you are being extremely helpful, Peter. Thank you. Have you any idea how the teacake came to be on the floor?"

"I suppose it must have slipped off one of the waiters' trays."

"With or without its plate?"

"I didn't see a plate on the floor."

"Do you know who Mrs Furzgate was with when she fell? Had she come to the hotel to meet a person or persons?"

"I have no idea. But I do know that several members of the Women's Compton Poppleford Bridge Club were having tea in the restaurant that afternoon. Perhaps she was with them."

"Perhaps she was. That's extremely interesting, Peter. Thank you. Oh dear, Pembers, we need to scarper."

Over Peter's shoulder Churchill could see the maid walking towards them with a man in a green plaid suit.

"Back the way we came, Pembers. Run!"

Chapter 11

HOLLYHOCK LANE WAS a delightful cobbled street lined with small houses. A climbing rose trailed over a wall, its pink blooms filling the air with a pleasant scent.

"I've got a bit of a hobble this morning, Pemberley," said Churchill. "My ankles are quite strained after leaving Piddleton Hotel at pace yesterday."

"I must say that you move quite quickly for a—"

"A large lady?"

"No, I didn't quite mean—"

"No need to pussy foot around, Pembers. I know what you intended to say, and I don't mind at all. In fact, I'm rather proud of my running ability. People usually underestimate my speed, and more fool them, I say!"

"Mr Crumble almost caught us."

"Until he was foiled by his trousers. It must have been quite a rip for us to have heard it from twenty yards away!"

They both laughed.

"I expect Mrs Crumble had to spend her evening sewing them up again," said Pemberley.

"More fool her if she did. She should make him do it

himself, and a pig's ear he'd make of it, no doubt. Oh look, here's our man." Churchill and Pemberley approached a thin grey house where a short, dusty-looking man in a pinstriped suit stood on the front step trying different keys in the lock.

"You can always spot a solicitor, Pembers," whispered Churchill. "They have a closed look about them that suggests they know far more than they're letting on."

"Well they do, don't they?"

"I suppose they do. But they like us to think it, too. Solicitors must spend many hours in front of the looking glass perfecting their smug expressions."

Churchill paused and waved at him. "Good morning Mr Verney!" she said cheerily. "Did Mr Cavendish mention we'd be joining you this morning?"

"Yes, he did warn me," replied the solicitor, his eyes narrowed behind a pair of thick spectacle lenses. "I'm trying to find the right key." He searched through the large bunch in his hand.

"You clearly administer a great number of properties, Mr Verney," said Churchill.

"Yes, I do."

"All of them belonging to deceased individuals?"

"Not all of them, no. Ah, this might be the one." He tried the key in the lock and uttered a quiet curse word when nothing happened. After a few further attempts with different keys the door creaked open and they were greeted by a waft of shuttered-up air.

They stepped into a small hallway housing a steep wooden staircase leading up to the first floor. On the ground floor was a small living room and kitchen area. Threadbare rugs lay on the floorboards and there were two worn easy chairs in the living room. The kitchen was small yet functional.

"She didn't have a lot of space, did she?" Pemberley commented.

"She didn't have a lot of anything," said Churchill. "I'd say Mrs Furzgate was as poor as a church mouse. How long did she live here?"

"Her entire life," replied Mr Verney.

Churchill noticed a dull bronze telescope sitting on an occasional table.

"That could do with a bit of spit and polish," she said. "I wonder if Mrs Furzgate used it to spy on her neighbours."

"She might well have done," replied Pemberley.

"I think it's purely ornamental," said the solicitor.

"Did you know Mrs Furzgate well?" Churchill asked.

"Not personally. I merely handled her affairs."

"Do you believe she may have been murdered?"

The solicitor gave a dry laugh. "No, I don't. What a preposterous idea!"

"Perhaps she kept poking that telescope at someone and they finally cracked," suggested Churchill.

"Highly unlikely," retorted Mr Verney.

"Do you know of anyone she might have fallen out with?" asked Churchill.

"No. And even if I did I'm bound by client confidentiality."

"Even though your client is deceased?"

"Even though she's deceased."

"I see. Well, I don't think there's much else to look at here is there, Pembers? Why is there a section of tea chest leaning against the fireplace?"

Pemberley stepped over and picked it up.

"It has some writing on it," she said, turning it over so that Churchill could read it. The letters had been neatly painted on in red paint.

"'No More Dirty Money'," read Churchill. "Interesting. I have to say that I agree with that sentiment. One often wonders which filthy places the coins in one's purse have lingered in; greasy palms, dust-filled trouser pockets and that sort of thing. The thought alone is making my hands itch for a bar of Sunlight soap. Thank you for your time this morning, Mr Verney, but we must be on our way. If you think of anything useful that doesn't breach client confidentiality you'll let me know, won't you? I would leave you with a carte de visite but they're still at the printers. You know where to find us, though; just above the bakery. I bought Atkins' business."

"Ah, poor Atkins," mused the solicitor. "He and I used to go shooting together."

"How lovely. Good day to you, Mr Verney."

"Mrs Furzgate's home yielded no clues did it, Pemberley?" said Churchill as they enjoyed a cup of tea and a slice of fruit cake back at the office.

"No, but dead ends are common in detective work."

"Absolutely. We private detectives must cope with them all the time. Dead ends must be suffered! I'm tempted to write down that piece of wisdom and stick it to the wall." She took a sip of tea. "Is your cardigan blue or green today, Pembers?"

"It was emerald once, but it's been washed rather a lot since then."

"It's definitely lost its hue," said Churchill. "Not to mention its shape."

"No, that's me," replied Pemberley. "I've lost my shape."

Churchill was about to ask for clarification when she

heard footsteps on the stairs. "Hark, Pembers! Someone's coming!"

Her heart sank as the brown-whiskered Inspector Mappin entered the room.

"Inspector!" said Churchill with forced enthusiasm. "My fellow *ship*! How can it be that we're not passing in the night? It's the height of day. Are we perhaps colliding?"

"Something like that," replied the inspector as he removed his hat and sat down in front of Churchill's desk.

"Do sit down," she said. "Oh, you already have. How about some tea? Would you like a slice of fruit cake?"

"No, thank you. I'm on duty."

"You've used that excuse before, Inspector. Does being on duty preclude you from enjoying elevenses?"

"I'll keep my visit brief, Mrs Churchill, and have a cup of tea and a biscuit when I return to the station."

"Very good, Inspector. What can I do for you?"

"Mr Bernard Crumble of the Piddleton Hotel has paid me a visit."

Churchill sighed. "I might have known."

"He informed me that two elderly ladies made quite a nuisance of themselves at his hotel yesterday afternoon."

"We were there yesterday afternoon weren't we, Pemberley? We didn't notice any old ladies being a nuisance. In fact, everyone was exceedingly well-behaved and pleasant until that rude, bearded man in the gaudy suit threatened to set his dogs on us."

"I'm told that you caused an obstruction at the foot of the staircase, Mrs Churchill, and subsequently caused damage to a cupboard door."

"Mr Crumble makes such a fuss about things. I don't have time for fussy people."

"Can you confirm that his complaint is accurate, Mrs Churchill?"

"It's not how I would describe it. Surely it's only fair to hear my side of the story, Inspector?"

"Of course. And what is your side of the story?"

"Well, Miss Pemberley and I were there as part of our investigation into the tragic death of Mrs Furzgate."

"Investigation? But there's nothing to investigate! Her death was clearly an accident."

"That's not what her godson believes, and he has charged us with getting to the bottom of it."

Inspector Mappin groaned and put his head in his hands. "Don't tell me. Mr Cavendish?"

"Yes, the very same, as a matter of fact."

"He's asked you to investigate his godmother's death? Even though a professional police investigation has deemed it an accident?"

"Subject to the coroner stating it as such."

The inspector laughed. "Knowing Mr Graves, the coroner, I'm extremely confident that he will find her death to have been an accident."

"The coroner is a friend of yours, is he?"

"Yes, we play tennis together."

"Do you indeed? And I suppose Atkins played tennis with the coroner as well, did he?"

"He did."

"Good," Churchill replied through clenched teeth. "It's a nice sociable game, isn't it, tennis?"

"In summary then, Mrs Churchill, you have confirmed that Mr Crumble has cause for complaint about your conduct yesterday afternoon?"

"He strikes me as the sort of man who always has cause for complaint, don't you think, Inspector? Have you ever seen the man smile? He looks like a chap who permanently has the hump."

"A woman has just died in his hotel, Mrs Churchill."

"I realise that. But just think of her godson, poor Mr Cavendish! Imagine his grief at losing his godmother in that manner! He has far more reason to be miserable than Mr Crumble."

"Let's settle this matter here and now," said the Inspector. "Mr Crumble has issued a lifetime ban to you and your secretary from ever setting foot in his hotel again."

"Pfft," snorted Churchill. "We don't ever want to go there again anyway, do we, Pembers?"

"Well the iced fancies were rather nice," said Pemberley.

"No, they weren't," retorted Churchill. "The fondant was too thin."

"And he demands a sum of twenty pounds to repair the cupboard door," continued Inspector Mappin.

"*Twenty pounds!*" Churchill's jaw almost hit her desk. "But the door can be repaired with a few tacks and screws, and a little bit of wood and a saw, or however it is you fix doors. I shall go up there and fix it myself for a twentieth of the cost!"

"The door must be replaced. The damage was quite extensive."

"A replacement door for *twenty pounds*. Mr Crumble routinely buys his doors from Fortnum and Mason of Mayfair, does he?"

"No, just from the carpenter's yard in Compton Poppleford."

"We're in the wrong business, aren't we Pembers? We should be running the carpenter's yard and selling doors to inept hotel owners for extortionate sums of money!"

"And then there's the matter of the torn trousers," said Inspector Mappin.

"Mr Crumble's unmentionables are nothing to do with me," replied Churchill. "I didn't go anywhere near them."

"Mr Crumble states that his trousers ripped while he was in the process of chasing you out of his hotel," said the inspector.

"He should wear a pair that fits him properly. Either that or reduce his waistline. And there's no need for you to glance at my waistline in that manner, Inspector. At least my clothes fit me properly!"

"Two shillings for repairs to the trousers."

"Two shillings! Can't Mrs Crumble repair them?"

"There is no Mrs Crumble."

"That explains a few things."

"Mr Crumble is a bachelor and must therefore pay his tailor to repair the trousers."

Churchill laughed. "He has a tailor? You could have fooled me. That green suit looked like something he might have bought second-hand from one of the clowns at Chipperfield's Circus."

"There's no need to be rude, Mrs Churchill," the inspector scolded. "Mr Cavendish asked you to carry out this investigation, did he not?"

"Yes."

"Well why don't you bill him for the door and the trouser repairs? Include it in your expenses."

"Now there's a thought!" A smile spread across Churchill's face. "It turns out you can have the capacity for good ideas after all, Inspector."

"Good. So that's settled, then. Now, when we last met, Mrs Churchill, you assured me that you weren't one of those meddling types."

"Absolutely not, Inspector."

"So stop meddling."

"I'm merely carrying out my job!"

"In which case you need to be professional about it, just as my friend Atkins was."

"Inspector Mappin, I take offence at the suggestion that you consider my conduct to be unprofessional."

"Trampled geraniums, broken doors and ripped trousers speak for themselves, don't they, Mrs Churchill?"

"Three unfortunate incidents, Inspector, which won't happen again."

"I'm glad to hear it."

"I shall return to my night-time sailing. You won't notice me at all."

"Very good. Let's keep it that way."

"You have my word."

Chapter 12

"SMITHY MIGGINS," said Churchill as she and Pemberley walked along the high street. "He's the chap who wrote the story about Mrs Furzgate's demise in the *Compton Poppleford Gazette*. It's possible that he knows a little more about the incident than was reported and would be a useful person to speak to. Do you know anything about him?"

"He wears a pork pie hat and a scruffy raincoat."

"Sounds like your archetypal news reporter."

"Always scribbling in his notebook and smoking a cigarette."

"Quite typical."

"Drinks like a fish."

"Predictable. Ink-stained fingers?"

"I should think so. Enjoys flower-arranging."

"For a moment I thought you said he enjoys flower-arranging."

"He does."

"Not entirely what I expected, in that case."

They had reached the offices of the *Compton Poppleford Gazette*: a red-brick building with white sash windows.

"How do you get in the place, Pembers?"

"Around the back."

The two ladies walked down a short passageway at the rear of the building, passing a yard containing several overgrown shrubs at one end. A sign on the office door read: 'No Beggars or Peddlers Allowed'. Churchill knocked and a tall woman with dyed red hair and painted eyebrows answered.

"Good afternoon! I'm Mrs Churchill of Churchill's Detective Agency."

"You're the lady who bought Atkins' business, aren't you?" The woman's manner was cold and haughty.

"Ah, so you've heard of me, then. All good I hope."

The woman said nothing, so Churchill cleared her throat.

"Please may I speak with your reporter, Smithy Miggins?"

"He's out on a story."

"When will he be back?"

"Who knows how long a story will take?"

"I don't know. Who indeed?"

"I don't know, either; it was a rhetorical question."

Churchill found herself struggling to warm to the woman. "Perhaps when Mr Miggins returns you could ask him to come and see me," she said. "Do you know where Atkins' former premises are?"

"Everyone knows where they are."

"Good. Well he may find me there."

"May I ask what it's regarding?"

"I'm investigating the death of Mrs Furzgate."

"Oh, *her*."

"Did you know her?"

"Everyone knew her."

"Good, well it's reassuring to hear that everyone knows

so much about everything in this village. That should make my job a little easier."

"I shall pass your message on to Mr Miggins. He may not get back to you, however. He's a very busy man."

"I'm sure he is, madam."

"My name is Mrs Duckworth."

"What a pleasure it is to make your acquaintance, Mrs Duckworth."

"Did you notice the way I lied to that dreadful woman, Pembers?" said Churchill as they walked back along the high street. "I told her it was a pleasure to make her acquaintance even though it wasn't at all. I have the stomach for many unpalatable things in life, but I find rudeness indigestible. Don't you?"

"It is both unsavoury and inedible."

"I'm pleased you agree, Pemberley. Now then, that Peter Brown fellow at Piddleton Hotel mentioned the Women's Compton Poppleford Bridge Club. Tell me about them, Pembers. Who's in charge there?"

Pemberley groaned. "A formidable lady who goes by the name of Mrs Trollope."

"I see. And her second-in-command is...?"

"Mrs Duckworth."

"That rude woman we just spoke to?"

"Unfortunately, yes. There's something rather superior about ladies who play bridge isn't there? It must be their high intellect."

Churchill chuckled. "High intellects don't worry me, Pembers. As a bridge player myself I'm quite at home with the bridge ladies. Hit me with some more names."

"There's Mrs Cranster, Mrs Goggins, Mrs Higginbath, Mrs Murgatoss-Bynes and Mrs Fazackerly-Bowes-Grant."

"Good work, Pemberley. I think we need to be brave and pay these ladies a visit. But if we're going to meet them on their own turf we'll need to brush up on our bridge skills."

"But I have no idea how to play it."

"Don't worry, Pembers, I'll give you a quick lesson. Come round this evening about seven."

Churchill and Pemberley sat at the dining room table in her cottage that evening. They had a glass of brandy each and a plate of Homewheat Chocolate Digestives to share.

"Now then, my trusty assistant, bidding four hearts means you plan to take ten tricks, with hearts as trumps," said Churchill.

"Did you make that draught excluder yourself, Mrs Churchill?" Pemberley asked, pointing at the sausage of stockings lying across the bottom of the door.

"Yes, I did. No matter how many gaps I plug in this place it's still chilly. Even in the middle of summer! I've complained to Farmer Drumhead about it, but he's still rather distracted by his mother's death. I'm not surprised she popped her clogs living in this place; the draughts are enough to carry anyone off. Now concentrate, Pembers. Do you have any hearts in your hand?"

"No."

"I thought you said you did?"

"Did I? This game is terribly confusing."

"Lay your cards on the table and let me have a look at them."

"I didn't think you were supposed to see them." Pemberley clasped them protectively to her narrow chest.

"Not ordinarily, but I need to help you understand what's in your hand."

"You're not trying to cheat?" asked Pemberley warily.

"No, Pembers, we're not even playing a proper deal! We need four people for that."

"Remind me what a trick is."

"I'm still trying to explain the principle of trumps," said Churchill through clenched teeth. "Just show me your cards before my head explodes."

Unable to wait any longer, Churchill reached across the table and snatched the cards from her secretary's hand.

"Let's have a look at this... You have five hearts here, Pemberley!"

"Do I?"

"And you have fifteen cards, when I only dealt you thirteen. Where did you get the other two from?"

"Oh, I don't know, Mrs Churchill. I don't think I'm cut out for bridge. Can we stop now?"

"We have to, for my patience has left me. It would be quite dangerous to continue."

Chapter 13

A TALL, familiar-looking woman with dyed red hair and painted eyebrows answered the door to Mrs Trollope's large house the following afternoon.

"Mrs Duckworth!" said Churchill cheerily. "Are you Compton Poppleford's official door-answerer by any chance?"

"No, I'm not."

"There was no need to answer; it was a rhetorical question. Miss Pemberley here telephoned Mrs Trollope this morning to request a meeting with your bridge club, and she invited us to her rather fine home this afternoon. What a delightful place it is, too." Churchill glanced up at the large, white-stuccoed facade. "I take it Mrs Trollope is at home?"

"They're all out on the lawn," replied Mrs Duckworth sourly. "Follow the path along the side of the herbaceous border and enter beneath the ornamental arch at the end."

"Thank you, Mrs Duckworth."

Churchill and Pemberley did as they had been instructed.

"Mrs Trollope has a resplendent herbaceous border, doesn't she, Pembers?" said Churchill. "And what a lovely display of delphiniums. It's a bit of luck that the bridge club is meeting here today. It means we can ask them all what they remember of that fateful day at Piddleton Hotel."

They reached the ornamental arch. "Oh, look! There they all are on the lawn." Churchill felt the need to whisper. "And what an extensive lawn. Mrs Trollope must have a man who comes in to cut it. In fact, she must have a team of gardeners for this place."

They walked across the lawn toward a group of ladies who were sitting about on deckchairs. Somehow Mrs Duckworth had got there before them.

"She wasn't going to let us take the shortcut through the house, was she?" Churchill whispered.

She fixed a grin on her face as they drew near the group of mature ladies, all of whom were staring at them, stony-faced. The tension of the moment reminded Churchill of her first day as a new girl at Princess Alexandra's School for Young Ladies.

"This is Mrs Cranster, Mrs Goggins, Mrs Higginbath, Mrs Murgatoss-Bynes and Mrs Fazackerly-Bowes-Grant," said Mrs Duckworth.

"Good afternoon, ladies!" said Churchill, keen to break the ice. "And what lovely weather we're having. I'm sure I read that the forecast this afternoon was for rain. They never can get it right, can they?" She glanced hopefully at a nearby table, upon which sat a jug of lemonade, a large bowl of strawberries, a jug of cream and a cake stand straining beneath the weight of iced fancies.

"Welcome to my home, Mrs Churchill. I have heard a lot about you."

Startled by the voice coming from behind her,

Churchill spun round to see a slightly built lady of about sixty wearing a floral summer dress and a large straw hat. She had sharp green eyes and her lips were stained a dark red.

"How lovely to meet you, Mrs Trollope. You've heard about me, have you? Goodness! Should I be worried?"

The old lady walked past her without answering and sat down in a striped deckchair.

"Do take a seat," she said when she was settled. "You don't want to make the garden look untidy."

"Of course not!" laughed Churchill nervously. "That wouldn't do at all, would it?" She approached a deckchair, which appeared worryingly low-slung. "If I sit myself in this one I might never get out of it again!"

"Nonsense, Mrs Churchill. If we can get out of them again, so can you. It's all in the hips."

"My hips are what concern me," said Churchill as she carefully lowered herself into the chair. Once she was seated her knees were level with her bosom.

"Goodness, Pembers," she whispered to her secretary, who had taken the chair next to her. "My derrière is well and truly jammed now. You'll have to get behind me and push me up out of this thing once we're done."

"Everything all right, Mrs Churchill?" asked Mrs Trollope as she placed a cigarette in a silver holder and lit it.

"Perfectly fine, thank you, Mrs Trollope. What a pleasant afternoon it is and what a delightful garden you have here! And what a pretty dovecote. How many doves do you have roosting in there?"

"Just the two." Mrs Trollope puffed out a large cloud of smoke. "They tell me you come from London."

"Yes, latterly. Although I originally hail from the Home Counties."

"And now you're a private detective, I believe."

"That's right. I bought the detective agency from the late Mr Atkins."

"And you have already been tasked with your first case."

"Indeed! I'm currently working on two investigations." Churchill realised, with a lurch in her stomach, that she hadn't been following Zeppelin for several days. She hoped Mr Greenstone hadn't noticed that she had neglected his case.

"London, you say? Whereabouts did you live?"

"Richmond-upon-Thames."

"I don't suppose you came across my good friend Lily there? Known in wider circles as Lady Worthington."

"What a small world! Yes, I'm extremely good friends with Lily. In fact, I mentioned her to Miss Pemberley only recently, didn't I, Pemberley?"

"Did you?"

"Yes, when I said I wouldn't be recommending that dreadful Piddleton Hotel to her."

"Ah yes, I remember now."

"What's wrong with Piddleton Hotel?" asked Mrs Trollope.

"It's run by a terribly rude man. Dreadful manners. And sartorially challenged. What was that clown suit he was wearing the other day, Pembers? Terrible, wasn't it?"

"Mr Crumble?" ventured Mrs Trollope.

"That's the one."

"He's Mrs Higginbath's nephew."

Churchill glanced over at Mrs Higginbath, a broad lady with long grey hair. Then she turned back to Mrs Trollope again, her mouth hanging open all the while.

"Nephew?" she said in a weak voice. "Well what a

coincidence! I see no resemblance at all." The truth was that Churchill had now noticed an uncanny similarity between Mrs Higginbath and her nephew, who both had the same scowling, square face and hairy chin. "Perhaps I caught him on a bad day," continued Churchill. "Maybe I should visit on another day when he's in a better mood. Actually, on second thoughts he won't let me."

"What's the problem with my nephew?" asked Mrs Higginbath.

"I'm not allowed in his hotel any more. It was my fault entirely; I angered him."

"We like Piddleton Hotel, don't we ladies?" said Mrs Trollope, puffing out another cloud of smoke. "We hold our monthly meetings there. Would you and Miss Pemberley like some refreshments, Mrs Churchill?"

"I would love a little refreshment. Thank you."

Fortunately for Churchill, Mrs Goggins brought the lemonade and cake to her chair so she didn't have to try and climb out of it. The conversation returned to Lady Worthington and much talk ensued about dinner parties, art exhibitions and the opera.

"I like to try and get up to London at least three or four times during the season," said Mrs Trollope. "I adore Dorset, but it's so terribly provincial isn't it?"

"Terribly," agreed Churchill.

"But you've only been living here for a week," commented Pemberley.

"A week is plenty of time for one to decide whether a place is provincial or not," retorted Churchill.

"Well, I like it here," said Pemberley.

"I like it here too," said Churchill. "We all *like it here*, but there's no escaping the fact that it's provincial."

"What do you mean by that exactly?" asked Pemberley.

"Rather quiet. Sleepy," replied Churchill, unsure what the word actually meant.

"Unsophisticated," clarified Mrs Trollope, "and rustic. Can you believe I dined with a lady last week who spooned her soup *towards* her?"

"What a faux pas," said Churchill. "She could have spilt it all over her blouse."

"Poor breeding," added Mrs Trollope.

"Perhaps she'd been brought up by wolves," suggested Churchill.

"'As all ships go out to sea, I spoon my soup away from me.' Do you recall that rhyme from your childhood, Mrs Churchill?"

"I certainly do."

"I don't," said Pemberley.

Mrs Trollope gave her a look of pity before clapping her hands together to attract everyone's attention. "Right, ladies! It's time to get our cards out!"

It took every bit of strength Pemberley, Mrs Goggins and Mrs Fazackerly-Bowes-Grant could muster to haul Churchill out of her deckchair.

"Rather unforgiving around the thighs those things, aren't they?" muttered Churchill to Pemberley as she rubbed her sore hips. "And so unnecessarily low to the ground."

They followed Mrs Trollope up to the house and were shown into a large, pleasant drawing room with a high ceiling and tall windows that looked out over the garden. Four green baize card tables had been set up in the room.

"Mrs Churchill, you and Miss Pemberley must come and join myself and Mrs Duckworth," said Mrs Trollope. "We want to see what you're made of. You do play bridge, don't you?"

"Play bridge?" replied Churchill. "We barely do anything else, do we, Pembers? Apart from solve crimes, that is."

"Nothing like a good deal to provide some respite from all that crime-solving, Mrs Churchill," said Mrs Trollope.

Chapter 14

THE AFTERNOON of bridge reached its conclusion at six in the evening. As the ladies got up to leave the room Churchill noticed something unusual about Pemberley's gait.

"Why are you limping, Pembers?"

"I'm not entirely sure, but it might have something to do with you repeatedly kicking me in the shin."

"I didn't kick you that hard!"

"Perhaps not, but it had a cumulative effect and now I'm struggling to walk without pain. I couldn't understand the need for it."

"Some of those bids you were making were quite beyond the pale, Pembers!"

"We still won though, didn't we?"

"By some miracle we did, but I can't for the life of me think how or why."

"And haven't you forgotten something rather important?"

"What's that then, Pemberley?"

"The reason we came here in the first place."

"Goodness, you're right! We completely forgot to ask them about Mrs Furzgate, didn't we? I say, Mrs Trollope!"

"Yes, Mrs Churchill?"

"This is rather embarrassing, but I've been enjoying your hospitality so much I'd quite forgotten the purpose of our visit."

"What might that be, Mrs Churchill?" The old lady lay her head on one side like an attentive dog.

"Mrs Thora Furzgate."

A noticeable flicker of disdain passed across Mrs Trollope's face.

"Did you know her well?" asked Churchill. "I understand you were at Piddleton Hotel when she fell down the stairs and tragically died."

"Were we?" asked Mrs Trollope.

"Yes, we were," said Mrs Duckworth.

"I remember her being there," said Mrs Trollope, "but I thought she fell down the stairs after we left."

"No, we were definitely still there," said Mrs Duckworth. "Don't you remember all the kerfuffle?"

"I definitely remember the kerfuffle, but there always seemed to be a lot of that whenever Furzgate was around. She also seemed to have a disagreement with one of the waiters while we were there."

"Was she with your group?" asked Churchill.

"No, she wasn't," replied Mrs Trollope.

"She was trying to be," Mrs Goggins piped up. "She was always asking to join the bridge club, wasn't she?"

"She was indeed," said Mrs Trollope.

"But she was no good at bridge?" asked Churchill.

"Oh, she was a reasonable enough player, but if we'd admitted her we would have ended up with an odd number of players, and that wouldn't be right considering that bridge is played in pairs. We didn't want anyone being the odd one out."

"She did say she didn't mind being the odd one out," added Mrs Goggins.

"Was that your only reason for refusing to admit her to the bridge club?" asked Churchill. "Because you didn't want an odd number?"

"That was the official reason," said Mrs Trollope, "but unofficially it was because the woman was a pain in the rear end."

"In what way?"

"Did you ever meet her?"

"Yes."

"Then you don't need me to explain."

"Did you speak to her when you saw her at Piddleton Hotel?"

"Yes. She was there on some misunderstanding. She seemed to think she was a member of the bridge club when, in actuality she wasn't."

"Were any cross words exchanged between you?"

"They weren't particularly cross, were they Ducky?" she asked Mrs Duckworth.

"No. They were *exasperated* words," confirmed Mrs Duckworth.

"Did you tell her to sling her hook?" asked Churchill.

"The conversation wasn't quite that rude," said Mrs Cranster, "but the implication was there."

"And what was her response?" asked Churchill.

"She was rather argumentative about it," replied Mrs Trollope, "but that was the woman's nature, of course. It was never easy to be rid of her."

"It wasn't," said Churchill. "I can vouch for that."

"In the end I had to ask Higginbath to escort her from the table."

Churchill glanced at Mrs Higginbath, who had refused to have much to do with her since the conversation about her nephew.

"Did you have to use much force, Mrs Higginbath?" asked Churchill.

"Not much," the haughty woman replied. "She knew she couldn't match my strength."

"Things became physical, did they?"

"No, not really."

"A shove didn't accidentally turn into a tumble down the stairs?"

"No, it didn't!" exclaimed Mrs Higginbath.

"No!" declared Mrs Duckworth.

"Now hold on!" protested Mrs Trollope.

Everyone began talking at once and Churchill realised that she had pushed her questions a little too far. She held up her hands in resignation.

"Sorry, ladies, I do apologise! I know you had nothing whatsoever to do with Mrs Furzgate's fall down the staircase. Forget that I said anything about it."

The room had fallen quiet and the glances she was receiving were mainly hostile. She decided to explain matters in greater detail.

"Mrs Furzgate's godson, Mr Cavendish, thinks his godmother may have been killed because she knew something she shouldn't have."

"That's a fair enough assumption," said Mrs Trollope. "She was an exceptionally nosy woman, and it was only ever going to be a matter of time before her curiosity got her into trouble."

"After all, it killed the cat, didn't it?" said Mrs Goggins.

"Which cat?" asked Churchill. "Mr Cavendish didn't mention a cat."

"It's a saying," said Mrs Goggins. "You could say now that curiosity killed Mrs Furzgate."

"Did it indeed?" said Churchill. "So you agree with Mr Cavendish's theory? What could Mrs Furzgate possibly have known that she ended up paying for with her life?"

The women shrugged.

"What sort of matters was she gossiping about at the time of her death?" asked Churchill.

"You would receive a quicker answer if you were to ask what sort of matters she *wasn't* gossiping about," said Mrs Trollope.

"I see. So what sort of matters was Mrs Furzgate *not* gossiping about shortly before she died?"

Everyone turned to look at one another with blank faces, and Churchill wondered whether she was encountering what she had often heard described as a wall of silence. Having found the bridge ladies so welcoming that afternoon she was rather baffled by their lack of assistance.

"There was the business with Mr Smallbone," said Mrs Goggins, causing everyone to turn and look at her.

"Mr Smallbone who runs the bric-a-brac shop?" asked Churchill.

"I'm so terribly glad to hear you call it that," said Mrs Trollope. "The chap is so insistent that he only sells antiques. Have you seen the clutter in there?"

"I have indeed," replied Churchill. "Dreadful tat. But what's the connection with Mrs Furzgate? Was she gossiping about him?"

"She was," piped up Mrs Goggins again. "She had accused him of selling fakes and forgeries."

"Did she tell him this directly or was it something she only said to other people?"

"Both," said Mrs Duckworth.

"It was hardly an original accusation," said Mrs Trollope.

"That's one thing you could say about Mrs Furzgate," said Mrs Cranster. "She had a habit of saying what everyone else was thinking."

All the bridge ladies except Mrs Trollope nodded in agreement.

"I can only assume Mr Smallbone was upset by the allegation," said Churchill. The ladies nodded again. "Let's imagine that he was so upset he decided to murder Mrs Furzgate as an act of revenge. It's possible she had evidence he was selling fake antiques, and that would have strengthened his motivation to silence her even further."

Mrs Trollope nodded vehemently. "I like this theory, Mrs Churchill."

"Did you see him at Piddleton Hotel on the day Mrs Furzgate died?"

"No."

"Ah. Well that scuppers our latest theory. If he wasn't at the hotel that day he can't have pushed Mrs Furzgate down the stairs."

"Unless he was in disguise," said Miss Pemberley.

"Disguise?" replied Churchill. "You think Mr Smallbone would go to the trouble of disguising himself so he could push someone down the stairs?"

"He could have disguised himself as a guest, or a waiter or even as a lady," said Pemberley.

Churchill laughed. "I should think his rather distinctive moustache would have given him away, Pembers. These ladies would have recognised him in an instant."

"Then you can't treat him as a suspect," said Pemberley sulkily. "We're back to square one."

"Oh dear. How I hate square one," said Churchill.

"Perhaps he hired an assassin," suggested Mrs Murgatoss-Bynes.

"He might have done!" said Mrs Trollope.

"Did you see anyone who looked like an assassin when you were at the hotel that afternoon?" asked Churchill.

"No."

"Oh."

"But that doesn't mean to say there wasn't one," said Mrs Trollope. "Perhaps the assassin was wearing a disguise."

"I like that theory, Mrs Trollope. I like it very much." Churchill felt her spirits begin to lift again. "Pembers, I think we need to go and speak to Mr Smallbone. Thank you, Mrs Trollope, and all of you, for your help today. I think we're one step closer to finding Mrs Furzgate's murderer."

Chapter 15

"I SEE you've managed to remove the 't' from the glass door, Pembers," said Churchill. "We're down to 'kins's Detective Agency' now. Nice steady progress."

"There's a lot of scraping involved," replied Pemberley.

"And it looks like Mr Smallbone has just opened up for the day," said Churchill, surveying his bric-a-brac shop from the office window. "We should get in there before any customers turn up."

"Do you think Mrs Trollope told us everything she knew about Mrs Furzgate?" asked Pemberley.

"Of course! Why wouldn't she?"

"It felt as though she was holding something back."

"Nonsense!" said Churchill, turning away from the window to face her secretary. "I know Mrs Trollope's type; there are thousands of them up in London."

"Oh dear, are there?"

"Yes! She's that certain sort of *sort*. You know?"

"I don't think I do."

"Yes, you do. A good sort. You may have noticed that

we got on like a house on fire. Mrs Trollope wouldn't keep anything from me, I feel sure of it. It's not the done thing among ladies like ourselves."

Pemberley raised a sceptical eyebrow as Churchill turned back to the window.

"Smallbone's putting up the trestle table outside his shopfront. He clearly hasn't heard the forecast for rain later."

Pemberley joined Churchill at the window.

"His antiques are about to get rather soggy," said Pemberley.

"Shall we go and have a chat with him about the deceased busybody?"

"Good morning, Mr Smallbone!" said Churchill as they approached him. "What a lot of toasting forks you have there."

He took a pause from his work of laying them out on the trestle table.

"Them's companion sets. *Antique* companion sets."

"Are they indeed? I can only see forks."

"I've got pokers inside."

"Sounds uncomfortable."

"And shovels in there 'n' all."

"What about brushes?" asked Pemberley.

"And brushes as well. They goes for ten shillin's each, but if you buys a complete set it's yours for two quid."

"*Two pounds* for a fireside companion set?" Churchill said scornfully.

"I could do two for three pounds and ten shillin's. That sound any better?"

"Not really."

"How's about three for five quid?"

"No."

"What are you ladies doing 'ere, then? I've got a nice copper bed warmer just come in. Fancy a look?"

"We've come to speak to you about Mrs Thora Furzgate," said Churchill.

"I ain't got time for that now. I'm workin'."

"Laying out toasting forks on a table, you mean?"

"I got customers to see to."

"Where?" Churchill peered in through the door of his shop. "I don't see any customers, Mr Smallbone."

"They'll be along 'ere shortly."

"Which gives you a few moments to speak to myself and Miss Pemberley about Mrs Furzgate."

"No it don't. Goodbye."

Mr Smallbone stepped in through the doorway of his shop.

"Why won't you speak to us Mr Smallbone?" Churchill probed.

He slammed the door shut on the two ladies and glared at them through the window.

"Would you look at that, Pembers! What a rude man!" declared Churchill.

"I 'eard that!" Mr Smallbone called through the window.

"Good! You were supposed to!" shouted Churchill in reply. She bent down and pushed open the letterbox. "Can you tell us if you were at Piddleton Hotel on the day that Mrs Furzgate died?"

"No I weren't! Why would I 'ave been?"

"Because you bore a grudge against Mrs Furzgate."

"It weren't no grudge. She were the one what accused me of wrongdoin'!"

"What exactly did she accuse you of, Mr Smallbone?"

Churchill began to feel a sharp pain in her back from all the bending over.

"I ain't sayin'. Now go away!"

Pemberley bent down and joined Churchill in shouting through the letterbox. "Did she accuse you of selling fake antiques, Mr Smallbone?"

"I don't sell no fake antiques!" He pressed his nose and thick moustache up against the window glass and glared at the two women.

"Then why did she make the accusation?" shouted Churchill.

"'Cause she 'ad a screw loose!"

"Did she buy something from you she wasn't happy with?"

"Yeah, she bought a nineteenth-century telescope with a two-and-three-quarter-inch objective lens. It 'ad an equatorial mount an' all."

"What on earth is that?" asked Churchill.

"It's when the mount is fitted with a polar axis that can be lined up to point at the north celestial pole," clarified Pemberley. "In layman's terms it means the telescope can follow the stars as they move across the sky."

"How do you even know that, Pembers? And what does that have to do with anything?"

Her secretary shrugged in reply. Churchill could feel her patience leaving her and hammered angrily on the shop door.

"Mr Smallbone, can you please open up so we can continue our conversation on a more conventional footing?" she shouted. "I'm rather tired of having to bend over to bellow through a letterbox."

Mr Smallbone did as she requested but regarded them both with a sulky face.

"It sounds as though Mrs Furzgate bought a rather

expensive telescope from you, Mr Smallbone, what with its equator thingummy."

"Equatorial mount," corrected Pemberley.

"She got it for a song," he replied. "I practically gave it away to 'er. I only wish I'd 'ung onto it and sold it to someone who was willin' to give me a proper price."

"How much did you sell it to her for?"

"Fifty pounds."

"Good grief!"

"Practically gave it away, as I said. And then she 'ad the nerve to come back 'ere and tell me it weren't even an antique. She demanded a thirty-pound refund!"

"And did you refund her?"

"No chance! And that's 'ow all the trouble started."

"*All the trouble*, Mr Smallbone?"

"Yeah, she called me a crook an' a thief. An' a miscreant an' a reprobate. She even called me a *wastrel*."

"Mrs Furzgate must have eaten a dictionary for lunch that day," chuckled Churchill.

"It ain't a laughing matter," he replied.

"No, it certainly isn't, especially if this trouble you describe ultimately led to her murder."

"Murder?! What you talkin' about, Mrs Churchill? She slipped and fell down the stairs."

"Her godson, Mr Cavendish, believes she was murdered."

"What, like someone's pushed her?"

"That's what he thinks."

"Well none of this trouble led to me pushin' 'er, if that's what you're wonderin'. I weren't even there!"

"But did you perhaps hire an assassin to do the deed?" asked Pemberley.

Mr Smallbone's moustache bristled defensively. "A

what now? An *assassin*? Me hire an assassin? Over a thirty pound refund?"

"She called you a wastrel, Mr Smallbone."

"Yeah, but it ain't an insult a man would murder somebody over. I got bigger fish to fry."

"Such as what?"

"What d'you mean?"

"What are your bigger fish?"

"My bigger fish?"

"That require frying? It was you who used the phrase, Mr Smallbone. It's rather an empty one if there's no meaning behind it."

"You're wastin' my time now. Are you gonna buy anythin'?"

"We are merely carrying out an investigation on behalf of Mr Cavendish. I shall make a note of everything you've told us this morning and return with any further questions, if I may."

"Only if you buy summat."

"Do you ever think of anything other than money, Mr Smallbone?"

"Have you been and 'arassed Bodkin yet?" he asked.

"Mr Bodkin the baker? Should we?"

"Yeah. All I done was sell Mrs Furzgate a telescope. He was 'er lover."

Churchill's mouth made a repetitive gasping motion as she tried to comprehend what Mr Smallbone had just told her.

"*Lover*, you say?"

Mr Smallbone nodded.

The revelation left Churchill feeling unsteady on her feet, so she rested up against the door frame for support. "Pemberley, did you know about the relationship between Mrs Furzgate and Mr Bodkin?"

Pemberley's eyebrows were raised halfway up her forehead. "No! I had no idea, Mrs Churchill."

"Me neither. However, it explains why Mr Bodkin was so keen to leave when she visited us that time. I can only guess there had been some sort of rift in their relationship by that stage."

"Perhaps one of 'em 'ad spurned the other," suggested Mr Smallbone.

"Perhaps. Well, we'll need to go and ponder on that one. Thank you for your time, Mr Smallbone."

"I don't s'pose you fancy a look at the bed warmer before you go?"

"That almost sounds like a proposition, Mr Smallbone. No thank you."

"You'd better go and find out what Bodkin was keepin' warm in 'is oven for Mrs Furzgate, eh?"

"That's quite enough, thank you, Mr Smallbone. Goodbye."

Chapter 16

"I SHALL NEED a little fortification before we speak to Mr Bodkin about his love affair with Mrs Furzgate," said Churchill, biting into a cherry bun. Pemberley poured her a cup of tea. "Thank you, Pembers. You are a love."

"I thought I had a good idea of who was with who in this village," said Pemberley, "but I knew nothing of the relationship between Mrs Furzgate and Mr Bodkin."

"It seems our Mrs Furzgate had a few secrets of her own. Is Mr Bodkin a married man?"

"Yes." Pemberley's tone was deeply disapproving.

"Goodness me! It's quite shocking then, isn't it?" Churchill picked up another cherry bun. "I wonder how Furzgate even went about it. It's not the usual sort of thing for a woman of her age. Where does one even start if one wishes to begin such a dalliance? Once one becomes a widow there's usually an assumption that those dallying days are behind one."

The second cherry bun remained poised in Churchill's hand as she ruminated over this. It had never occurred to her to form a romantic attachment with anyone other than Detective Chief Inspector Churchill.

"And we now know where Mrs Furzgate's telescope came from," said Pemberley.

"She paid quite a bit for it, didn't she? That explains why there wasn't really anything else of any value in her home. All the money went on that thing, with its equator whatsit. I say, we haven't yet received a visit from the reporter Smithy Miggins, have we?"

"Mrs Duckworth probably didn't even pass on the message."

"I suspect you're right, Pemberley. Despite answering her fair share of doors, she strikes me as the sort of woman who believes message delivering is beneath her."

"Is that someone coming up our stairs?"

"I do believe it is, Pembers."

Churchill shifted uncomfortably in her seat as Mr Greenstone shuffled into the room with his hat in his hand.

"Oh, hello," he said.

"Mr Greenstone!" said Churchill, placing the cherry bun back on her desk and rising to her feet. "How lovely to see you again! How's Zeppelin?"

"I came here to ask you the same question."

"Did you now? Do take a seat, Mr Greenstone. Would you like some tea and cake?"

"No, thank you. I've just eaten my breakfast."

"Have you indeed? My husband was a late riser too given half a chance. He was never given a quarter of a chance though!"

Churchill laughed at her own quip, while Mr Greenstone took a seat across the desk from her with his shoulders slumped.

"So you're still no closer to finding out who's been feeding my cat?" he asked.

"Not yet, Mr Greenstone. However, I have been conducting some reconnaissance around your home."

"I know. I saw you, didn't I?"

"That's right! You did indeed. And the reconnaissance phase will continue until I have ascertained who has been feeding Zeppelin."

"I haven't seen you around there recently, though."

Churchill chuckled awkwardly. "We do happen to have other clients, Mr Greenstone, and we need to ensure that each case is given an equal amount of attention."

"If you're busy you can refund me the ten pounds and I'll find someone else who can help."

"No, no, Mr Greenstone, there's no need for that. We will find out who's feeding your cat. Just a few days more is all we require."

"I see. So it won't take much longer, then?"

"No, we're almost there with it. Look, we even have Zeppelin up on our incident board!"

"So you have. His face doesn't look quite like that, though."

"It's merely an artist's impression. If you have a recent photograph we could use that instead."

"I do." Mr Greenstone's face brightened. "I'll bring it in!"

"Marvellous."

"I do hope you manage to find the person who's been feeding him. It's terribly upsetting when he sniffs at the food I give him, then turns his nose up at it and walks out the door."

Mr Greenstone's eyes were damp.

"We'll find the culprit, Mr Greenstone. Don't you worry. Pop off home and find a nice photograph of Zeppers for our incident board, and I'll get right onto it."

Mr Greenstone popped his hat back on his head and shuffled away.

"Pembers, get out there and find out who's feeding that cat," said Churchill once Mr Greenstone had left. "I'd forgotten all about him. I'm going downstairs to speak to Mr Bodkin."

"What does the cat look like?" asked Pemberley.

"There's a picture of him on our incident board."

"But that's an artist's impression. Which *I* drew!"

"Well, he's grey and quite fat. Well-padded, I should say, not fat. You'll find him, Pembers. Now shoo."

Chapter 17

"GOOD MORNING, Mrs Churchill. The usual elevenses?" asked Mr Bodkin as he tucked six eclairs into a paper bag.

Churchill pursed her lips and surveyed the baker in the light of Smallbone's unexpected revelation. She concluded that somewhere beneath the bald head, thick eyebrows and generous dusting of flour lay the heart of a Lothario.

"Are you all right, Mrs Churchill?" he asked, holding his hand out for the money.

"I'm fine, thank you, Mr Bodkin. May I speak to you in private, please?"

"I've already offered you a generous discount, Mrs Churchill, and while you're a much-respected, loyal customer, I can't be increasing it any further, I'm afraid. I've got a business to run."

"It's not that at all, Mr Bodkin. It's about another matter."

Mr Bodkin glanced about him, as if evaluating all the work he had to get done. "Just for a minute or two then, Mrs Churchill. That's fourpence for the eclairs."

After paying him, Churchill followed Mr Bodkin into

the bakery at the back of the shop, where a young, gangly man with a cigarette in his mouth was kneading dough.

"Hop it for a minute will you, Bodger?" said Mr Bodkin. "Mrs Churchill and I need to have a private discussion, apparently."

The youth leered suggestively before leaving the bakery through the door at the back.

Churchill looked around for somewhere to sit or something to lean against, but everything was covered in a thick layer of flour. She looked down at her crimson twinset and noticed she already had some on her bosom. Brushing it briskly away only added more flour, which had somehow found its way onto her hands.

"This is a rather floury place, Mr Bodkin."

"It's a bakery."

"I need one of those white coats so I don't get it on my clothes. I suppose it's rather too late for that now."

She noticed Mr Bodkin was politely averting his eyes from the flour all over her chest.

"What can I help you with, Mrs Churchill?"

"It's something of a rather sensitive nature regarding the late Mrs Furzgate."

The baker groaned. "Please don't ask me about that woman."

"I'm afraid I must, Mr Bodkin. Her godson, Mr Cavendish, has asked me to investigate her death."

"Why on earth has he done that?"

"He believes her death was suspicious."

"I've got nothing to say on the matter. I must get back to work, Mrs Churchill."

"Do you have something to hide, Mr Bodkin?"

"Why would I have something to hide?"

"It only makes you seem suspicious, you know."

"Does it?"

"Yes, so you may as well just come out with it."

"Come out with what?"

"The details of your close relationship with Mrs Furzgate."

Mr Bodkin groaned again. "How do you know about *that*?"

"I never reveal my sources, Mr Bodkin."

"Our love affair has nothing to do with anyone else."

"I'm trying to find out the motive behind the killing."

"But she fell!"

"I know, but Mr Cavendish believes she was murdered."

"The chap's a fool."

"You may be right about that. But do you really think her death was an accident?"

"Of course it was."

"Can you think of a reason why anyone would want to cause her mischief?"

"Quite a few, really. She wasn't universally liked."

"I noticed you ran away from her when she visited our office last week. Why was that, Mr Bodkin?"

"'I didn't want to see her."

"Why not?"

"We'd had a falling out."

"About what?"

"It was a trivial matter, but the long and short of it was that I had called for an end to the affair."

"What was her reaction to that?"

"She was upset!"

"In what sort of way? Weepy upset or angry upset?"

"Oh, angry upset! She threatened to tell everyone. Even my wife!"

"And did she do so?"

"No, thankfully she died before she had a chance to tell her."

"*Thankfully*, Mr Bodkin?"

"I didn't quite mean that I was thankful for it; I was dreadfully upset, as you can imagine. But I can't deny the grief was accompanied by a slight relief that my wife would be none the wiser."

"So it was a rather convenient death for you, Mr Bodkin?"

"That would not be a fair way to describe, it Mrs Churchill, but it did put an end to a potentially sticky situation. I miss Thora, though; I *really* miss her. She was a damned attractive woman."

Churchill recalled the short, myopic woman in the tweed coat and wondered for a moment whether they were discussing the same person.

"My wife and I have slept in separate bedrooms for thirty years," he added.

"Mr Bodkin, I have no wish to hear about your domestic arrangements."

"I felt the need for—"

"Tra la la!" Churchill began to sing a tuneless song as loudly as she possibly could. "I don't wish to hear about it, Mr Bodkin!"

The baker stopped talking and sighed.

"Were you at Piddleton Hotel when Mrs Furzgate fell down the staircase?" asked Churchill.

"No, of course I wasn't. I was working here."

"Do you have an alibi?"

"Bodger will tell you I was here. If he can remember that is; the man has a mind like a sieve. But why would I need an alibi? You don't think I had anything to do with it, do you? Anyway, you're just some woman who bought

Atkins' business. You're not even a police officer. I don't have to answer to you!" He squared his jaw.

"Very well, Mr Bodkin, but it may harm your defence if you do not mention when questioned something you later rely on in court."

"What do you mean by that?"

"Nothing, really. But it sounds good, doesn't it? My dear husband used to say it a lot."

"If you think someone murdered Thora you should speak to those awful bridge-playing women. Mrs Trollope bore Thora a grudge after she scuppered her plans to become mayor of Compton Poppleford."

Churchill caught her breath on receipt of this new piece of information. "I happen to know the bridge ladies quite well," she said. "But I didn't know Mrs Trollope had made a bid for mayor. That is most interesting to hear."

"You won't tell my wife, will you?" asked Mr Bodkin.

"About Mrs Trollope's bid to become mayor?"

"No! About me and Thora."

"No, I won't. But I think you should tell her yourself."

"Never! She would leave me for good."

"Would that be such a bad thing Mr Bodkin? After sleeping in separate bedrooms for thirty years it would free you up to dust your flour wherever you wished."

Chapter 18

CHURCHILL SPENT a pleasant afternoon updating her incident board and reading through Atkins' files. As she worked, she basked in the gratifying realisation that her humble detective agency was beginning to take off. *It's all working out rather well*, she envisaged writing in her next letter to Lady Worthington. *I have a number of extremely important clients.*

The important clients hadn't contacted her yet, but she felt sure they would once the news of her impending success with the Thora Furzgate case spread like wildfire.

Pemberley returned to the office shortly after four o'clock.

"What perfect timing, Pembers! You're just in time for tea, and I've been reading about the most fascinating case in Atkins' files. It's the one where his train got stuck in a snowdrift in Yugoslavia and some boorish American chap got stabbed to death in the night. Atkins was trapped on the train with the murderer and a whole host of eclectic travellers!"

"Ah yes, I remember that one," said Pemberley as she

sank down into the chair behind her desk. "He was detained on the continent for a good few days on that occasion."

"I imagine he was! How did you get on with the cat?"

"No sign of him," she replied wearily.

"No sign? But you were gone for five hours!"

"I know! I walked the length and breadth of Compton Poppleford looking for that pesky cat."

"Did you check to see if he was inside Mr Greenstone's home before you began? Zeppelin may have been asleep on the armchair in there the entire day."

"I didn't think of that. Perhaps he was. Why do you have white powder all over your erm, your…" Pemberley cleared her throat awkwardly. "Your, ahem, thorax."

"*Thorax*, Pembers?"

"I should have said chest area."

Churchill looked down. "Oh, my bosoms, you mean? That's nothing. It's just flour from when I went to see Mr Bodkin." She tried to brush it off again.

"What on earth did he do to you?" asked Pemberley with a horrified expression on her face. "He didn't try to…?"

"Oh no, Pembers, the man's quite harmless. But it seems impossible to pay him a visit without finding oneself covered in flour. He denies having anything to do with Mrs Furzgate's death, but then again he would, wouldn't he? I'd say the chap has a strong motive for murdering her, as he didn't want her telling his wife about their fling. He did, however, mention that Mrs Furzgate ruined Mrs Trollope's bid to become mayor. Do you know anything about that?"

"Yes, I remember it well."

"It would have been a useful bit of background for me to have had in advance of our meeting with the bridge ladies."

"Would it?"

"Indeed it would, Pembers! It gives Mrs Trollope a motive for wanting poor Thora to be bumped off. Having cleared the lady of all suspicion I now have to consider her a potential suspect. It's quite a time-consuming endeavour having to unpin and then repin her picture to the incident board."

"I would leave her up there until you can be absolutely certain."

"Yes, that's exactly what I plan to do now. Thank you, Pemberley. Now, explain all this business about Mrs Furzgate ruining Mrs Trollope's dreams of becoming mayor."

"It was something to do with corruption."

"Mrs Trollope is corrupt?"

"*Allegedly.* But only according to Mrs Furzgate."

"It's no wonder Trollope refused her entry to the bridge club! I feel terribly narked that no one dared breathe a word of this scandal to me. Corrupt in what manner?"

"She is said to have received money from disreputable sources."

"Really? Which sources?"

"Mrs Trollope's son, Timothy, was caught up in a bit of bother. He's escaped to the Bahamas now."

"If you're going to escape anywhere then the Bahamas is probably the best place to go. What sort of bother?"

"Some sort of counterfeiting or smuggling; I can't remember exactly which. I think there may have been a bit of blackmail thrown in as well."

"Mrs Trollope's son, eh? Who'd have thought it? He didn't receive any mention during our bridge match, did he? I wonder why. I still don't understand what all this has to do with Mrs Furzgate."

"Apparently, Mrs Trollope's mayoral campaign was

funded by a rather nefarious friend of her son's. The allegation was that this friend used the funding as an opportunity to launder money."

"Did he, indeed? I can't say I'm up to comprehending all the detail of that, but is it safe to say that Mrs Trollope received some dodgy cash?"

"Yes. Her mayoral campaign was muddied by laundered money, allegedly. Nothing was ever proven, but Mrs Furzgate enjoyed making rather a song and dance about it all. She raised a petition and organised a march along the high street: Compton Poppleford Village People Against Corruption!"

"Good for Thora. Much as I used to like Mrs Trollope, I must take Furzgate's side on this one. And the painted piece of tea chest we saw at her home makes perfect sense now: *No More Dirty Money*. It must have been a sign she made for the march, Pembers! The next time you hold a wealth of information about someone you will tell me about it, won't you?"

"Oh, I hold a wealth of information about a lot of things. I just don't always know when it's relevant to begin spouting about it."

"Well I'd say this piece was relevant about two days ago, and now I feel there's a good deal of catching up to do. But never mind; at least I know it now. Update the incident board with it, will you? I need a custard tart and some thinking time."

The throb of a motor car's engine interrupted her thoughts, prompting Pemberley to glance out of the window.

"Oh, it's him again," she said reproachfully.

"Him? Who's him?"

"Our man about town, Cavendish."

"Oh, him."

"You're not going to flirt with him again, are you?"

"Flirt, Pemberley? I've never flirted with anyone in my life. I don't need to flirt. People are drawn to my natural grace like butterflies to pollen."

"Or flies to—"

"Stop right there, Pembers! There's no need to finish that sentence."

Chapter 19

"CIAO, MRS CHURCHILL!" said Mr Cavendish as he breezed into the office leaving a trail of expensive eau-de-cologne in his wake.

Churchill felt a flutter in her chest as he grinned at her. His teeth were whiter than she remembered, and his thick blond hair had a pleasing lustre to it.

"Ciao indeed, Mr Cavendish! How very continental of you. I must say you've taken me quite by surprise. If I'd known you planned to visit us today I would have bought extra eclairs."

"There's no need for eclairs, Mrs Churchill, I am quite satisfied with your good self."

"Are you really? Goodness, well that's quite something then, isn't it?"

"Indeedy." He placed his boater on the hat stand and sat down opposite her.

"Some tea please, Miss Pemberley!" Churchill called out. "You must be here for an update on my investigation, Mr Cavendish."

"That I am, my formidable detective. What have you managed to find out so far?"

"Well, Miss Pemberley was just telling me about the fine work your godmother did in organising the Compton Poppleford Village People Against Corruption march. That was extremely worthy of her."

"Ah, yes. She was a lady with strong opinions."

"You must have been very proud of her."

"I was, yes. She was no pushover."

"The only problem with taking a stand is that it can upset the applecart, and I fear her anti-corruption march may have angered one of the local mayoral candidates."

"Oh, yes. That business with Mrs Trollope, you mean?"

"Yes. I have my eye on that lady. A possible suspect, if you ask me."

"If that old fish murdered my godmother I'll—"

"Let's not jump to conclusions, Mr Cavendish. I must say that when I first met the woman I had a favourable opinion of her, but now that I've heard about her dirty money my mind is less convinced on the matter. But let me look into it before you begin exacting your revenge on innocent parties."

Pemberley placed a tea tray on Churchill's desk.

"Thank you for the tea, Miss Pemberley. I have also spoken to Mr Smallbone—"

"*We*," interrupted Pemberley.

"I'm sorry, Miss Pemberley?"

"We both spoke to Mr Smallbone, didn't we, Mrs Churchill?"

"Yes, my secretary is quite correct. We *both* spoke to Mr Smallbone and we *both* spoke to Mrs Trollope and her bridge ladies. Isn't that right, Miss Pemberley? I can see that my secretary wishes to make that clear to you, Mr

Cavendish. We spoke to Mr Smallbone, who told us about an altercation he had with your godmother about a telescope."

"A telescope?"

"Yes, Mr Cavendish. It had an…"

"An equatorial mount," said Pemberley quickly.

"What's that?" asked Mr Cavendish.

"It's fairly irrelevant to the investigation," Churchill said.

"If that rickety old conman murdered my godmother I'll shove that telescope—"

"There's no need to do anything of the kind yet, Mr Cavendish! As I've already said, I need to look into it. Miss Pemberley, would you mind sipping your tea at your desk? I'm hearing a rather distracting slurping noise in my left ear."

Pemberley walked over to her desk, her shoulders slumped.

"And then there's Mr Bodkin the baker, of course."

"What's he got to do with it?" asked Mr Cavendish.

"Ah, now this is where the investigation becomes a little delicate. How equipped are you at handling delicate information, Mr Cavendish?"

"Extremely well equipped, I'd say. Hit me with it, Mrs Churchill."

"Are you sure, Mr Cavendish? Bear in mind this is your godmother we're talking about. I wouldn't be surprised if you feel rather uncomfortable about the whole aff—"

"I'm as ready as I'll ever be, Mrs Churchill. Come on! The suspense has got me by the throat and is beginning to throttle me."

"Well, it seems your godmother enjoyed a brief love affair with Mr Bodkin the baker."

"Did she indeed?" Mr Cavendish raised his eyebrows. "That's my gal!"

"*Gal?* This is your godmother we're discussing, Mr Cavendish."

"Was she not entitled to a love affair?"

"I suppose she was. I don't see any reason why not, other than that Mr Bodkin is a married man."

Mr Cavendish gave a lascivious laugh. "Well, well, what a pair. You seem rather disapproving of their fling, Mrs Churchill. Is a lady of advanced years not permitted to enjoy herself?"

"No, I mean yes. Of course she is permitted to do so."

"Older ladies surely have passions as strong as their younger counterparts, am I right, Mrs Churchill?" Mr Cavendish grinned.

"I wouldn't know," she replied curtly, "which is silly, really, being one of those aforementioned ladies myself."

"Do you not have passions yourself, Mrs Churchill?"

The uneasy silence was broken by Pemberley choking on her tea.

"Of course I have passions," Churchill replied boldly, staring the young man directly in the eye.

Pemberley continued to splutter.

Mr Cavendish gave Churchill an appreciative smile. "Good," he said, "and so you should. Now perhaps you understand my godmother a little better."

"I do. Perhaps a little too well, but that's important for the investigation, I suppose. Are you all right over there, Miss Pemberley? Your face resembles a strangled tomato."

Her secretary nodded.

"Look what you've done to my staff, Mr Cavendish. Poor Miss Pemberley is quite incapacitated."

"Oh dear! Please accept my apologies, Mrs Churchill.

I've been told I have that effect on ladies." He gave her a mischievous wink.

"I see." Churchill turned her attention to drinking tea.

"I may jest, but on reflection I think the baker's the guilty party. I'm sure of it, in fact." His face reddened with anger. "I shan't waste any time dashing downstairs and baking his doughy face to a crisp!"

"Please calm down, Mr Cavendish! This is all conjecture. I have merely identified three possible suspects, and there may be more to add to the list. If you're going to get this het up about it all I shall have to desist from updating you on my progress."

"Oh no, Mrs Churchill, please don't desist. I like our updates." Mr Cavendish pushed out his lower lip sulkily.

"Then behave yourself." Churchill drained her tea. "Now, young pup, I must be pressing on with something else. You're not my only client, you know."

"You're not throwing me out of here, are you, Mrs Churchill?"

"No, no, of course not, Mr Cavendish. But I do have work to be getting on with. See those filing cabinets along that wall? They're crammed full of important cases that require my attention."

"Naturally. I shan't detain you a moment longer." He stood to his feet. "And many thanks for all the hard work you've put into this investigation so far. Would another twenty pounds be suitable recompense?"

He removed his wallet from his pocket.

"Oh, Mr Cavendish, there's no… Well, yes, I suppose it would. This is a substantial investigation."

"It certainly is. And your help is invaluable."

"Thank you, Mr Cavendish."

"And thank *you*, Mrs Churchill. Adieu."

"Adieu to you."

"Adieu, Miss Pemberley," he said as he picked up his hat.

"Goodbye," she replied.

"That fellow is incorrigible, Pembers," Churchill muttered as his footsteps descended the stairs.

Chapter 20

COMPTON POPPLEFORD LIBRARY WAS A SMALL, crooked building leaning up against the town hall on the high street.

"This is a cosy little place, isn't it, Pembers?" said Churchill, glancing around at the well-stocked shelves. "I really should make more time for reading. Do you make time for reading? Actually, don't answer that; it's obvious you do given that you're a walking encyclopaedia. I suppose I'd better go and sort myself out with a reading ticket."

Churchill walked over to the librarian's desk and rang the little bell.

"Do they man this place, Pemberley? Hullo! Anybody here?"

She rang the bell again.

"That's enough!" scolded a voice from behind a book-shelf. "Did you think I hadn't noticed you walking in here?"

"That's exactly what I thought," replied Churchill,

glancing around to find out where the voice had come from. "Where are you?"

"Here."

A lady with a square face and long grey hair stepped out from behind the shelves.

"Oh, you made me jump!" Churchill's heart sank as she realised who the librarian was.

Mrs Higginbath.

Churchill smiled obsequiously as the librarian walked over to the desk and positioned herself behind it.

"Mrs Higginbath!" she began. "May I apologise once again for the small misunderstanding I had with your nephew, Mr Crumble, at Piddleton Hotel? It was such a small incident that I've practically forgotten all about it. I do hope he has done the same."

Mrs Higginbath said nothing.

Churchill turned to Pemberley in the hope she might add something to the conversation and ease the awkward atmosphere, but Pemberley was absorbed in *Ghosts of the West Country and Other Terrifying Tales*.

"I'd like to apply for a reading ticket, if I may," Churchill said.

"A reading ticket, Mrs Churchill?" replied Mrs Higginbath. "Ah yes, that's quite simple. All you need is a letter of recommendation."

"Jolly good. That sounds easy enough, then."

"I should add that the person recommending you will need to have been a resident of this parish for at least eight years."

"Excellent, well I should think Miss Pemberley would be perfectly qualified to recommend me."

"And needs to have known you personally for at least ten years."

"I'm sorry… For a moment there I thought you said ten years."

"I did."

"Really? A resident of this parish who has known me for ten years? But that's impossible! Miss Pemberley has only known me for ten days!"

Mrs Higginbath shrugged.

"This library is a valuable asset for me in my detective work," continued Churchill. "I imagine Mr Atkins had a reading ticket, didn't he?"

"He did, yes."

"Can't I just piggyback on his ticket? I bought his detective agency, didn't I?"

"'I'm afraid not, Mrs Churchill. We don't allow ticket piggybacking here."

Although Mrs Higginbath's face remained impassive, Churchill felt sure the librarian was enjoying every moment of this standoff.

She took her purse out of her handbag. "Would a shilling or two see my way?" she asked quietly.

"Are you trying to bribe me, Mrs Churchill?"

"Bribe? No!" Churchill shoved her purse back into her handbag. "You see, I'm not quite sure how things are done down here in Dorset. In London there's often a fee for these things. That's why it's such an expensive place to live. Miss Pemberley!"

Her secretary looked up from the ghoulish book.

"Help!" Churchill mouthed silently.

Pemberley sauntered up to the desk.

"Have you any bright ideas about how I can get a reading ticket for this place, Miss Pemberley?"

"You could borrow mine."

"Ah yes, there's a thought." Churchill turned back to

face Mrs Higginbath. "I shall borrow my secretary's reading ticket."

"The borrowing of reading tickets is forbidden, Mrs Churchill."

"Why doesn't that surprise me? Righty-ho, I'm bored of this conversation now. Where might I find back issues of the *Compton Poppleford Gazette*, Mrs Higginbath?"

"You're not permitted to find them, Mrs Churchill. You don't have a reading ticket."

"Let me rephrase my question. Where might *Miss Pemberley* find back issues of the *Compton Poppleford Gazette*?"

Mrs Higginbath sighed. "In the newspaper cupboard next to the fireplace."

"Right then, Pembers," said Churchill, her head buried in the newspaper cupboard. "When did all this business with the Compton Poppleford Village People Against Corruption march occur?"

"It was last autumn. November, I think."

Churchill leafed through the papers and pulled out all the relevant copies.

"Here we are," she said, laying them out on a nearby table. "Let's have a look at how the corruption allegations were reported."

As she began leafing through the newspapers she noticed Mrs Higginbath glaring at her.

"On second thoughts, Pemberley, *you* look through the newspapers seeing as you're the one with the reading ticket. I'll peer over your shoulder. We don't want to rile Medusa over there."

Half an hour later Churchill had read all she could about Mrs Trollope's mayoral bid. The Compton Poppleford Village People Against Corruption march had received only a two-sentence mention.

"Are you sure you're correct about this wayward son and money laundering business, Pemberley? Everything I've read about Mrs Trollope is complimentary; in fact, one of the editorials states that the *Compton Poppleford Gazette* is 'saddened' that she was unsuccessful in her bid. And why was so little written about the march? I think you may have your wires crossed."

"There's no doubt that Mrs Trollope's son Timothy escaped to the Bahamas with a pile of dirty money. The funds were channelled in various ways, meaning the paper trail became so confused it was lost altogether. Everyone said that profits from those same funds were used to fund Mrs Trollope's mayoral campaign."

"And you're sure about that?"

"Yes, everyone was talking about it, and it's the reason her bid was unsuccessful. Mrs Furzgate was especially vocal, as you know, and the march was the nail in the coffin for Mrs Trollope's aspirations."

"So the *Compton Poppleford Gazette* was simply selective in its reporting at the time?"

"It seems to have been."

"You think there was some sort of cover-up?"

"It seems that way, doesn't it?"

"The plot thickens, Pemberley. I think I need to speak to the editor of this newspaper and find out what he knows."

"Mr Trollope? I'm not sure how much he'll be willing to tell you."

"Did you just say the name Mr Trollope?"

"Yes."

"Any relation to Mrs Trollope?"

"Yes, he's her husband."

"You mean to tell me the editor of the *Compton Popple-ford Gazette* is married to Mrs Trollope?"

"Yes."

Churchill groaned. "Well that explains the newspaper's biased reporting of the affair!"

She folded the newspapers angrily and crammed them back into the cupboard.

"You could have told me this sooner, Pemberley, and saved us an entire morning!"

"I'm sorry, Mrs Churchill. I didn't realise exactly what you wanted to look up in the library. Perhaps if you'd—"

"Told you sooner? Yes, I take your point, Pemberley. Next time I'll explain my plans in advance so we can avoid any profligate use of time." She folded her arms and sighed. "Marvellous. So what's the next step?"

"You could try speaking to Nightwalker."

"Mr? Mrs?"

"Neither. Just Nightwalker."

"Nightwalker? That's the unfortunate individual's name?"

"Yes."

"And who is this Nightwalker?"

"A contact of Mr Atkins'. He's some sort of investigative journalist."

Churchill felt a smile spread across her face. "Excellent! An investigative journalist is just what we need. This Nightwalker fellow presumably knows all about Mrs Trollope and the dodgy money."

"I'm sure he does."

"Perfect. Let's get straight back to the office and telephone him."

"Oh no, you can't do that."

"Why not?" Churchill hissed exasperatedly. "Isn't that what Atkins did?"

"No. To contact Nightwalker you must place an enigmatic message in the classified section of the *Compton Poppleford Gazette*."

Churchill groaned again. "Why is everything as difficult as swimming through mud?"

"It's not so very difficult, Mrs Churchill. I placed several messages for Nightwalker on behalf of Mr Atkins."

"Did you, Pembers? Oh good. Then let's go and do it now before my patience leaves me completely and ends up on the next train back to London."

Chapter 21

"HELLO, pussy cat! Why don't you show Auntie Churchy where you fetch your extra meals from?"

Zeppelin did nothing but stare back at Churchill from beneath the hydrangea in Mr Greenstone's garden.

Churchill popped a butter toffee into her mouth and wondered when she would hear from the mysterious Nightwalker. Pemberley's obscure message had been printed in the classified section of the *Compton Poppleford Gazette* the previous day.

Will Lady who took wrong umbrella from Butcher's Shop, Tuesday afternoon, kindly return?

Pemberley had assured a sceptical Churchill that this was the message that had been agreed between Atkins and Nightwalker, and that she had used it successfully on many occasions.

Zeppelin began to lick his right shoulder.

"You're looking rather too comfortable there, puss," said Churchill with the toffee still in her mouth. "That's the sort of cleaning a cat does when he's preparing himself for an afternoon nap."

She watched Zeppelin for a while longer, then sighed as he curled himself into a ball and went to sleep.

"Mrs Churchill?"

She turned to see a lady wearing a large summer hat.

"Hello, Mrs Trollope! What a pleasant surprise!"

"What are you doing on Greenstone's lawn?"

Churchill was taken aback by the sharpness of the comment and the hostile glint in the old lady's eyes.

"Watching his cat, Mrs Trollope."

"Greenstone knows you're here, does he?"

"If you're wondering whether I have his permission to stand on this lawn, then yes, I do. I'm currently conducting an investigation on his behalf."

"That's all right, then. Just thought I'd check." Mrs Trollope sucked on her silver cigarette holder and blew a plume of smoke in Churchill's direction. "I hear you've been visiting the library."

"You heard correctly, Mrs Trollope. I'm not sure it's a particularly interesting topic of conversation, though. Surely something more exciting than that must have occurred in Compton Poppleford since we last met."

"If only it had, Mrs Churchill. You took a keen interest in some back issues of the *Compton Poppleford Gazette*, I hear."

"Goodness! Next time I have something to broadcast to the village I'll ensure that Mrs Higginbath knows about it first. Yes, Mrs Trollope, I perused some copies of your husband's fine publication. Would you like a butter toffee?"

"No, thank you. May I ask what you were researching, Mrs Churchill?"

"You may ask, but please don't take offence at my refusal to answer your question, Mrs Trollope. It was part of my investigative work, you see, and I must respect my client's confidentiality."

"Mrs Higginbath told me there was some discussion between Miss Pemberley and yourself about the Compton Poppleford Village People Against Corruption march."

"Mrs Higginbath has the ears of a cocker spaniel, doesn't she? I'm afraid I'm unable to comment any further, Mrs Trollope."

Churchill turned away, fixed her eyes on the sleeping cat and hoped Mrs Trollope would grow bored and saunter away.

"Mrs Furzgate tried to discredit me, that's for sure," continued Mrs Trollope, "but if you think that gives me a motive for having her murdered you are sorely mistaken."

Churchill spun round in mock surprise. "*Murder*, Mrs Trollope? *Motive?* Whoever suggested such a thing? I fear you have put two and two together and made five. Forget five; fifty-five! Scratch that; five hundred and fifty-five!"

"Good, well I certainly hope that's the case. Suspecting I had anything to do with Mrs Furzgate's death would be little more than tomfoolery, wouldn't it, Mrs Churchill?"

"It would indeed, Mrs Trollope. I can't understand why anyone would even begin to consider it. It's a daft idea. Preposterous. Farcical!"

"Indeed it is. Well, it's reassuring that we're singing from the same songsheet, Mrs Churchill."

"We are, Mrs Trollope. And what a tuneful song it is."

"Good," replied Mrs Trollope. "Let's ensure that it doesn't become discordant."

. . .

"Curse Mrs Trollope!" fumed Churchill as she returned to the office with a large box of custard tarts.

"Oh dear," replied Pemberley. "What's she done now?"

"Seen right through my investigation, that's what! She knows that I suspect her. You haven't spoken to her, have you?"

"No, not since we played bridge with her the other day."

"Are you sure, Pemberley? This isn't one of those moments where it transpires that you did speak to her and tell her everything about the investigation after all?"

"Quite sure, Mrs Churchill. Why would I do that?" Pemberley asked, her brow crumpled.

"Very well. Please don't take offence, my trusty assistant. It simply means that Mrs Trollope is good at deducing things. And can you believe that Mrs Higginbath reported every detail of our library visit to her? She even knew which articles we'd been looking at!"

"You do have a rather loud voice, Mrs Churchill."

"Meaning?"

"Meaning that Mrs Higginbath could hear every word you said. Sometimes a little discretion is required."

"I can assure you that I am extremely discreet, Pembers!"

"I'm talking about *quiet* discretion. The sort of whispered discretion people can't overhear in libraries."

"Point taken, Pembers. I'm aware that subtlety isn't always my strong point."

"I think we need to create our own code language, which only you and I understand."

"Not a bad idea, Pemberley, albeit a rather time-consuming one. I'll just whisper when needs be and hopefully that will suffice. Would you like a tart?"

Pemberley took one and Churchill followed suit.

"What colour is your pullover, Pembers? I can't decide between mustard and butterscotch."

"Cream."

"Cream? What nonsense. It's undoubtedly a shade of yellow."

"That's because I accidentally washed it with a brown skirt. Anyway, let's forget about that. Nightwalker will be at the Pig and Scythe pub at eight o'clock this evening."

"You've heard from him? How wonderful! Thank you, Pembers. Would you like to accompany me? I'll need your help in identifying the man."

"I have no idea what he looks like."

"You've never met him? Oh, I see. Well perhaps you can accompany me anyway, seeing that I don't know where the Pig and Scythe is."

"You won't find me setting foot in that place."

"Why not, Pembers?"

"It's full of rustic types."

"Oh, come now. The great unwashed are quite harmless."

"I'm not so sure about that. You'd better be careful in there."

"Don't you go worrying about me, Pembers. The club-house at the Richmond-upon-Thames Ladies' Lawn Tennis Club can also be a nest of vipers, but I have lived to tell the tale."

Chapter 22

SITUATED next to the village's abattoir, The Pig and Scythe was a beamed building with mullioned windows. Churchill pocketed the map Pemberley had drawn her and ducked her head as she stepped in through the low-slung door.

The dingy bar fell silent as she entered. She felt sawdust beneath her feet, and an odour of stale hops and urine hung in the air. Each face she glanced at was sunken and lined, and every cap and jacket was coated in a layer of grime.

She forced a bright smile and walked toward the bar, where a wizened man with an eye patch had just spat onto a tankard and was polishing it with a filthy cloth.

"Good evening!" she said brightly before leaning forward to whisper the code words to the barman in the discreet tone Pemberley had advised. "I hear the express left Wimborne Minster fifteen minutes late."

The barman raised an eyebrow, then moved his one visible eye to the extreme left, indicating the direction in which Nightwalker sat.

"Marvellous," replied Churchill. "I'll take a drink with me, if I may. A glass of Richebourg Grand Cru, please. Twenty-three if you have it."

"Scrumpy?" replied the barman.

"Is that all you have?"

"Yep."

"I suppose a glass of that will do instead." Churchill grinned self-consciously, wondering when the locals around her would resume their conversations.

Carrying her greasy tankard, Churchill walked between the tables in the direction of the barman's indicative gaze. Her bosom attracted stares from all angles, and she realised she was the only woman in the entire establishment. Churchill deduced that most of the men present were labourers or members of the criminal class. But somewhere there had to be an investigative journalist. She hoped his appearance would make his identity obvious.

Slumped in the corner of the room was a man with a loosened tie and a shabby felt hat tipped over his face. He appeared to be asleep, but she assumed this was a clever ruse.

Churchill perched herself on the rickety wooden stool across the table from him and felt relieved to hear the background chatter start up again.

"Nightwalker?" she whispered.

There was no reply. *Perhaps he is actually asleep*, she thought to herself. Not daring to say his name again, Churchill rummaged in her handbag for something she could prod him with. She happened upon a crochet needle and used it to give him a gentle poke in the chest.

The effect was immediate.

"Orff!" yelped the man, springing up from his position and clasping his ribs. His hat fell from his head and he emitted a string of curse words, which Churchill surmised were Anglo-Saxon in origin.

The pub fell silent again and the man examined his shirt as if he expected to find blood.

"Did you just… *stab me?*"

He was about forty with a heavy brow, sharp blue eyes and rough stubble on his chin.

"No, I merely gave you a soft prod with this," said Churchill, holding up the crochet hook.

"Is that so? In that case I hope I'm never on the end of a hard prod," retorted the man, retrieving his hat from beneath the table and pulling it back onto his head.

"I believe you were expecting me," said Churchill. "I'm the detective who bought Atkins' business."

"Yes, I was expecting you," he replied, wincing as he rubbed at his ribs.

"So it's safe for me to assume you are—"

"Don't say the name!" he interrupted.

Churchill smiled knowingly. She was beginning to enjoy this clandestine meeting. It made her feel as though she were a proper private detective.

"What can you tell me about Trollope?" she asked. She lifted her tankard to take a sip of scrumpy but paused when she noticed unidentifiable flakes floating about in it.

"Mr or Mrs?"

"The latter. Actually, let's begin with the son."

"Nasty piece of work, Timothy Mervyn Trollope. About twenty-eight years of age now, thirty tops. Educated at Harrow. Dropped out of Sandhurst."

"Dropped out? Oh dear."

"Kid took a job with Hobart and Hampden in the City of London."

"Ah yes, the bank."

Nightwalker nodded. "Summarily dismissed two years later for embezzlement."

"Was he imprisoned for the offence?"

Nightwalker shrugged. "Should've been, but word is he had some dirt on the chairman."

"Goodness! I wonder what the dirt was."

"Got into customs after that."

"Working for the government?"

"Yeah, until he started taking backhanders off his old friends in the City."

"Young Timothy Trollope sounds like quite a sort. Would you excuse me for a moment while I go and exchange my drink? It's got things floating in it."

Nightwalker leaned forward and peered into her tankard.

"Supposed to be like that."

"These bits are intentional?"

"Never had scrumpy before?"

"No, I can't say I have. I'm from London. Originally the home counties. Do you think these bits are pieces of apple?"

"Guess so." Nightwalker pulled a pouch of tobacco from his jacket pocket. Churchill took a tentative sip and discovered that scrumpy tasted far better than it looked.

"I hear young Timothy moved to the Bahamas," she said.

"Yeah, the kid accumulated so much grubby cash he didn't know what to do with it. A friend from his Harrow days got him set up with a shell company in Nassau." Nightwalker sprinkled a neat line of tobacco into a cigarette paper and began rolling it.

"And Timothy's dodgy money funded his mother's mayoral campaign."

Nightwalker nodded. "That's what they say. Folks got

suspicious when they saw the size of her campaign team. And she didn't just rent an office; she hired out an entire building. Her hospitality bill must have been through the roof. Seems every businessman from here to Blandford Forum was wined and dined."

"She must have spent a lot of money on the campaign."

Nightwalker nodded again. "This is Compton Popple-ford we're talking about. You can't get showy round here or people start gassing."

"Is it possible that Mrs Trollope used her own money? Or her husband's, perhaps?"

Nightwalker lit his spindly cigarette and puffed out a cloud of smoke.

"Not a chance. She was the daughter of a teacher; there was no wedge in that family. And you don't get too much dough as the editor of a small-town newspaper neither. Whatever money they had they spent on the kid's education. Whole lotta good that did him."

"I've always considered Harrow to be overrated. I'm assuming the large house the Trollopes own was also bought with the son's ill-gotten gains."

"Most likely," replied Nightwalker. "Furzgate put paid to Trollope's mayoral plans, though, didn't she? The local busybody done good."

"Do you think she paid for it with her life?"

"Might have done."

"Mrs Furzgate's godson thinks she was murdered and has asked me to investigate."

"Cavendish?"

"The very man."

"Watch you don't go upsetting no one."

Churchill laughed. "It's too late for that, Mr Night-walker! I've already upset plenty of people, I'm afraid."

He grimaced and sucked hard on his crooked cigarette.

"Tread carefully, Mrs Churchill. You don't want to be going the way of Furzgate."

"Does Mr Trollope publish any of your articles in the *Compton Poppleford Gazette*?"

Nightwalker gave an empty laugh. "No chance of that. My work's too close to the truth for the likes of him. The *CP Gazette* ain't a newspaper, lady. It's a propaganda machine."

"So I'm beginning to discover. Who'd have thought such skulduggery existed in a little old place like Compton Poppleford?"

"The little old places are the worst, Mrs Churchill, that's why I'm here." He grinned for the first time, revealing a crooked row of tobacco-stained teeth. "Crooks come to villages like this thinking they can hide from the big wide world. Take Smallbone, for instance."

"Mr Smallbone who runs the bric-a-brac shop?"

Nightwalker nodded. "Not many folks know this, but he was detained for ten years at Her Majesty's Pleasure."

"Whatever for?"

"Murdering his business partner."

"Smallbone *murdered* someone?"

"It was some years back, and the partner was as bent as a two-bob note. Ask Smallbone about the missing years and he'll tell you he was working at his uncle's whisky distillery on the Isle of Bute. But some of us know better."

"And to think I bought a vase from that man! Not to mention the desk!"

"He's served his time. I'd say he was a reformed character if he wasn't passing off junk as priceless antiques."

"That's exactly what Mrs Furzgate accused him of!"

"She was no fool, that woman."

"It seems not, though it's a shame she acted like one.

Who do you think might have been behind her murder? Mrs Trollope? Or Mr Smallbone?"

"No idea. I'll leave that for you to find out. You're the detective, Mrs Churchill."

"Is there anything you can tell me about Bodkin the baker? I hear he had a love affair with Furzgate."

"One word. *Ruthless*. Ask yourself why he owns the only bakery in the village."

"Why does he own the only bakery in the village?"

"Ask yourself that question." He squashed the stub of his cigarette into the ashtray.

"I could ask, but I don't know the answer yet."

"You'll find out, Mrs Churchill." He handed her a folded slip of paper. "Don't read this till you need to speak to me again."

"What is it?"

"The code you'll need for our next meeting, should you ever need one."

"We're finished already?"

"I never stay too long in one place, Mrs Churchill. Good luck. And mind what you do with that crochet hook!"

Chapter 23

"I'M EXTREMELY pleased with our incident board now, Pembers." Churchill stood in the centre of the office to admire it. "I like all the pins and lengths of string we've added; it looks pleasingly elaborate. That's a flattering picture of Mrs Trollope. Where on earth did you find it?"

"I cut it out from her advice column."

"She has an advice column? Don't tell me... in the *Compton Poppleford Gazette*?"

"Yes. It's called 'Ask Mrs Trollope'."

"Of course it is. And what sort of advice does she dish out?"

"General housekeeping advice. How to clean silver and when to treat the dog for fleas; that sort of thing."

"Invaluable, no doubt."

"Oh, it is. I've picked up some very useful tips from it."

"I was being sarcastic, Pemberley. Does our moustachioed bric-a-brac friend over the road ever talk about a stint at his uncle's whisky distillery on the Isle of Bute?"

"He does! Says they were the best ten years of his life."

"Does he really? It seems the man is an accomplished liar."

"Really? How so?"

"He was in prison, Pembers."

"*Prison?*"

"That's what Mr Nightwalker told me."

"It's just *Nightwalker*, Mrs Churchill; it's a code name. You don't need to say the Mr."

"Well this night-walking chap told me Smallbone murdered his business partner and served a ten year sentence for it."

"Good grief! He never mentioned that!"

"He's not going to, is he, Pembers?"

"I thought I knew this village so well, but it seems as though everyone has dark secrets."

"It seems so."

"Oh, while I remember, some post has arrived for you, Mrs Churchill." Pemberley rummaged through the clutter on her desk to find it.

"Some post for me? I do believe this is the first piece of official post sent to me since I became a private detective, Pemberley."

"It's quite a moment, isn't it? Here it is." Pemberley held out the envelope. "The first piece of official post for Churchill's Detective Agency." She smiled proudly.

"You can go ahead and open it, Pembers."

"Can I?"

"Of course you can. You're my secretary, and before long I shall be receiving so much post I'll need you to open it for me. Didn't you open Atkins' post?"

"Yes I did."

"There you go, then. You may open my post too. There are no secrets between us, Pemberley."

"Thank you, Mrs Churchill."

Pemberley eagerly ripped open the envelope and pulled out a letter.

"Oh, it's one of those," she said as she read it.

"One of what?"

"One of those letters where someone's cut out each letter from a newspaper and stuck them onto the page to form words."

"How terribly laborious. Why've they done that?"

"To remain anonymous."

"It's an anonymous letter, Pemberley? A tip-off, perhaps? Let me see it."

Churchill snatched the letter from her secretary's hands.

Dear Mrs Churchill

It was me what pooshed Mrs Furzgate down the stairs.
Mr Bodkin

"Good grief, Pemberley!" The letter trembled in Churchill's hand as she read it. "This is more than a tip-off; it's a confession! Mr Bodkin claims to have murdered Mrs Furzgate!"

"It must have taken him ages to cut out all those letters," said Pemberley. "Why did he bother when he could have just written the letter himself?"

"He obviously wanted to disguise his handwriting."

"But why? He's put his name on it."

"You're right, Pembers. Perhaps he did so out of habit."

"If he'd wanted to remain anonymous he wouldn't have done it. He would have just put 'Anonymous' or something like that."

"Perhaps he couldn't spell anonymous," suggested Churchill. "His spelling isn't exactly top notch, is it?"

"But that wouldn't be a reason to include his name, would it? If he couldn't spell anonymous he could have put 'Anon'."

"Perhaps he's wishing he had now."

"There's something not quite right about that letter."

"Well, there's only one thing for it. We'll just pop downstairs and ask him about it."

"No! You can't do that!" said Pemberley.

"Why not? The man works just beneath our feet. In fact, I don't know why he went to such great lengths in paying postage for this letter. He could have just pushed it under the door. Perhaps he can explain that as well."

"No, Mrs Churchill, the man has admitted to committing a criminal act. You must involve the police!"

"Inspector Mappin? Over my dead body!"

"I'm sorry, Mrs Churchill, but you must. The letter you hold in your hand is legal evidence."

"But this is my investigation, Pembers. I'm not handing it over to some lazy policeman who hasn't done an ounce of work on this case and will take all the credit for it!"

"It's what Mr Atkins would have done, Mrs Churchill."

"Would he indeed?"

"Yes, and he was extremely professional."

"Well, professionalism is a common trait among us private detectives. We're certainly much more professional than the police force."

"So you'll show Inspector Mappin the letter?"

"Well, I suppose it is legal evidence, Pembers. I'd better take it down to the police station."

. . .

"Hmm, interesting," said Inspector Mappin as he examined the letter from Mr Bodkin. His shiny walnut desk was positioned beneath a poster offering a three-pound reward for a stolen plough. The poster next to it was a reminder for people to cover their mouths and noses while sneezing.

"Envelope?" He held out his hand.

"Envelope *please*," corrected Churchill as she reluctantly handed it to him.

"Hmm."

"Well?" asked Churchill impatiently.

"I wondered if I would recognise the handwriting on this envelope, but I don't think I do."

"It's Mr Bodkin's, Inspector. He signed his name in the letter."

"If Bodkin wrote this," said Inspector Mappin, "why is there no flour on the letter or the envelope? Have you been to his bakery? There's flour everywhere."

"I can vouch for that, Inspector. Perhaps he wrote it at his home."

"Have you been there? His house is also covered in flour."

"Do you suspect that Mr Bodkin isn't the author of this letter, Inspector?"

"I can't say either way, but it's important that we keep an open mind."

"Absolutely. That's what I always say."

"There's only one thing for it, and that's to put it to the chap himself. Thank you for bringing this to my attention, Mrs Churchill. Leave it with me."

"Leave it with you, Inspector? But the letter was addressed to *me*."

"It's a confession to a crime, Mrs Churchill. I will take it from here."

"But you'll require my assistance, Inspector Mappin."

"No, I shouldn't think so."

"You can't just push me off my own case!"

"I'm not pushing you off anything, Mrs Churchill, tempting though that may be."

"What did you just say?"

"I shall keep you informed, Mrs Churchill."

"That wasn't what you just said. It was about pushing me off something."

"It was you who said that. Goodbye, Mrs Churchill. I need to bicycle over to Bodkin's and have a word. Having confessed to the crime, he may be considering his escape and I'd like to catch him before he gets away."

Inspector Mappin got to his feet and put on his hat.

"Very well, Inspector, but you'd better keep me informed. Or else."

"Or else what, Mrs Churchill?"

"I'll think of something."

Chapter 24

A SHORT WHILE later Churchill arrived back at her office, gasping for breath.

"Is his?" She couldn't finish her sentence, having to keep her mouth open in order to get as much air as possible into her lungs.

"What's happened, Mrs Churchill?" Pemberley leapt up from her chair, her eyes wide with concern.

Churchill held up a hand as a signal for her to wait. She had never been so exhausted in her entire life.

"Inspector Mappin," she said quickly before taking in another big gulp of air.

"What has he done to you, Mrs Churchill?"

"Nothing. Is his bicycle?"

"Are you having a heart attack? Shall I fetch Doctor Norris?"

Churchill shook her head. "His bicycle. Is it outside?"

Pemberley peered out of the window.

"No."

"Lemme know when it's there."

Churchill collapsed onto her chair and tried to slow her

breathing. Still unable to close her mouth, her heart was pounding in her head.

"I took a shortcut," she explained to Pemberley between gasps. "He told me he would speak to Bodkin, so I ran through the park. I beat him!"

"Well done Mrs Churchill, but at what cost? I'd better make you a restorative cup of tea."

"While I remember, Pembers," puffed Churchill. "Can you visit the library for me," she paused to get her breath, "and borrow all the books you can find about the Isle of Bute?"

"Of course." Pemberley got up from her desk, looking out of the window as she did so. "Oh, Mappin's here now. He's just leant his bike up against the lamppost."

Churchill staggered to her feet and felt a dizzying rush to her head. "I need to get down there."

"I think you need to rest, Mrs Churchill. You look very unsteady on your feet."

"No, no. I must be there when he speaks to Bodkin. It's my case, Pembers. I'm not letting him steal it!"

Churchill lurched out of the door and stumbled down the stairs. She burst through the door of the bakery to find Inspector Mappin standing at the counter. Mr Bodkin stood behind it with a concerned expression on his face.

"Mrs Churchill!" exclaimed Mappin. "How did you get here so fast? You were at the station just fifteen minutes ago."

"I can move surprisingly quickly when I need to, Inspector." Her mouth opened and closed like a gasping fish, and the police officer gave her a bemused look.

"I'm afraid Bodkin's not available to serve customers at the present time. I need to have a word with him, and I don't think you need me to explain the matter it concerns." He gave her a surreptitious wink.

"What do you need to speak to me about, Inspector Mappin?" asked the baker.

"I'll explain in just a moment, Mr Bodkin. I'm waiting for this customer to leave the premises."

"Well, I shan't," retorted Mrs Churchill. "I wish to buy some jam tarts."

"Mr Bodkin will fulfil your request once I have finished speaking to him."

"But how will he do that? Aren't you here to arrest him?"

"*Arrest me?!*" exclaimed Mr Bodkin. "What on earth for?"

The police inspector sighed. "Mrs Churchill, I'd appreciate it if you kept your mouth shut on this matter."

"What am I being arrested for?" the baker asked again. "Tell me what's happening here, Inspector!"

"Let me explain out the back," replied the inspector. "We can have a quiet word without any interruptions."

"I'm not going out the back with you if you're going to arrest me."

"Have I made any indication that I'm about to arrest you, Mr Bodkin?"

"No, but *she* has." The baker pointed at Mrs Churchill.

"And what authority can Mrs Churchill possibly have on the matter?" Inspector Mappin replied. He turned aside to Churchill. "Do you see now what happens when you meddle? My work here has been complicated no end by your presence."

"I just came in for some jam tarts, Inspector."

"Mr Bodkin," said Inspector Mappin. "Perhaps your assistant can see to Mrs Churchill's jam tarts while we talk out the back?"

"But are you planning to arrest me, Inspector?"

"I would like to speak to you about a matter that has

been brought to my attention. Let's put a stop to all this dilly-dallying and get on with it."

"But—"

"NOW!" barked Inspector Mappin so loudly that Churchill felt her feet briefly leave the floor.

Mr Bodkin sulkily called out for Bodger, who sauntered in with a cigarette in his mouth. The baker instructed his assistant to serve Mrs Churchill her jam tarts, then he and Inspector Mappin stepped into the room at the back of the shop, closing the door behind them.

"How many tarts d'you want?" asked Bodger.

Churchill lowered her voice to a whisper. "If I give you a shilling will you allow me to step behind the counter and listen at that door?"

The youth stared back at Churchill.

"Five," he replied.

"*Five shillings?* What impudence!"

"Five or no listening at the door."

Churchill scowled at the youth as she pulled her purse out of her handbag and handed him five shilling coins. "I hope you feel proud of yourself robbing an old widow."

Bodger gestured toward the door to indicate that she could take up her position there.

"And six jam tarts please," she said, hurrying to the other side of the counter.

Pressing her ear to the door, Churchill could just about hear the voices of Inspector Mappin and Mr Bodkin.

"Is this someone's idea of a joke?" said Bodkin.

"You tell me," replied the inspector.

"You don't need me to tell you anything! A seasoned police officer like yourself should immediately recognise this letter as a prank."

"Where were you on the second of July, Mr Bodkin?"

"Are you asking me where I was when Mrs Furzgate

died? How preposterous! I've already had Mrs Roly-Poly from upstairs here asking me questions about her."

Churchill pursed her lips.

"What questions?" asked Inspector Mappin.

"Just general nosiness; you know what she's like. I don't understand why people keep asking me about that Furzgate woman."

"Because of your love affair, perhaps."

Bodkin groaned. "Why does everyone keep mentioning that? And I take objection to the description *love affair*. It was nothing more than a brief dalliance."

"But where were you when Mrs Furzgate fell down the stairs at Piddleton Hotel?"

"I was here, Inspector! Where else would I have been?"

"And the lanky youth who works here, what's his name?"

"Bodger."

"Bodger can vouch for the fact that you were here, can he?"

"Probably not. He can't remember what he had for breakfast most days."

"Is there anyone else who could provide an alibi?"

"All my regular customers."

"And who are they, exactly?"

"I don't keep a list, Inspector! Just ask around the village. Why am I having to tell you how to do your job?"

Churchill smiled at this comment.

"So you deny that you wrote this letter."

"Of course! I've been framed, and by someone who can't spell at that. At least I know how to write my words properly."

"That's your defence? Your spelling capability?"

"Yes."

"May I visit your home and have a look round?"

"And look for what?"

"Newspapers with letters cut out of them; that sort of thing."

"Inspector, has it occurred to you that if I'd gone to the trouble of cutting out individual letters from a newspaper and gluing them onto a piece of paper, I'd also have gone to the trouble of disposing of my source of letters? I'm offended that you think I'd be so empty-headed as to leave cut up newspapers lying about."

"Mr Bodkin, you can see my dilemma here, can't you? I've been presented with this letter, which may or may not have been created by you, and I need to follow it up. Will you permit me to look around your home?"

"If you must. But you'll have to get past the wife first. I really don't understand this, Inspector. I thought Mrs Furzgate's death was an accident. No one even considered foul play until that dumpy busybody from London started nosing around."

"I have to follow up this letter, Mr Bodkin. You may wish to remember my loyalty during the Greenstone affair."

"Meaning?"

"Sooner or later someone is going to request the truth."

"Are you trying to blackmail me, Inspector?"

"No, I'm merely asking for your co-operation in this matter."

"We've known each other for many years and I appreciate your discretion with that whole Greenstone business. But do you honestly think I could have sent a cack-handed letter such as the one you hold in your hand?"

There was a pause.

"No, I don't," replied Inspector Mappin.

"Good."

"Unless it's a bluff."

"What do you mean?"

"This letter is so unlike something you'd send that perhaps you did send it hoping everyone would assume you didn't when actually you did."

"That's not a bluff, it's a double bluff."

"Are you sure? I'd just call it a bluff."

"Either way, Inspector, I didn't send it. You're welcome to visit my wife and attempt to search my home, but you'll be lucky if you get past the front door. I need to get back to my work now. Hopefully Bodger's served Mrs Roly-Poly with her jam tarts and she's long gone."

Churchill heard footsteps approaching the door and darted over to the other side of the counter as quickly as she could before it opened.

Inspector Mappin emerged, covered in a light dusting of flour.

"You still here, Mrs Churchill?" he asked.

She peered intently at the coconut macaroons. "Sorry, did you say something, Inspector?"

"I asked if you were still here."

"No I'm not. Does that answer your question?"

Inspector Mappin gave a large sigh.

Chapter 25

"EVEN STOUT WALKING shoes aren't up to the task when you need to run somewhere," said Churchill, removing her shoes and wiggling her sore toes. "What do you know about the Greenstone affair, Pemberley?"

Pemberley paused at her typewriter. "The Greenstone affair? I can't say I know anything about it."

"Might it have something to do with our client, Mr Greenstone?"

"Possibly. Where did you hear about it?"

"While I was earwigging on Inspector Mappin and Mr Bodkin, Mappin mentioned that he'd given Bodkin his loyalty during the Greenstone affair."

Pemberley thought about this for a moment. "Well, Mr Greenstone used to own a bakery, but he had to close it down due to all the complaints."

"Complaints about what?"

"The quality of his offerings. I didn't really understand it because I visited his bakery a number of times over the years and I was more than happy with his goods. In fact, they were often better than Bodkin's. But many customers were clearly unhappy because the affair warranted a two-page spread in the *Compton Poppleford Gazette*. Greenstone never recovered from that."

Churchill bit slowly into a jam tart as she thought about this.

"Mr Nightwalker told me Bodkin was ruthless, and he told me to ask myself why he was the only baker in Compton Poppleford. Now I'm beginning to understand."

"You don't think that—"

"Bodkin was behind the closure of Greenstone's bakery? Yes, I do. And given that the editor of the *Compton Poppleford Gazette*, Mr Trollope, is a man of dubious moral character I don't doubt that he was financially recompensed by Bodkin for printing those slurs."

"But that's terrible!" exclaimed Pemberley. "Poor Mr Greenstone!"

"Poor Mr Greenstone indeed. Mr Nightwalker was right on another matter, too. He said the little old places like Compton Poppleford are the worst. And to think that Mappin, an officer of the law, knew about it and kept his mouth shut. Tut, tut, tut."

"Well, Bodkin will get his comeuppance now that he's been arrested for Mrs Furzgate's murder."

"Only he hasn't, Pemberley. The man is still as free as a bird. Bodkin claims he's been framed and Mappin is carrying out some further investigations. There's something not quite right about the whole affair. I feel certain there's some mutual back-scratching going on here, Pembers. It has a whiff of the old boys' network."

"I suppose the old girls' network would be Mrs Trollope and her bridge ladies."

"Yes, I think you're right there."

Pemberley sighed. "I've always wanted to be a member of a network."

"You can be a member of something with me, Pembers!"

"Such as what?"

"A sleuthing network, just you and me. How does that sound?"

"It sounds very good, Mrs Churchill. I like it!" Pemberley raised her jam tart as a toast.

"Bodkin claims he's being framed for Mrs Furzgate's murder," said Churchill. "Perhaps Mr Greenstone is the real culprit."

"That would be fairly unlikely unless he knew that Bodkin was behind the campaign to close his bakery down."

"There's only one way to find out, isn't there?" replied Churchill, putting on her shoes. "Let's go and ask him."

"Zeppelin used to be so loyal," sniffed Mr Greenstone as he slumped in his armchair nursing a cup of tea. "I often think of our time together and try to identify the moment when it began to go wrong, but I just don't think I can. It was such a gradual change that it was barely noticeable."

"Indeed," said Churchill impatiently. "You'll be pleased to hear that we've managed to narrow down our list of suspects to this street, the neighbouring one and the row of houses on the other side of the duck pond."

"That's still quite a number of suspects," he replied sadly.

"Inspector Mappin and his wife have been ruled out," Churchill said.

"I knew they would be; Inspector Mappin's wife hates cats. How much longer will it be before you have the case solved, Mrs Churchill?"

"Oh, not long now, Mr Greenstone. Most likely within the next few weeks or month. Perhaps two months if the case develops a complication."

"What sort of complication?"

"A complication like Zeppelin just sitting under the hydrangea and not moving. I spent two hours watching him earlier this week and he didn't move once."

"He does that sometimes."

"He does indeed. And that's a complication, you see, because how on earth can I find out who's feeding him if he doesn't lead me to them?"

"Perhaps you could ask him nicely to take you there," suggested Pemberley.

"Thank you for your contribution, Miss Pemberley. Now then, Mr Greenstone, I hear you used to run a bakery."

"Yes, I did."

"How wonderful. Bakeries really are my favourite type of shop."

"They were mine once, too."

"Oh dear. What happened?"

"I had to close down."

"That's a terrible shame, Mr Greenstone. Was there a specific reason for that unfortunate turn of events?"

"The customers stopped coming."

"Oh no, that really is a shame. Did any of them give any indication as to why they had stopped visiting your bakery?"

"Not really, no."

"Oh. Did something happen that forced their hand?"

"A lady called Mrs Murgatoss-Bynes claimed she was poisoned by my fruit scones."

"That sounds like a preposterous claim. She's one of Mrs Trollope's friends, isn't she?"

"I believe so."

"Yes, I've met her. I know the type. She was expecting a refund, was she?"

"Not particularly, no. I don't really know what she was expecting. But she made quite a song and dance about it, and then told her story to the local newspaper."

"Sounds like she made quite the tempest in a teapot about the whole affair! Fancy doing such a thing, eh, Miss Pemberley?"

Her secretary nodded in agreement.

"You'd have thought the editor of the *Gazette* would have thought twice about publishing a story so lacking in newsworthiness," added Churchill.

"You would, wouldn't you?" Mr Greenstone turned his sad gaze on her. "But I don't think he gave the impact on my business much thought."

"Oh, come now, Mr Greenstone! I do believe this is Mr Trollope we're talking about. He knows full well that printing such a damning article about a local business would put its customers off. If you ask me, Mr Trollope knew exactly what he was doing!"

"Then why did he print it?"

"Your guess is as good as mine, Mr Greenstone. However, this story does make me wonder what the other baker in town, Mr Bodkin, made of you having to close down."

"Oh, he was grinning like a Cheshire cat for weeks."

"I bet he was!"

"I detest the man."

"I don't doubt that you do, Mr Greenstone."

"We were both apprenticed to old Mr Wallop. He was a fine baker. Bodkin always resented the way my buns rose higher than his."

"He should have worked harder at his craft rather than

wasting his time harbouring resentment. I really can't abide people like that."

"Yet he's the one with the monopoly on baked goods in this village, Mrs Churchill, and I'm not."

"Through no fault of your own, Mr Greenstone! You were badly wronged."

"I'm pleased to hear you say that, because I've often thought the same thing."

"Have you ever felt vengeful about it?"

"What do you mean?"

"Have you ever been tempted to exact your revenge on the people who brought you down?"

"Oh, yes."

"Really?"

"Yes. I've attempted to take my revenge in the past."

"How so? Sending the odd poison pen letter, maybe?"

"Oh no. But I did push a lighted rag through the letterbox of the *Compton Poppleford Gazette*'s offices."

Churchill gasped. "You committed an act of *arson*, Mr Greenstone?"

"Yes."

"And what happened?"

"It sort of fizzled out on the doormat. I didn't put enough paraffin on it."

"Did you try anything else?"

"No. The lighted rag satiated my need for vengeance in the end. I don't suppose they really noticed it when they arrived for work the following morning."

"I see. So you didn't send a poison pen letter?"

"No. I don't really have a way with words. And my spelling's not very good, either."

"I see. I'm enjoying our little chat here this afternoon, Mr Greenstone. I find it helps a great deal to get to know one's clients a little better. One of my other clients is Mr Cavendish, godson of the dearly departed Mrs Furzgate."

Mr Greenstone seemed disinterested and focused on sipping his tea.

"Did you know Mrs Furzgate at all, Mr Greenstone?"

"Everybody knew her," he replied after a pause. "In fact, she left you with no choice in the matter. She had an ability to thrust herself hook, line and sinker into people's lives."

"Mr Cavendish believes her death was not an accident," Churchill ventured, hoping this might be enough to encourage Mr Greenstone to admit that he was behind the letter sent to frame Mr Bodkin. "Mr Cavendish believes she was murdered."

"Does he?" replied Greenstone. "Well that doesn't surprise me. She was rather irritating."

"If Mr Cavendish is correct there are a number of possible suspects. Mr Bodkin for instance." Churchill stared at Mr Greenstone intently to gauge his reaction, but there was none. "And Mr Smallbone. And the Trollopes."

"Ah, Mr and Mrs Trollope," he piped up. "They're probably behind it somehow."

"Do you think so Mr Greenstone? Have you any evidence to suggest they may have been involved?"

He shook his head. "No, although my niece once did some secretarial work at the *Compton Poppleford Gazette* and there are a lot of secrets in that place, let me tell you."

"Such as?"

"I don't know. Secrets are secret, aren't they? But Veronica, that's my niece, told me that Mr Trollope is sitting on a big stack of them."

"Is he really?" said Pemberley. "That must be jolly uncomfortable."

"I should like to meet with Mr Trollope," said Churchill.

"Oh, I wouldn't bother," said Pemberley. "He's not a nice man at all."

"No, he's not," agreed Mr Greenstone.

"I see. Well perhaps there's another way of finding out what he knows. I feel a plan formulating, Pembers."

"What about Zeppelin?" asked Mr Greenstone.

"There's no need for your cat to concern himself with Mr Trollope," replied Churchill.

"I didn't mean that," Mr Greenstone replied. "I meant when are you going to find the time to work on Zeppelin's case? It seems to me that you're rather distracted by this Mrs Furzgate business."

"Don't for one minute think we've forgotten about dear Zeppelin, Mr Greenstone. A professional detective always solves her cases. Just you wait and see."

Chapter 26

"WE DIDN'T MANAGE to elicit a confession from Mr Greenstone about that letter, did we, Pembers?" The two ladies walked down a lane toward the high street.

"Can we be sure it was him who sent it?"

"He admitted that his spelling wasn't up to scratch, but other than that there's nothing to suggest he's behind it."

"Who else could it have been?"

"I don't think Bodkin would be stupid enough to send it, unless he's double bluffing as Inspector Mappin suggested. I'm inclined to think the letter may be from the murderer himself."

"Or herself?"

"Indeed, or herself. And he or she is trying to pervert my investigation by shining the spotlight on someone else."

"Clever."

"Not *that* clever, Pembers, seeing as the culprit can't spell properly."

"But sometimes people can be clever in different ways. While they may not seem too clever on the face of it, they may be clever in another respect."

"Hmm, I sort of see what you mean, Pembers. Let's pass by the *Compton Poppleford Gazette*'s offices shall we?"

"I hope you're not planning to speak to Mr Trollope. He can be rather cantankerous, and he's quite scary, too."

"I'm not going to speak to him directly; I have a more subtle plan. We need to conduct some surveillance."

"Why are there so many flies about this evening?"

"Stop flapping, Pemberley, you'll get us noticed."

"But they're not bothering you; it's only me they're interested in."

"You must have sweet-tasting skin, Pembers."

"Why does everybody say that? What does it actually mean?"

"Shush. Here comes someone now."

The two women ducked behind the shrubs in the yard as the door of the *Compton Poppleford Gazette* offices opened. A miserable, hatchet-faced man in brown tweed with bicycle clips around his trousers emerged.

"Is that our man Trollope?" Churchill whispered to Pemberley.

"Yes, that's him."

Mr Trollope glanced around before walking over to a brick outhouse, unlocking the door and disappearing inside.

"What's he doing?" whispered Churchill.

Her question was answered when Mr Trollope emerged a few moments later wheeling a bicycle out. He leant it against the wall, locked the door of the outhouse and went back inside the office building.

"Now what's he doing?"

Just a short while later Mr Trollope appeared again, this time carrying a briefcase, which he placed in the basket at the front of the bicycle. Then he locked the office door, climbed onto his bicycle and cycled away.

"Ah ha!" said Churchill, trying not to wince from the pain in her knees as she stood up straight.

"What do you mean by that?"

"We've identified his routine. What I want you to do, Pembers, is hide behind this bush for the next week and ascertain whether this routine of his is one he carries out every evening."

"But what about the flies?"

"Tell them to buzz off." Churchill chuckled at her own joke as they headed off.

Chapter 27

THE BELL above the door of Mr Smallbone's shop gave a pleasing tinkle as Churchill stepped inside. He looked up immediately.

"I ain't permittin' you in 'ere if you's gonna ask me questions about 'er again," he warned.

"Who's *'er*? The cat's mother?"

"Mrs Furzgate."

"Oh, her. No, I'm not. I thought I'd come in here for a little peruse instead. I don't often find the time for a little peruse."

Churchill began inspecting the piles of bric-a-brac around her while Mr Smallbone regarded her warily.

"You's makin' me suspicious," he said.

"Me?" Churchill laughed. "You don't need to worry about me, Mr Smallbone."

"Reckons I do. If you's in 'ere to cause mischief you can go on an' leave now."

"You're willing to turn away a paying customer?"

"You're gonna buy summat are you?"

"I might do if I see something that catches my eye."

"Like what?"

"A paperweight. I'm looking for a paperweight so that when Miss Pemberley opens the window the papers don't get blown off my desk."

"That can be right annoyin'."

"Can't it just?"

"The paperweight section's over 'ere," he said.

"Oh, you have a dedicated section for paperweights. How perfectly charming."

Mr Smallbone walked over to an old desk that had various heavy items resting on it. Churchill sauntered over and examined them.

"This is a pretty one with the flowers inside it," she said. "How do glass-blowers achieve that effect? Quite marvellous. Shame about the chips, though."

"You 'ave to expect wear and tear of antiques on account of 'em being so old."

"Indeed. Now this one's interesting. Is it a brass lizard?"

Mr Smallbone nodded.

"How much?"

"Five quid."

"Good grief. Really?"

"It's antique, Mrs Churchill."

"Course it is. And here we have several more glass paperweights and an elephant. Is that real ivory?"

Mr Smallbone nodded again.

"And what's this? It looks like a cog of some sort."

"That there's an antique cog."

"Naturally. And I suppose that's antique grease on it as well?"

Mr Smallbone peered closely at the dirty cog sitting among the paperweights. His moustache twitched.

"Thinkin' about it, the cog ain't meant to be there. Must of been left over from when the boiler got replaced."

Churchill gave a polite laugh. "Goodness me, you are funny, Mr Smallbone." She glanced around the shop. "You must have been running this place for a long time given the amount of knowledge you have about antiques. Let me hazard a guess. Thirty years?"

"Almost forty."

"Nearly forty years! What a thought that you've been in this very shop every single day for forty years."

"Yeah, it's been a long time."

"Every single day? You must have missed one or two over the years?"

"Nope, I've been 'ere every day. Never missed a single one. Never been too ill fer work."

"Gosh, what a remarkable constitution you must have, Mr Smallbone, to never be ill and to have been in this shop *every single day* for forty years!"

"Yeah, 'part from a gap of a few years, that is."

"A gap?"

"Worked at me uncle's whisky distillery on the Isle of Bute fer a bit, I did."

"Really? How interesting! What made you decide to do that?"

"Jus' fancied a change."

"I know exactly what you mean, Mr Smallbone. Doesn't one feel much better when one has a change of scene?"

"Yeah."

"Which distillery does your uncle own?"

"Eh? Which what?"

"Which distillery?"

"Oh, it's got the family name, Smallbone." He scratched at his moustache.

"Is it really? I don't recall there being a Smallbone distillery on the Isle of Bute."

"You've been there, 'ave you?" His eyes widened in alarm.

"Yes, I lived there for a few years. Like you, I fancied a change of scene."

"Oh."

"Which place is it near? Kerrycroy? Ambrismore? Glecknabae?"

"Dunno, it was ages ago now."

"Perhaps it was Rothesay, with the castle."

"There might've been a castle there."

"Glenmore Bay is rather pretty, don't you find?"

"Oh, yeah."

"Did you go to Glenmore Bay?"

"Proberly."

"You should know whether you did or not because you surely can't have missed the pier there, which is the longest in Scotland."

"Oh yeah, longest pier in Scotland it is."

"You walked along it, did you?"

"Yeah, can't miss it, as you said Mrs Churchill."

"Except that I was telling a porky pie."

"A what?"

"I was fibbing, Mr Smallbone. There is no such place as Glenmore Bay on the Isle of Bute and I have no idea where Scotland's longest pier is, but it certainly isn't there."

Mr Smallbone's face turned pale.

"What are you playin' at?"

"I could ask the same of you. Did you really spend ten years on the Isle of Bute?"

"How did you know it was ten years?"

"A little bird told me."

"Miss Pemberley?"

"I never reveal my sources. But I don't believe that you spent ten years on the Isle of Bute. Where were you?"

"None of your business. I knew you'd come 'ere to cause mischief. I told you! I said you was up to no good." He poked his forefinger at her.

"I heard that you were serving time for murder."

Mr Smallbone dashed over to the door and locked it. Then he turned to face Churchill, his eyes wide with horror and his moustache trembling.

"Ain't no one, and I mean *no one*, in Compton Popple-ford as knows about all that. If I 'ear you've breathed a single word—"

"Don't panic, Mr Smallbone, my lips are sealed. As a private detective I know how to be discreet. As far as I'm concerned you've served your time."

"I 'ave. I *'ave* served me time. And he 'ad it comin', you know."

"Did he indeed?"

"Yeah, 'e were a crook. And a thief and a liar. 'E double-crossed me, 'e triple-crossed me, 'e—"

"Mr Smallbone, I don't doubt you have an elaborate justification for putting an end to another man's life, but I'm not here to be judge and jury all over again."

"So what are you doin' 'ere? I'm confused, Mrs Churchill. You said as you wanted to buy a paperweight and now you're diggin' up things you ain't got no cause to dig up. What d'you want from me? Money, is it?"

"Do I look the blackmailing type, Mr Smallbone?"

"I dunno. But I want you to get out me shop and never come back. But you're always knockin' about, ain't you? You works in that office just across the road so's you can look outta your window and down to my shop any time you want. Woah, it gives me the shivers, it really does!"

"Mr Smallbone, I shall have to splash some cold water

over you if you don't calm down this very minute! Now take some deep breaths."

Astonishingly, Mr Smallbone did as he was told. Churchill realised the man had become putty in her hands.

"I gather this man you despatched was an unpleasant character," she said.

Mr Smallbone nodded.

"Now I have no desire to go into the detail of how you carried out the deed, but I think that if it was possible for you to do away with a crook who was more than likely able to defend himself, it would have been even easier to push a defenceless old lady down the stairs."

"Oh no," groaned Mr Smallbone. "We ain't back to 'er, are we? You don't give up, Mrs Churchill."

"She accused you of selling fake antiques."

"That she did."

"And the accusation must have annoyed you. In fact, it was probably more than mere annoyance; there was a very real risk that she could have ruined your business of almost forty years."

"She could 'ave."

"And a little shove down the staircase at Piddleton Hotel would have easily put an end to the problem."

"I know what this looks like. I'm a convicted murderer who was bein' pestered by the local busybody. It would of been easy to do away with 'er, and I can't deny I didn't consider it. But I didn't do it! Not this time. Perhaps after another few months of it I might 'ave done, but it weren't nothin' to do with me."

"I appreciate your honesty, Mr Smallbone."

"Good."

"Just one more question."

"Oh, hell. What now?" Mr Smallbone stood, slumped and defeated, by the locked door.

"Did you send a letter to me claiming that Mr Bodkin had pushed Mrs Furzgate?"

"No. Why would I do summat like that? 'E murdered 'er, did 'e?"

"He says that he did no such thing."

"Course 'e did."

"Well, yes, he doesn't wish to implicate himself any more than you do. How do you spell 'pushed', Mr Smallbone?"

"How do you spell it? Pushed? Why you askin' me that for?"

"Just answer the question, Mr Smallbone. Then I'll buy a paperweight from you and leave."

"P-U-S-H-E-D."

"Thank you."

Chapter 28

"WHAT AN INTERESTING PAPERWEIGHT," said Pemberley as Churchill placed the brass lizard on her desk. "Did you buy it from Mr Smallbone?"

"I did indeed, Pembers, and I talked him down to a pound from five. Thank you for finding *The Isle of Bute Illustrated Guide Book* in the library for me; it came in most useful. Mr Smallbone actually believed I'd been there!"

"Did he come clean?"

"Just about. He's admitted to one murder, at least, but I can't tell whether he is also responsible for Mrs Furzgate's demise. He's adamantly denying it, of course, and he knows to spell pushed with a 'u' rather than double 'o'. He's also terrified people will find out about his misdemeanour, so we've got a hold over him now, Pembers."

"Poor Mr Smallbone."

"What? Why would you feel sorry for him?"

"I really don't know. I suppose I shouldn't. It's just that he looks rather sad most of the time."

"He's only got himself to blame. Now, how are you getting on with your surveillance of Mr Trollope?"

"I've observed him for two evenings now, and his routine has matched exactly that of the evening when we both watched him."

"Good, good. He strikes me as a creature of habit, so continue watching him, Pemberley, and we'll decide when to strike. Currant bun?"

"Thank you, Mrs Churchill. I'll go and put the kettle on."

The throb of a motorcar outside made the window panes rattle.

"There's only one man with an engine that loud," said Churchill.

A moment later Mr Cavendish breezed in through the door with his bright, bouncy hair and white teeth.

"Surprise, surprise, Mrs Churchill!" he said with a broad grin.

"It isn't much of a surprise at all, Mr Cavendish. I heard your engine throbbing long before you set foot in here."

"Oh dear. Is it really that loud?" He placed his hat on the hat stand.

"I'm afraid so, and that being the case you'll need to try harder if you want to surprise me. I hope you're not one of those menace drivers, Mr Cavendish."

"Who, me?" He deftly unbuttoned his jacket with one hand and took a seat at her desk.

"Yes, you, Mr Cavendish. One of those chaps who races through the villages scattering chickens and blowing off young ladies' hats."

"Mrs Churchill, do I look like a chap who would do such a thing?"

"I think you do, Mr Cavendish."

"You look ever so stern when you pull that face, Mrs Churchill. I feel like a naughty schoolboy."

"And so you should, Mr Cavendish. So you should. I've a good mind to put you over my knee and—"

"Tea, Mr Cavendish?" Pemberley interjected.

"Thank you, Miss Pemberley. Do continue with your sentence, Mrs Churchill."

"I forget what I was about to say now. I suppose you're here for one of our little update meetings?"

"Indeed I am, Mrs Churchill. They are the highlight of my week!"

"Then you must have an extremely dull social calendar."

Mr Cavendish laughed. "Not at all. Quite the contrary, in fact."

"Then I consider myself very flattered by your visit."

"You should!" He winked. "So, has there been any progress with the case?"

Churchill told him about the letter purporting to be from Mr Bodkin. Mr Cavendish listened intently and sipped his tea.

"And Bodkin is the chap my godmother had a love affair with, is that right?" he asked when she had finished.

Churchill nodded.

"The man is clearly guilty, then!" Mr Cavendish stood to his feet. "I've a good mind to pop downstairs and punch his lights out!"

"Steady on, Mr Cavendish. I'm more inclined to believe the letter was sent to me by someone wishing to frame Mr Bodkin. It may even be from the murderer himself!"

"Or herself," interjected Pemberley.

"Or herself."

"So how do we find out who sent it?" asked Mr Cavendish, sitting down again.

"That's what I'm working on at this very moment.

Unfortunately, Inspector Mappin is in possession of the letter. He seems to think he's in charge of the whole thing now. However, I plan to visit him to ask how his investigation is progressing. Perhaps you would like to accompany me."

"I can think of nothing I would enjoy more. When are you planning on going?"

Churchill consulted her desk calendar and then looked at her watch.

"How about now?"

"I'm ready when you are, Mrs Churchill."

"We're off to the police station, Miss Pemberley," said Mrs Churchill, picking up her handbag. "I shall have my cup of tea on my return. Woman the fort, if you please."

Churchill sank down into the passenger seat of Mr Cavendish's car and rested her handbag on her lap.

"Well, this is all rather swanky," she said. "And it's surprisingly comfy, too. Those dials look rather complicated. You can understand them all, can you?"

"One or two of them. I think the others are decorative."

"Oh dear, really? Don't you think you should —"

The engine started with a loud roar.

"Chocks away!" Mr Cavendish shouted over the noise.

"Chocks? An automobile requires chocks, does it? I thought that was just for aeroplanes."

"Hold on to your hat!"

Three minutes later Churchill staggered out of Mr Cavendish's car beside the police station. Her legs felt weak and her head spun.

"Oh dear," she said, patting her hair. "My shampoo and set is quite ruined."

"You go on in and see Inspector Mappin," said Mr Cavendish. "I'll jog back and fetch your hat. I did warn you to hold on to it."

"I held on to it as best as I could, Mr Cavendish! Was there any need to go around the corners like that?"

Churchill walked into the police station slowly with the sensation of extreme speed still coursing through her veins.

Everything was peaceful inside. So peaceful, in fact, that Inspector Mappin had fallen asleep behind his desk. Churchill stood and watched him for a moment; his head was tilted back against his chair and his mouth wide open. He wasn't an attractive sleeper.

"Inspector Mappin?" she ventured. He stirred slightly, smacked his lips together, then resumed his snooze with his mouth open.

Churchill rummaged in her handbag for her crochet needle and found it just as Mr Cavendish stepped into the room with her hat in his hand.

"Voila, Mrs Churchill," he said. He presented it to her then glanced at Inspector Mappin. "Good heavens! The chap's fallen asleep on the job."

"He certainly has. A prod to the ribs with my crochet hook should sort him out."

"No wait, don't," said Mr Cavendish, a mischievous grin spreading across his face. He lowered his voice to a whisper. "We can have some japes! Let's put something in his mouth. Come on, what have we got here?" He searched the desk. "How about a paperclip?"

"I have no time for your schoolboy humour, Mr Cavendish," scolded Churchill.

"Or I could roll a piece of paper into a ball and bowl it in! Come on, help me find a scrap of paper."

Inspector Mappin stirred and his eyes flickered open.

"Wh-what?" He shook himself awake. "When did you get here? And what are you doing with that paperclip, Cavendish?"

"Nothing, Inspector Mappin."

"And the metal implement, Mrs Churchill?" asked the inspector, eying the crochet needle warily.

"I was about to prod you with it, Inspector Mappin. You shouldn't be sleeping on duty."

"I wasn't asleep! I was merely deep in thought."

"Pitiful excuse." Churchill placed the crochet hook back in her handbag and sat down.

"Mr Cavendish and I are here to find out what progress you've made in identifying the sender of the mysterious letter."

"Oh, that. What's it got to do with Cavendish?"

"He just happens to be Mrs Furzgate's godson, and he's also my client. Besides, the letter you have in your possession was sent to me, so it's actually *my* letter."

"I need to hold on to it for now, Mrs Churchill."

"You do that, Inspector. How are your investigations going?"

"Well, Mr Bodkin, the man the letter was supposedly sent by, denies sending it."

"Of course he does!" said Mr Cavendish. "But the chap has already incriminated himself, so how can he deny it? Why hasn't he been arrested, Inspector? Why is he not in your police cell at this very moment?"

"Because there's no proof he sent it," replied Inspector Mappin.

"Of course he sent it!" retorted Mr Cavendish. "The fellow signed his name!"

Churchill began to suspect that what she had known

for a long time was true: Mr Cavendish wasn't especially bright.

"The fact Bodkin's name is on the letter suggests that he didn't send it," she explained.

"What?" Mr Cavendish's brow crumpled. "I don't understand."

"Why would he send such a letter were he guilty of the murder?" Churchill asked him. "Why confess at all?"

"Because he feels guilty."

"But why go to the trouble of cutting out all those little letters?" asked Churchill. "Why not just write the letter in his normal handwriting? Or why even go to the trouble of writing a letter at all? Why not just walk into this police station and confess?"

"That's a good point well made," said Inspector Mappin, "for a meddling busybody."

"I knew that it would be too much to expect unadulterated flattery from you Inspector," said Churchill.

"Ah, but I am being complimentary, Mrs Churchill," he replied. "Perhaps you have your head screwed on the right way after all."

"Of course I do."

"Having carried out my own investigations," continued the inspector, "I can wholeheartedly say that this strange letter is merely a clumsy attempt to frame Mr Bodkin."

"You and I are in agreement, Inspector, but the question remains, who sent it? Have you found out yet?"

"No."

"So that's the stumbling block. The letter is not from Bodkin, but we have no idea who it is from. Have you dusted it for fingerprints, Inspector?"

"I have, but that's of little use to me unless I take the fingerprint of every man in this village."

"And woman."

"I suppose so. That would double the workload, wouldn't it?"

"So what now, Inspector?"

"Well, *that*, I suppose. The fingerprints."

"It's not terribly feasible, is it? What if someone refuses to allow you to take their fingerprints?"

"Then they must be the guilty party!"

"And what if five people refuse? Does that make them all guilty parties?"

"Well, it would suggest they'd all been up to no good and had something to hide, so they're probably guilty of something. It might give me the opportunity to clear up a few cold cases."

"I think it's a flawed plan, Inspector. Surely people have the right to object to you taking their fingerprints."

"But if they do there's got to be something fishy about them. They should respect law and order!"

Churchill sighed. "In the meantime I shall continue with my own investigation."

"I don't think you should, Mrs Churchill. This is a police matter now."

"Since when? You didn't even believe Mrs Furzgate's death was murder until a few days ago!"

"Investigations often undergo a sudden change, and I am viewing matters differently now. I adapt my approach according to the evidence that presents itself."

"Good." Churchill got to her feet. "Well, I think it was rather a waste of our time coming here, Mr Cavendish. Inspector Mappin clearly hasn't made any progress."

"I've ruled Bodkin out," said the inspector indignantly.

"Good. Well that's a start, I suppose. I don't know about you, Mr Cavendish, but I've heard enough."

"So have I!" he agreed. "Besides, the culprit is quite

clearly Bodkin! You've ruled out the wrong man, Inspector!"

"Leave the detective work to me, Mr Cavendish," said Inspector Mappin.

"No, I'll be leaving it to Mrs Churchill. She knows what she's doing. Would you like me to drive you back to your office, Mrs Churchill?"

"No thank you, Mr Cavendish. I'd prefer to walk."

Chapter 29

"NOW THEN, my trusty assistant, run through Mr Trollope's routine for me again. I want to make sure we have this right."

Churchill and Pemberley were walking along the high street toward the offices of the *Compton Poppleford Gazette*.

"He leaves the office at six o'clock, then walks over to the outhouse and unlocks it," said Pemberley. "Then he walks inside, retrieves his bicycle and wheels it out."

"How long is he in the outhouse for?"

"It usually takes between ten and twenty seconds. Then he rests his bicycle against the wall of the office, walks back to the outhouse and locks the door. Once he's done that he goes back inside the office to fetch his briefcase. He comes out with it, locks the door of the office and places his briefcase in the basket on the front of his bicycle. Then he climbs onto it and rides off."

"So we strike while he's in the outhouse," said Mrs Churchill. "We have a window of between ten and twenty seconds to get inside the offices. It won't be easy, but it's not impossible."

"Surely he'll see us when he returns for his briefcase," said Pemberley.

"Is there a cupboard we can quickly dive into?"

"How should I know?"

"Have you not been inside the offices before?"

"No."

"Oh, for some reason I thought you had. There must be a cupboard we can hide in while he fetches his briefcase."

"You know how I hate cupboards."

"That's a good point. We don't want to cause damage to any more doors. Perhaps we can dive under a desk."

Pemberley said nothing, but the manner in which she eyed Churchill's portly figure suggested she wasn't entirely convinced by the idea.

"You think me incapable of diving under a desk, Pembers?"

"Diving under a desk in a matter of seconds requires nimble movements."

"I can be nimble. And quick," retorted Churchill. "I can even jump over a candlestick."

"Why would you do that?" asked Pemberley with a puzzled expression on her face.

"It's just an old rhyme, Pembers. Are you sure Trollope is definitely the last to leave? There's no one left in the office afterwards, is there? And no one else who leaves with him?"

"No, my surveillance suggests otherwise on all counts."

"Good, then let's get a move on. Mr Trollope will be fetching his bicycle soon, and we don't want to miss our window of opportunity."

"I'm not sure about this at all," said Pemberley. "I don't think we have enough time to run into the office and hide ourselves. What if there's nowhere to hide at all and he sees us?"

"Then we play dumb. We tell him we saw the door had been left open and we wanted to check if there was anyone about in case the door had been left open by accident. We're just two helpful citizens ensuring that everything's all right. Does that sound like a good plan?"

"I suppose so."

"He'll be snappy with us, of course, because he seems that type, but if we pretend to be two bewildered old women who aren't really sure what's going on I'm sure he'll overlook the incident. I've used this ruse a number of times."

"I'm not so sure it would work on him," said Pemberley.

"How else are we going to find out all the secrets Trollope's sitting on, Pembers? We may find evidence that leads us directly to Mrs Furzgate's killer. We might uncover evidence of a whole host of other nefarious activities at the same time. Someone has to stand up to the Trollopes, and we know Inspector Mappin is hardly the man to do it."

"I don't think I want to stand up to the Trollopes. I think I'm quite happy as I am," Pemberley replied meekly.

"Goodness, that's no way to be. Where's your backbone, woman? Think of dear Mr Greenstone and the way he was forced out of his business. And poor meddlesome Mrs Furzgate pushed down the stairs. I won't pretend I enjoyed my brief meeting with Thora Furzgate, but do you think she deserved to die?"

Pemberley shook her head.

"Exactly," said Churchill. "Of course she didn't. There's one thing I cannot stand, and that's a bully. And we have two of them in the shape of Mr and Mrs Trollope. The sooner I get to the bottom of the hold they have over this village, the better. And unfortunately, Pembers, that means taking a risk now and again. As a dear old aunt of mine used to say, 'You can't make an omelette without breaking a few eggs.' Are you with me or are you not?"

"Of course I'm with you. This is what Churchill's Detective Agency is all about!"

"That's the spirit! It certainly is what Churchill's Detective Agency is about, and we'll show Compton Poppleford that we're a force to be reckoned with!"

Churchill strode off proudly down the high street with Pemberley scurrying along beside her.

Chapter 30

"HE'S TAKING his time this evening," whispered Churchill as she leant against the wall of the *Compton Poppleford Gazette* offices, just around the corner from the door Mr Trollope was due to appear from.

"It's not quite six o'clock yet," replied Pemberley.

"Whisper, Pembers! Do you want him to hear you?"

"Sorry," whispered Pemberley. "It's not quite six o'clock yet."

"I know it's not; I heard you the first time!" hissed Churchill. Feeling uncharacteristically nervous, she could feel her heart thumping heavily in her chest.

They waited a moment longer and then Churchill heard the unmistakeable sound of a door opening.

"That's the door!" whispered Pemberley.

"I know, I heard it."

Pemberley peered carefully around the corner, trying to reveal as little of her head as possible.

Churchill held her breath as she waited for the signal that it was time to move. Slowly, almost excruciatingly so,

Pemberley's arm raised up, and then she beckoned with her hand that the time had come.

Churchill sprang up as if an electrical current had shot through her stout walking shoes. She barrelled around the corner toward the door. Unfortunately, Pemberley was standing in her way. She pushed past her secretary, heading for the open doorway as quickly as she possibly could. A quick glance at the outhouse reassured her that Mr Trollope was momentarily out of sight.

As Churchill stepped into the doorway she realised Pemberley had done the same thing, only the doorway wasn't wide enough for both of them at the same time. They were jammed in, stuck together and unable to move.

"Step back!" Churchill hissed, flailing her arms and handbag helplessly in front of her.

"I can't! I'm stuck!" whimpered Pemberley.

Churchill's heart was pounding so heavily she feared it might stop altogether. Mr Trollope was about to emerge with his bicycle to find them stuck in his doorway.

Churchill used all the strength she could muster to squeeze past the door frame, which gave a creak as she finally burst free like a cork from a bottle.

The office was disappointingly small with just four desks inside. Each desk had a typewriter and a telephone on it. The briefcase was resting on the largest desk.

Churchill headed for the desk furthest away from the door. She moved the chair and hurled herself beneath it, hitting her head on a drawer as she did so. She just had time to pull the chair back into position before two legs with bicycle clips around them came into view.

Mr Trollope.

Surely he had seen them, Churchill thought to herself. *What had happened to Pemberley?*

Churchill's chest felt fit to burst as she held her breath.

Her head throbbed with pain from her altercation with the drawer.

Mr Trollope's feet paused beside the large desk and Churchill surveyed his polished brogues as she listened to the sound of rustling papers. She urged him to hurry up and prayed he wouldn't notice her. Unable to hold her breath any longer, she reluctantly allowed herself to exhale and then quietly inhale again. She felt sure her knees would never forgive her for squashing them into such a position.

What if he happened to peer under the desk and see her here? What excuse could she possibly come up with? She realised she would probably have to feign insanity.

Churchill tried not to exhale too loudly in relief as she heard the briefcase snap shut and watched Mr Trollope's brogues make their way towards the door. Once the door was closed and the key had turned in the lock, a grin spread across her face. She slowly pulled herself up from beneath the desk and tried to stretch out her legs, wincing with pain at the knees.

She peered out from behind the desk, but there was no sign of her secretary.

"Pemberley?" she whispered cautiously.

A shuffle came from the far end of the room in reply.

"Pembers?"

Churchill was relieved to see her gangly secretary clamber out from beneath another desk. Her spectacles were crooked, but she appeared otherwise unscathed. She peered cautiously out through the window, which overlooked the rear yard and outhouse where Mr Trollope kept his bicycle.

"All clear," she said quietly.

"We did it!" enthused Churchill as she stretched her arms above her head.

"What was all that business in the doorway?" asked Pemberley. "You should have let me go first. I was in front of you!"

"But you were moving too slowly; I had to get past."

"And then you jammed us in! We should have maintained our positions and stayed one behind the other. Imagine what might have happened if we were in the military!"

"Military precision isn't really a skill of mine, Pembers. What's important is that we did it!" Churchill gestured around the room and chuckled. "It's an Aladdin's cave!"

"Do you think so? There doesn't seem to be much in here."

"It's an office, so it's a functional, comfortless space. But there are filing cabinets and cupboards here, Pembers, all holding a multitude of secrets, no doubt. And to think we have all night to explore them!"

Pemberley's face fell. "We have to stay here all night?"

"Not if we discover the full hoard of secrets before then. Let's get on with it." Churchill pulled a paper bag out of her handbag. "I brought provisions. Can I interest you in an Eccles cake, Pemberley?"

"Thank you."

"Isn't it marvellous that Mr Trollope didn't see us? He had no idea!" Churchill chuckled again and bit into her cake.

"I'm still worried he might have seen us," said Pemberley, holding her uneaten Eccles cake in her hand. "What if he's cycling home at this very moment with a nagging thought that he heard or witnessed something suspicious? It might be enough to make him turn around and come back."

"Nonsense, Pembers, if he'd noticed anything he would have lingered here and perhaps looked under the desks. He wouldn't have left as he did and locked the door behind him."

"That's another thing that's bothering me."

Churchill sighed. "What now, Pembers?"

"The locked door. How do we get out?"

"I'm sure it's the sort of door one can open from the inside." Churchill strode up to it and examined the lock. She tried the handle and the door remained steadfast. "Or perhaps it isn't."

"Oh no!"

"Shush, Pembers, the door's the last of our worries. There must be another door somewhere or, failing that, a window we can climb out of."

Churchill walked up to the windows, which overlooked the high street, and peered closely at them.

"Yes, I thought so. These are straightforward sash windows. It'll be easy to clamber out."

"They don't look big enough," commented Pemberley.

"Big enough for what?"

Pemberley didn't reply, but gave Churchill the same look she had when hiding under desks had cropped up.

"You'd be surprised what I can fit through, into and under, Pembers. Now, enough of this procrastination. We need to start looking for secrets."

"What if all the drawers and cupboards are locked?"

"Try one of them. Have a go on that one over there."

Pemberley walked over to one of the filing cabinets and pulled out a drawer.

"Does that look locked to you, Pembers?" asked Churchill.

"Not especially."

"Good. Luckily for us, Mr Trollope doesn't seem to be too particular about security. It shows how confident he's become that no one will ever find him out. Let's stop fretting and get to work. I'll begin with A," said Churchill, walking over to the first drawer of the filing cabinet.

"Why A?"

"Because it's the first letter of the alphabet!"

"Why not try F?"

"F? Why the devil would I start with F?"

"F for Furzgate."

"Oh, I see what you mean! We should think of the names of people Trollope may have done some mischief to and look them up first. Excellent idea. In which case, you do G for Greenstone."

"But G is just beneath F. We'll be bumping into each other as we did when we got stuck in the door."

Churchill sighed. "Try S for Smallbone, then, or B for Bodkin. Just get on with it. I'll do G in a moment."

She began rummaging through the drawer of the filing cabinet marked F.

Chapter 31

AN HOUR later Churchill opened her handbag and brought out a flask.

"Tea, Pembers?"

"Thank you. A flask? That's very organised of you, Mrs Churchill."

Churchill produced two tin cups from her handbag, set them on a desk and poured.

"I suppose we shall lose the light soon," said Pemberley glancing through the window at the lowering sun.

"We still have an hour or so before we need to worry about that," replied Churchill.

"And then what will we do?" asked Pemberley. "We can't put the lights on or that will draw attention to us."

"I have a little police torch my husband used in the Met."

"It's not a bullseye lantern, is it? Those things can get terribly hot."

"No, Pembers. Now I've already told you there's no need to fret. Just leave these little matters to Churchy."

Pemberley choked and almost spat out her tea. "Goodness! What sort of tea is this?"

"It's got a little drop of whisky in it. Drink it up; it's fortifying."

"Are you sure it's just a drop?"

"Yes. A wee dram, as our Scottish friends like to call it."

"I know you told me not to fret, Mrs Churchill, but aren't you concerned that we haven't discovered any of Mr Trollope's secrets after an hour of searching?"

"Not *concerned*, Pemberley, but it does bother me a little. It seems his filing system is more complicated than we first thought. You'd think that a search under the letter F would reveal a file for Mrs Furzgate, wouldn't you?"

"Perhaps he has his own system."

"He clearly does, Pembers. That's rather typical of a man, I'm afraid. My husband often had his own complex system for things that should otherwise have been straightforward. But there's nothing for it other than to keep looking. We have all night."

Pemberley shuddered. "I have a horrible feeling in my waters."

"About what?"

"That someone's going to come back here. What if they find us? How would we even begin to explain ourselves? I don't think there's anything here that might be of use. I think we should leave while we still can. I should hate to be discovered; I couldn't bear it. We would be in ever so much trouble. They'd put us in a police cell!"

"That's enough, Pemberley! There's nothing to worry about. Mr Trollope hasn't the slightest intention of returning this evening, I'm absolutely sure of it. He's left for the day and taken his briefcase with him. I expect he and his lady wife, Mrs Trollope, are currently enjoying a comfortable evening at home. I wonder what the Trollopes do in the evenings at home."

"Play dominoes?"

"I imagine they hatch evil plans to take over the village."

"Over a game of dominoes, perhaps?"

"If you insist. Now let's get back to work."

Churchill drained her cup and prepared herself for another search through the files. Although she had been quick to reassure Pemberley, she was quietly worried about their lack of progress. Even worse was the concern that someone could discover them here.

"I think it's time for the little police torch, Pemberley," said Churchill as the room darkened. She rummaged around in her handbag.

"Can't we just leave?" protested Pemberley. "We've been here for almost three hours. I don't think Mr Trollope keeps any secrets in his office."

"Patience, Pembers."

"I'm afraid I've run out of patience."

"Here's the torch," said Churchill, turning it on. "Now we can crack on." She shone the torch into the filing cabinet. "Now, what's left to look at? More hieroglyphics, by the looks of things. I don't understand all these pieces of paper with wild scribblings on them."

She held a sheet of paper up to show Pemberley.

"That's shorthand," her secretary replied.

"Gobbledegook, more like. There are notepads filled with the stuff on that shelf behind you."

Pemberley reached up and grabbed one.

"This one belongs to Smithy Miggins," she said.

"That reminds me to give the chap a piece of my mind when I meet him. Fancy not returning my call! It's the height of rudeness."

Pemberley began to leaf through the notebook.

"You'll make neither head nor tail of it, Pembers," continued Churchill. "I'm au fait with a few languages, but this one is completely beyond me."

"It's not a different language; it's English in a shortened form."

"It could be double Dutch for all I know."

"This looks quite interesting," said Pemberley. "It's about Piddleton Hotel."

"How do you know that?"

"I can read shorthand."

"How?"

"I learnt it at St Hilda's Secretarial College."

"Did you indeed? But that's one of the most prestigious secretarial schools in the country!"

Pemberley shrugged.

"I see. So what does the shorthand say about Piddleton Hotel?" Churchill handed Pemberley the torch.

"I think it's the interview with Mr Crumble."

"Oh dear. Dreadful man."

"There's some discussion here about a man named Pierre."

"Pierre? Who's Pierre?"

"It looks as though there is an agreement in place not to mention him."

"I don't understand. Let me look at that, Pembers." Churchill peered closely at the notebook. "Oh it's no use, I can't understand it. What do you mean about this Pierre chap?"

"It seems he was dismissed for dropping the teacake at the top of the stairs."

"And so he should be. Hang on a moment! Pierre dropped the teacake?"

"Apparently so."

"On purpose or accidentally?"

"It doesn't say. But Mr Crumble was keen for it not to be mentioned."

"Why ever not?"

"Perhaps he didn't want it to become common knowledge that a member of his staff was responsible for Mrs Furzgate's death."

Churchill considered this for a moment. "So Pierre is our murderer." She thought some more. "But only if he dropped the teacake there with every intention of having Mrs Furzgate slip on it. If he dropped it by accident then it would merely be negligence."

"But he'd still be in trouble. Perhaps Mr Crumble could be sued for negligence."

"He'd probably be culpable whether Pierre dropped the teacake intentionally or accidentally. Do you know what, Pembers? It wouldn't surprise me a bit if Crumble greased Trollope's palm to keep this out of the newspaper."

"He did. I can see the sum of one hundred pounds written down here."

"The scoundrel!"

"Do you think Inspector Mappin knows about this?"

"If not he soon will. We'll show him that notebook, Pembers, and then everything will be out in the open. What a scandal!"

"Uh oh, someone's coming!" hissed Pemberley.

"Where?"

"I saw a light out in the yard. There's someone out there with a torch!"

A ball of panic rose up into Churchill's throat. "Are you sure?"

"Yes!"

"But why would someone come here at this hour?"

"I don't know, but they have!"

Pemberley turned the torch off.

"Pembers, we need to get out of here. Let's escape through the window!"

She picked up her handbag and dashed over to the window, which opened onto the high street. Fortunately, she was able to push it open quickly and quietly.

"Out this way Pembers!" she hissed.

She heard the sound of keys jangling outside the door.

"But you won't fit!" exclaimed Pemberley in a squealed whisper.

"Nonsense!"

With her heart thudding in her ears, Churchill threw her handbag out into the deserted high street and leant forward onto the windowsill. She swung her right leg up and pushed her knee out through the window at the same time as her shoulders. She pushed herself forward and prepared to meet the ground on the other side.

But then she stopped.

Her heart raced, knowing the door would open at any moment. She tried to shove her shoulders forward, placing her hands on the wall beneath the window for added lever-age, but her right knee remained wedged against the window frame, as did her left shoulder. She couldn't move forwards and she couldn't move backwards. Her skirt and petticoat had ridden up high on her left leg, which remained in the room, while her handbag lay on the pavement beneath her.

"What on earth!" came a man's voice from behind her.

His voice startled her so much that her hat fell off and rolled a short distance along the street. The lights flickered on and Churchill let out an enormous sigh of disappointment.

She began to think of a plausible explanation.

Chapter 32

"IT WAS A DRUNKEN DARE," Churchill explained to Mr Trollope as she sat on a chair in his office nursing her bruised knee and shoulder.

She smiled at the lean, hatchet-faced man who stood before her and felt her cheeks redden as she recalled how improperly close she had been to the editor as he stood astride her and forcibly dislodged her from his office window.

"But you're not even drunk!" he fumed.

"Not now I'm not. The argument with the window sobered me up very quickly indeed. But my secretary," she glanced around the room, wondering where Pemberley had got to, "told me she would pay me two pounds if I could climb through the window of your office. You shouldn't leave it unlocked, you know."

"That's all the temptation you need, is it? An unlocked window?"

"I'm afraid so, Mr Trollope. It's extremely childish, isn't it?" She giggled.

"I don't find it funny, Mrs Churchill, and what's more I

don't believe your foolish story. You broke into this office with the intent of stealing something, and when Inspector Mappin arrives I'll have him search your handbag."

"You may have a look in my handbag yourself, Mr Trollope. I have nothing to hide."

"It's my rule never to look inside a lady's handbag. I'll leave that to an officer of the law."

"You'll soon discover that I have taken nothing from your office, Mr Trollope, so there's really no need to make a big song and dance about all this."

"You may not have found the chance to steal anything, but you broke in and entered."

"I didn't actually enter; I got no further than the window. You can vouch for that yourself as you had to release me from it."

"You still broke in."

"But I didn't actually *break* anything. The window was unlocked. You admitted that yourself, Mr Trollope."

The door flung open and Inspector Mappin dashed in, breathless and perspiring. He was wearing his house slippers and a cosy cable-knit jumper. As soon as he saw Churchill his face assumed a deep scowl.

"Oh, it's you," he said. "What are you doing here, Mrs Churchill?"

She attempted to convince him with the same drunken dare story she had used on Mr Trollope.

"It's a feasible story, I suppose," said the inspector when she had finished.

"No it's not," said Mr Trollope. "It's piffle!"

"If it could be corroborated by Miss Pemberley the story may have legs," said the inspector. "Where is Miss Pemberley, Mrs Churchill?"

"I should think she's probably gone home," replied Churchill, concerned that she would have to get to

Pemberley before Inspector Mappin did. She still couldn't understand how her secretary had managed to disappear.

"She went home, leaving you stuck in the window?" Inspector Mappin asked.

"I think she got nervous when Mr Trollope arrived. She'd heard he can get incredibly cross."

"I can indeed!" Mr Trollope boomed. "It makes no odds whether you find this Pemberley woman or not, Inspector. The fact is, I found this woman jammed in my window, and I highly suspect she was sniffing about in my office!"

"Were you, Mrs Churchill?" asked Inspector Mappin.

"Was I what?"

"Sniffing about in here?"

"Do I look like a bloodhound, Inspector? Actually, don't bother replying to that, it would give you an excuse to be offensive. I don't sniff about places; I conduct my work with absolute professionalism. This unfortunate situation I find myself in has nothing to do with my work. It was merely a drunken dare, as I have explained."

"Search her handbag please, Inspector," said Mr Trollope.

"Of course."

Churchill watched as the inspector looked through her belongings.

"A flask of tea?"

"I always carry one with me."

"A paper bag with an Eccles cake in it?"

"You never know when you need one."

"A crochet hook? Ah yes, I've come across that before. Well, there don't appear to be any stolen items in the handbag, Mr Trollope."

"No secret documents?"

"No secret documents," confirmed the inspector.

"That's something, I suppose."

"Do you have secret documents, Mr Trollope?" asked Churchill innocently.

"You know I have. That's why you're here, isn't it?"

Churchill laughed. "If only I knew what you were talking about half the time, Mr Trollope!"

"She may not have stolen anything, Inspector," said Mr Trollope, "but I wish to press charges against this woman for breaking into my property."

"We've already discussed this," said Churchill. "I got no further than the window."

"So you say. But perhaps you had already been inside and were on your way out again."

"But how would I successfully get in through the window if I couldn't get out through it?" asked Churchill.

"Perhaps you got a better angle on the way in. Even if you didn't get in, you showed intent, and that's a crime, Inspector Mappin."

"I have to agree that a crime has been committed," said the inspector.

"Then you must arrest her, Mappin."

"Now hang on a minute," said Churchill. "Don't you need to corroborate my story with Miss Pemberley first?"

"There is that," said Inspector Mappin.

"She's just trying to buy time," said Mr Trollope. "Arrest her please, Inspector. She should not be on my premises."

"I wonder what our mutual friend, Lady Worthington, would make of this matter, Mr Trollope," ventured Churchill.

His eyebrows lifted. "You know Lady Worthington, do you?"

"Yes, she's a very good friend of mine."

"I think she would be rather disappointed in you if she knew what you'd been up to," said Trollope.

"Oh no, she knows me too well for that. This sticky little situation would come as no surprise to her whatsoever. She would laugh the whole affair off. That's one thing you can say about the upper classes; they're so good at laughing things off. Have you ever noticed that?"

"Can't say I have."

"Does Lady Worthington know you and your lady wife well?"

"Quite well, yes."

"How well?"

"Are you still trying to buy more time, Mrs Churchill?"

"I only asked how well Lady Worthington knows you, Mr Trollope. Does she know your son well?"

"My son? What does he have to do with any of this?"

"Does Lady Worthington know him?"

"No, I don't believe she does."

"Perhaps it's just as well he's in the Bahamas, in that case."

"What do you mean?"

"I mean that you wouldn't wish to risk Lady Worthington finding out about him."

"She knows he exists, if that's what you mean."

"Ah, but that's not all though, is it? She would take a dim view of his predilections, I imagine."

"What are you suggesting?"

"Embezzlement, bribery, blackmail… that sort of thing."

"Now hang on! What's this all about?"

"Lady Worthington wouldn't like to hear about such matters, would she?"

"And you'd tell her, would you?"

"Only if it were absolutely necessary."

Mr Trollope put his hands on his hips. "You're telling me that if I press charges in response to your breaking into my office you'll tell Lady Worthington all those dreadful lies about my son?"

"Are they lies, Mr Trollope?"

"Would you be prepared to tell Lady Worthington about them whether they are or not?"

"Only if my hand were forced."

"Then you're even more despicable than I first thought, Mrs Churchill."

"Am I to arrest this lady or not, Mr Trollope?" asked Inspector Mappin.

Mr Trollope waved his hand dismissively and took a seat behind the largest desk. "Do what you like, Inspector. I came here to do some prep for tomorrow's edition."

"I think Mr Trollope's just saved you a heap of paper-work, Inspector," said Churchill with a stifled sigh of relief.

Chapter 33

"WHAT HAPPENED to you last night, Pembers?" asked Churchill the following morning.

"I hid in the broom cupboard."

"I didn't know there was a broom cupboard in Mr Trollope's office."

"Neither did I until I knocked against the door and fell inside it. I spent three hours in there with the broom, the mop and a box of carbolic soap. Luckily, I had the little police torch with me."

"Mr Trollope remained in his office for three hours?"

"It was probably about two and a half, but I remained there a while longer just to be certain the coast was clear."

"Oh dear, Pembers. I think you did marvellously well considering you don't like cupboards. And at least you escaped the long arm of the law."

"So did you, Mrs Churchill. I heard everything from inside the cupboard and I thought you talked your way out of it rather well."

"I did, didn't I? However, it's not all sweetness and

light, Pemberley. The fact of the matter is that Mr Trollope discovered me in his office. My card is marked."

"And we didn't really discover any of Mr Trollope's secrets."

"No. We don't have much to show for our labours, do we? Nothing other than the name Pierre."

"But Pierre sounds like he could be crucial."

"You're right, Pembers, he does. Unfortunately, I think we'll need to visit our clown-suited friend Mr Crumble at Piddleton Hotel again to ask him about Pierre."

"Will he even speak to us?"

"Not willingly, I wouldn't have thought, but we'll do what we can."

Churchill and Pemberley stepped into the foyer of Piddleton Hotel and lingered beside a pedestal upon which stood a cheap plaster imitation of the Venus de Milo.

"Where do you think we'll find him?" whispered Pemberley.

"Oh there'll be no need to find him," replied Churchill. "It's a bit like standing in a field with a bull in it; he'll come charging over soon enough. And here he is!"

Mr Crumble had a dark look on his face as he marched across the foyer in a turquoise plaid suit.

"Out you go!" he ordered. "You two are banned from the premises, remember?"

"We remember, Mr Crumble," replied Churchill, "and we'd only be too happy to oblige, but unfortunately business necessitates our presence here today."

"You have no business with me. Now leave before I set the dogs on you!"

"Oh no. Not that threat again, Mr Crumble. I think your guests would be quite distressed to witness two defenceless old ladies being torn apart by a pack of hounds. You would lose custom, there's no doubt about it."

"It would be on the front cover of the *Compton Poppleford Gazette*," added Pemberley.

"It certainly would!" agreed Churchill. "It wouldn't be good publicity for this establishment, that's for sure. Although I suppose if you were to offer the editor of the *Gazette* the sum of one hundred pounds he might be persuaded to keep the story out of his paper."

The hotel manager glared at Churchill. "You're the most tiresome woman I have ever met. Please leave my hotel before I lose my temper."

"Do you still plan to set the dogs on us?"

"I said *leave*!"

Churchill saw his fists clench.

"Mr Crumble, we will happily leave your establishment as soon as you have told us who Pierre is."

"I've never heard of anyone with that name. Now toddle off."

"Are you sure?" asked Churchill. "Perhaps you'd like to think about it again?"

"There's no need. I have never met anyone who goes by the name of Pierre in my entire life."

"That's not what you told Smithy Miggins at the *Compton Poppleford Gazette*, Mr Crumble."

His face reddened.

"I have no idea what you're talking about, Mrs Churchill."

"On the day that Mrs Furzgate fell down the stairs, it was suggested that Pierre had dropped a teacake that appears to have been implicated in the case. He was a member of your staff, and you paid—"

"Ssshhh!" hissed Mr Crumble, looking around anxiously. "Follow me."

He led them down a floral-carpeted corridor into a dingy, wood-panelled office that smelt of tobacco smoke.

"Now, what's all this about?" he fumed once he had slammed the door shut. "Are you suggesting that I had something to do with Mrs Furzgate's death? It was an accident; a pure accident! I can't tell you how much it's consumed my daily life since she died here. I wish it had never happened!"

"We all wish it had never happened," said Churchill, "but you would make life much easier for everyone if you explained exactly how it occurred."

"How should I know? I wasn't there!"

"Tell us about Pierre and the teacake."

"And if I do, what next? Will you tell the police?"

"Oh goodness me, no! Inspector Mappin is about as much use as a chocolate teapot."

"So what then?"

"I'm a private detective, Mr Crumble, and I handle my investigations with the utmost discretion."

"Does that mean you won't tell anyone?"

"It all depends on how much of a bearing it has on the investigation."

"But if people know about Pierre they won't come and stay at my hotel!"

"I'm sure the matter can be handled with great delicacy."

"What does that mean?"

"Just tell us what Pierre did."

"I can't. I'll lose customers!"

"If Pierre was involved in the death of Mrs Furzgate we need to do something about it, Mr Crumble. We can't cover up for him any longer. If you're not going to tell me anything more about him the public will most certainly find out what's been going on here."

"You wouldn't!"

"I would, Mr Crumble. At the present time I only know some of the information. Tell me all of it and you will have my discretion. If I continue to know only some of it, I shall go around shouting rather loudly about it."

Mr Crumble groaned and rubbed his face with his hands.

"Fine. Pierre worked here for a few days and then I fired him."

"Why did you fire him?"

"Because he dropped the teacake which Mrs Furzgate slipped on."

"Accidentally or on purpose?"

"That's just the thing. I think he did it on purpose!"

"What makes you say that?"

"He was quite a clumsy, hopeless fellow anyway, but then I have always struggled to recruit good staff here."

"Perhaps you don't pay them enough."

Mr Crumble scowled. "Money is rather tight in the hotel trade these days."

"So what happened?"

"Well, from what the staff tell me there was a slight to-do between Pierre and Mrs Furzgate, and when he saw her walking towards the staircase he rolled the teacake across her path. I'm quite sure he didn't mean to kill her; I don't see why he would have wanted to go that far. But he wished to do her some harm, that much is clear. As soon as I heard what had happened I dismissed him."

"And paid to keep his actions quiet."

"We had to. Can you imagine the impact on the business if it were discovered that my hotel was responsible for the poor woman's death?"

"I must say I'm pleased the truth is finally out, Mr Crumble. Now where might we find this Pierre?"

"I have no idea."

"What did he look like?"

"He had curly brown hair and wore spectacles. He was French."

"Surname?"

'I don't know."

"Do you know of any Frenchmen in this village, Pemberley?"

"I know of a French lady named Madame Bellegarde, but other than that, no."

"Does Madame Bellegarde have a son?"

"She has three daughters."

"Do any of them happen to be married to a chap called Pierre?"

"No, they're all under the age of twelve."

"Does Madame Bellegarde have any brothers?"

"No, only sisters."

"Does she have a husband?"

"She's a widow."

"I see. You seem to know quite a bit about Madame Bellegarde, Pembers."

"She's my neighbour."

"Good. A neighbour with only female relatives."

"Yes."

"I shouldn't think it would do any harm to ask her about this Pierre fellow when you get the chance, Pemberley. I don't suppose you've ever seen a man matching his description at her property?"

"Never."

"Did Pierre give away any information about himself, Mr Crumble? Anything at all that could help us in tracking him down?"

"None at all. He spoke no English and I spoke no French."

"And never the twain shall meet," added Churchill. "Thank you, Mr Crumble, for your eventual compliance. It's a shame there had to be so much rudeness before we got to the crux of the matter."

"I trust you'll keep this secret as we agreed, Mrs Churchill. Any time you wish to stay here as my guest you will be most welcome."

"I might consider it once you've updated the decor, Mr Crumble."

Chapter 34

"PIERRE," mused Churchill as she and Pemberley walked back to the office. "Pierre, Pierre, Pierre. It sounds like he's our murderer, Pemberley. But how can we find out who he is? Are you sure you've never come across him before?"

"I'm very sure."

"We're going to have to ask absolutely everybody. Someone knows something, Pembers, they have to. Why don't you go back into the village and start asking people about this mysterious Frenchman? In the meantime, I'd better go and watch Zeppelin for a bit. If I'm not seen to be doing something Mr Greenstone may give the case to someone else. It's rather boring watching a cat, but it'll give me a chance to mull this one over. A little thinking time is what's needed. I feel the need to allow everything to ferment in my head."

Two hours later Churchill was jolted awake by the rustle of a bush. Unaware that she had fallen asleep, she stumbled to her feet and dusted the leaves from her skirt. She hadn't anticipated that the sunny spot beside Mr Greenstone's apple tree would be so comfortable.

To Churchill's relief, Zeppelin was still present, and she suspected it was he who had woken her as he uncurled himself from beneath the hydrangea bush and stretched out his hind legs.

Churchill popped a butter toffee in her mouth and quietly observed as the cat strolled over to the slate wall and hopped over it.

"Where are you taking Auntie Annabel now, Zeppy?" she asked as he paused to watch a butterfly. He flicked the end of his tail, then trotted off down Muckleford Lane.

"Not too fast, pussy cat!" she called out to him. "Auntie Annabel's bunions haven't quite recovered from the sprint to her office the other day. And she's still got a dodgy knee from the… Oh, good afternoon, Mrs Trollope."

The sour-faced lady fixed Churchill with her sharp green eyes, which blazed out from beneath the brim of her summer hat. Her thin lips were stained with lipstick the colour of blood.

"Would you please excuse me, Mrs Trollope? I'm following the cat who has just trotted past you."

"The cat can trot on for all I care," she said, blocking Churchill's path.

"I'm in the middle of an investigation, Mrs Trollope."

"So I gather."

"Please may I pass? I don't wish to lose sight of that cat."

"Oh, you'll find it again soon enough, I'm sure of that. Just like you found your way into my husband's office."

"There's no need for us to discuss that, Mrs Trollope. I ironed the matter out with your husband and the inspector at the time."

"What were you doing in there?"

"It was nothing more than a drunken dare, which I feel terribly ashamed about now."

Churchill moved to step past Mrs Trollope, but the stern-faced woman moved in the same direction and prevented her from passing. "Surely you must have carried out a few drunken dares you feel rather embarrassed about yourself, Mrs Trollope?"

"I've never been drunk in my life."

"No, I can't imagine you would have been."

"You threatened to tell Lady Worthington about our son."

"Only because your husband was about to have me arrested for a crime I didn't commit."

"You were in his office!"

"Mrs Trollope, while it's terribly pleasant to stop for a chat on a sunny afternoon, I feel this conversation is going around in circles somewhat. I thought we got on quite well when we first met, but sadly relations between us appear to have soured. I put it down to a clash of personalities, but I bear you no ill-will and am quite happy if you wish to be on your way. I do, in fact, need to be on my way myself as I have a cat to follow."

Mrs Trollope's eyes narrowed and she lowered her voice to a threatening whisper. "You've got yourself into something that is way over your head, Mrs Churchill. So far over your head that even a tall ladder couldn't get you out again."

"How about a tall crane?" asked Churchill.

"No chance!" she hissed, shoving her face up close to Churchill's. "You really have no idea what will happen to you if you continue on this fool's errand, do you?" She gave an empty laugh. "No idea at all! Oh dear, Mrs Churchill, you have a lot to learn."

"Well, you need to choose a lipstick shade that matches

your complexion, Mrs Trollope. Skin tone pales as you grow older, and red is just too harsh for you. It'd be all right on a twenty-year-old, perhaps, but not on the face of a mature lady."

"That's supposed to be a put down is it?" Mrs Trollope sneered. "Rather a weak one at that." Her eyes narrowed even further. "Now how about you do the sensible thing, Mrs Churchill, and keep your nose out of matters that don't concern you? If you persist with this nonsense someone is going to get hurt. *Seriously* hurt."

"Hospitalised, perhaps?"

"It would be beyond the capabilities of medical assistance."

Chapter 35

"I'VE BEEN WONDERING what Mrs Trollope might actually do to hurt someone," Churchill said to Pemberley as they each enjoyed a cream bun in their office the following morning. *'If you persist with this nonsense someone is going to get hurt,'* is what she said. Who will get hurt? And how? I detest empty threats."

"I think it all sounds rather menacing, and not particularly empty," replied Pemberley.

"But what could Mrs Trollope and her husband actually do? She's tiny and he's lanky-limbed. The pair of them would probably be blown over in a strong wind."

"Ninjutsu," said Pemberley.

"Bless you, Pembers," replied Churchill.

"I said ninjutsu."

"There's no need to be rude."

"It's a Japanese martial art dating from the fourteenth century. Mrs Trollope mastered it when she and her husband were travelling in Japan."

"The Trollopes lived in Japan? Oh golly, I've just

realised what I did there, Pembers. You told me the name of that martial art and I thought you were——"

"Sneezing. Yes, I realised that."

"Oh, how funny! It really did sound like a sneeze. How do you say it again?"

"Ninjutsu. Anyway, as I was saying, Mrs Trollope has mastered it, and that might be the way someone could get hurt."

"You think she would use that Japanese martial art thingummy against someone?"

"Why do you think Mrs Higginbath walks with a limp?"

"Oh goodness, Pembers! That's dreadful! No wonder everybody does what she says. What a bully."

"Please be careful, Mrs Churchill."

"You don't need to worry about me. Did I tell you about the time I was set upon at the clubhouse of the Richmond-upon-Thames Ladies' Lawn Tennis Club?"

"No. But *please* be careful, Mrs Churchill. I'm worried that you might be in way over your——"

"Head? Yes, I get it. Thank you, Pembers." Churchill drained her tea and began to feel rather despondent. "For some reason that cream bun didn't quite hit the spot. I'm going back down to Bodkin's for something else."

Mr Smallbone was buying crumpets when Churchill entered the bakery. She greeted him cheerily, but he only muttered a reply and quickly left.

Bodger stood behind the counter. There was no sign of Mr Bodkin.

"Good morning, Bodger. I would like four custard tarts, please. Oh, good grief, there's a *rat*!" Churchill leapt back several feet from the counter, the furry brown rodent having lodged itself part-way beneath it. "You must kill it, Bodger!"

"Where?" he shrieked, pulling Freddie Carnegie-Bannerman's cricket bat from the wall. He dashed out from behind the counter, brandishing it with intent.

"Where is the blighter?" he yelled. "I'll get 'im!"

"There!" screeched Churchill, pointing down at the floor.

Bodger swung the cricket bat and Churchill turned away as he brought the bat crashing down on the rat. She kept her eyes fixed on the cottage loaves in the window but heard the sound of splintering wood as Bodger killed the rat and did some considerable damage to the counter in the process. Eventually, he stopped.

"I think it's dead," he said quietly.

"Take it away; I can't look at it," replied Churchill. She had lost her appetite for custard tarts.

"I'll put it in the bin out the back," said Bodger. "Hang on a moment," he continued. "I don't think it's a rat after all. What *is* it?"

"It's too big for a mouse, that's for sure," said Churchill, still staring at the cottage loaves. "Don't tell me it's a hedgehog. I couldn't bear it if we'd killed a hedgehog. Oh, goodness. It's not a hedgehog, is it?"

She turned round to see Bodger holding the brown, furry thing at arm's length.

"There's something else in it, too," he said. "Something like broken glass."

Churchill took a step toward him, peering at the hairy object.

"I don't think it's a living creature," she said cautiously. "In fact, it looks like a hairpiece of some sort. Is Mr Bodkin known for wearing a toupee? I haven't ever seen him wear one, and besides, that shade doesn't match his eyebrows."

At that moment the door behind the counter opened and Mr Bodkin came striding out.

"What the devil's going on out here?" When he set eyes on Churchill he groaned.

"Do you wear a toupee, Mr Bodkin?" she asked him.

"What an impertinent question! Of course not! What are you doing with Freddie Carnegie-Bannerman's cricket bat, Bodger?"

"I was trying to kill what I thought was a rat," the lanky youth replied sheepishly, looking at the smashed panelling at the front of the counter.

"Couldn't you have used another bat? That one's priceless!"

"I think you should be more worried about the prospect of a rat on the premises, Mr Bodkin," said Churchill. "But don't worry, it's not a rat after all. We were quite mistaken. It appears to be a wig and... Is that a broken pair of spectacles?"

"I think so," replied Bodger, detangling the broken frames from the hairpiece.

"Let me have a look!" said Mr Bodkin, striding out into the shop.

"No, don't, there's no need," Churchill replied, aware that the baker would be exceptionally angry once he saw what had happened to his counter and precious bat. "I'll come back for the custard tarts later," she added swiftly, noticing his face had turned puce with rage as he surveyed the damage. She dashed out of the door as quickly as her legs would carry her.

. . .

"I'd stay away from the bakery for a while if I were you, Pembers," said Churchill as she sat back at her desk.

"I heard a dreadful din," Pemberley replied.

"It's nothing to worry about," said Churchill. "Bodger has attacked a wig and pair of spectacles with a cricket bat. I've left him and Bodkin to sort it out between them."

Loud shouts rose up through the floorboards from the shop beneath their feet.

"I hope they sort it out soon. It'll be difficult for us to concentrate on our work otherwise, won't it, Pembers? I'll go back for the custard tarts when it's all calmed down."

"Why was there a wig and a pair of spectacles in the bakery?" asked Pemberley.

"Oh, I don't know. Someone dropped them there, I suppose."

"But why?"

"Perhaps they fell out of someone's bag."

"But why would they be carrying them around in the first place?"

"I have no idea, Pembers. Live and let live, I say."

"But *why*?"

"You sound like a child asking why all the time. I don't know *why*, do I?"

"That's exactly what a detective needs to know," replied Pemberley. "The detective needs to ask why in order to understand a person's motive. Atkins used to do it all the time."

"Did he indeed? That must have been very annoying."

"It was how his highly inquisitive, intelligent detective mind worked. *Always ask why*, he would say to me."

"Oh, I see. When you talk about intelligent detective minds I know exactly what you mean. That's quite different, isn't it? Of course I always ask *why* when I'm investigating a case. I thought you meant why in the more general sense."

"What general sense?"

"Oh, I don't know, Pembers. What was the point of this conversation?"

"Why did someone leave a wig and a pair of spectacles in the bakery? And how?"

"We're on to how as well, are we? Well I suppose the *how* is that they fell out of someone's bag and the *why* could be… They were on their way to a fancy dress party."

"I'm not aware of any fancy dress parties taking place today."

"Well there might be, Pembers. You won't necessarily receive an invitation to every party in Compton Poppleford."

"Oh, I never receive invites to any parties in Compton Poppleford, but I usually hear about them."

"Oh, all right. Not a fancy dress party, then. How about some other costumed event, such as… I can't think of one."

"A disguise!" said Pemberley. "Perhaps someone was planning to use the wig and spectacles as a disguise."

"That's quite a common usage, I suppose."

"But why would someone want to disguise himself?"

"Presumably it's someone who doesn't wish to be identified. And – I'm warming to this now, Pembers – perhaps they don't wish to be identified because they're up to no good!"

"So a criminal could have left the wig and spectacles in the bakery."

"Yes. And yes! I know who it was, Pemberley. There was a criminal in there just before me. Smallbone was leaving just as I arrived. The wig and spectacles must have fallen out of his bag!"

"Was he carrying a bag?"

"He wasn't, no. Perhaps they dropped out of his pocket."

"Did he have big enough pockets?"

"I didn't look, Pembers! I don't make a habit of sizing up a man's pockets. I always give men's pockets a wide berth, in fact."

"Then we're no closer to the truth."

"Perhaps we don't need to be. We already have a rather complicated case to focus on. We don't want to be distracted by strange goings-on at the bakery, do we? It's just a shame we can't get any more custard tarts for the time being."

Added to the shouting downstairs was a series of loud thumping noises.

"I think we'd be foolish to ignore the wig and spectacles," said Pemberley. "Someone – possibly Mr Smallbone, who is a convicted murderer – has for some reason deposited a disguise in the bakery."

"You think he left it there intentionally?"

"I think he wanted to be rid of it. How could it have fallen out of his pocket accidentally?"

"He certainly would have noticed if it had, wouldn't he?"

"Exactly. And the fact that he deposited it there suggests he was finished with it."

"Mr Smallbone disguised himself with a brown curly wig and spectacles, then tried to rid himself of the disguise." Churchill pondered this. "Why didn't he just put them in the bin if he didn't need them any more?"

Chapter 36

"PEMBERLEY, YOU'VE SOLVED IT!" Churchill declared as she burst into the office the following morning. "You clever old stick, you! I woke up in the night and remembered what you'd said!"

"What did I say?" asked Pemberley, taking a pause from her typing.

"When we first met Mrs Trollope and the bridge ladies you suggested that Mr Smallbone might have disguised himself and pushed Mrs Furzgate down the stairs. Well, there you go. You were right! Mr Smallbone used the wig and spectacles to disguise himself as Pierre!"

"I suppose I could be right, but don't you remember your reply to me?"

"No, what was it?"

"You said that his rather distinctive moustache would have given him away."

"Oh yes, I remember that now," said Churchill, suddenly feeling deflated. "That was rather astute of me, wasn't it?"

She sat down at her desk. "There's a chance this Pierre character had a moustache, though," she said.

"I think Mr Crumble would have mentioned it in the description of Pierre if he had. Besides, nobody has a moustache quite like Mr Smallbone's."

"You're right, Pembers. It's a one-off."

"We've established something though, haven't we?"

"What's that?"

"The possibility that Pierre doesn't exist and was merely someone wearing the disguise you found at the bakery."

"That has to be it! The wig and spectacles were worn by the mysterious Pierre!"

"But why didn't Mr Crumble notice it was a disguise?"

"Because the man's a fool. Now all we need to do is find out who disguised himself as Pierre."

"Or *her*self."

"Really, Pembers? You think a lady could have made a convincing Pierre?"

"It's possible."

"I suppose anything's possible. But to begin with we can't overlook the fact that the wig and spectacles were found at Mr Bodkin's bakery, so once again the baker is under suspicion. Either someone is attempting to frame him or he's doing it himself to pretend that he's being framed."

"A bluff?"

"I think it's a double bluff."

"No, it's definitely a bluff."

"Bodkin and Mappin had this same disagreement. Anyway, it doesn't really matter. Come on, let's go and speak to him about the wig and spectacles. Hopefully he's calmed down after yesterday's counter-smashing incident."

The two ladies made their way downstairs.

"We're 'ins Detective Agency' now," said Pemberley. "Did you notice I had managed to scrape the *k* off the door?"

"I did, Pembers. Excellent work."

They stepped out into the street just as Mr Bodkin was leaving the bakery. Churchill stopped still as she crossed the road.

"He's off somewhere," she whispered. "Where could he be going?"

"I don't know."

"I think we need to follow him."

"But he'll see us!"

"We won't follow him in an obvious manner, Pembers. We'll merely walk a short way behind him and pretend to be deep in conversation about something or other whenever he turns around. After all, it's quite believable that we just happen to be walking behind him, isn't it?"

"On the high street it is, but if he heads off down an unbeaten track it may be a little harder to explain ourselves."

"We'll worry about that if and when it happens, Pembers. Come on, let's go. We don't want to lose sight of him."

The two ladies crossed the street and followed Mr Bodkin past the butcher's shop, Mrs Bramley's Tea Rooms, the bookshop, the hardware store, the haberdashery shop, and the Wagon and Carrot tavern.

"Where's he going?" asked Pemberley.

"Are you expecting an immediate answer to your question?" Churchill queried.

"It would be useful to know, wouldn't it? These shoes aren't particularly comfortable. If I'd known I would be walking a great distance this morning I would have put on another pair."

"Stop grumbling, Pembers, and keep up. Expect the unexpected."

"Oh dear. I don't like the sound of that."

"It's the bread and butter of detective work. Look, he's turned right by the clock tower. Keep up!"

They turned into a narrow street lined with beamed houses. At the end of it sat the church of St Barnabas.

"Is Bodkin a religious man, Pemberley?"

"I don't know."

"Perhaps he plans to pray his way out of his predicament," laughed Churchill. "Oops, look away! He's turned around."

The ladies stopped and inspected some petunias in a window box.

"Has he seen us?" Churchill asked through clenched teeth.

"I don't know. I'm looking away, like you told me to."

"All right, I'll do one of those sweeping glances of the general environs and gauge whether he's spotted us or not."

Churchill looked around as if taking in the scenery of the street. Without looking directly at Mr Bodkin she was able to see that he was no longer looking in their direction.

"It's safe again, Pembers, let's go. We'll need to hang back a little bit as this road is quieter than the high street."

"I knew it. He'll soon realise we're following him."

"Nonsense! Let's pretend we're going to the church. We can stride rather purposefully toward the churchyard without drawing any suspicion to ourselves, as if we had a perfectly valid reason for going there."

"I don't want to bump into the vicar, though. He'll want to know where I've been."

"When did you last attend church, Pembers?"

"About twenty-three years ago."

"Tut-tut. And it's still the same vicar?"

"Yes. I have to hide whenever I see him out and about. He never looks any older; he'll go on forever I think."

"He must be blessed. Come on, Bodkin's gone past the church now. We need to see where he heads off to next."

The two ladies scurried past the church just in time to see Mr Bodkin step into a doorway on the left-hand side of the street. The door closed behind him.

"Interesting," said Churchill. "Let's just slowly stroll past and take a sidelong glance at the property as we pass it. No need to draw attention to ourselves."

As they neared the building Churchill noticed a shiny brass plaque next to the door Mr Bodkin had just walked through. She paused to read it.

"Mr T. W. Verney, Solicitor at Law," she whispered to Pemberley. "How interesting. Why would Mr Bodkin be visiting Mrs Furzgate's solicitor?"

Chapter 37

CHURCHILL AND PEMBERLEY had a cup of tea back at the office to the sound of hammering from the bakery downstairs.

"It sounds like Bodkin's getting that counter fixed," said Churchill. "I think you should pop down for some iced fancies and mention to Mr Bodkin that you saw him going into a lawyer's office, Pemberley."

"Why me?"

"Because it's always me confronting him and I think he's bored of me. And he calls me Mrs Roly-Poly behind my back. Did you stifle a snigger just then, Pembers?"

Pemberley shook her head and tried to straighten her face. "But you're the detective, Mrs Churchill."

"Yes, that's true. But we're a team, aren't we? You may be my secretary in name, but you're actually much more than that."

"Am I?" Pemberley pushed her shoulders back proudly. "Thank you, Mrs Churchill. Just hearing you say that means a lot to me."

"You're welcome. I mean, it's obvious, isn't it? Now go and see Bodkin."

Churchill settled down with another of Atkins' files while Pemberley went downstairs to the bakery. The detective was soon absorbed by a case in which a German word had been written in blood on a wall when Pemberley returned empty-handed.

"Oh, crumbs. Is he out of iced fancies?" asked Churchill.

"No, the bakery is closed for refitting."

"But there were only a few splintered slats on the counter. Certainly nothing to warrant a complete refurbishment."

"Everything's being ripped out. A very nice workman showed me where the counter will be located, and there's going to be a storage display especially for bread rolls. He's having new ovens fitted, which will expand his bread product offering by two-thirds."

"Did you speak to Bodkin?"

"No, I didn't see him there."

"Bodger?"

"No."

"Any sign of the wig and spectacles?"

"No sign at all. The counter and most of the shelving has gone, so I don't suppose the wig and spectacles would have been left lying about."

"No, I don't suppose they would be. Darn it!" Churchill thumped her desk. "If I'd thought more quickly at the time I'd have taken the wig and spectacles from Bodger. Now the evidence is lost."

"Bodkin may have them somewhere?"

"He'll have disposed of them if they implicate him."

"Unless it was a bluff."

"A double bluff. Darn it and darn it again, Pembers. I

feel as though this investigation is slipping through our fingers."

A heavy throbbing sound from the street outside made her desk tremble.

"Drilling?" Churchill cried out. "What's Bodkin having done down there now? I swear our office will have collapsed into his bakery before the day is out!"

"It's not a drill," said Pemberley, looking out of the window. "It's Mr Cavendish's car."

Mr Cavendish bounded into the office moments later.

"Good morning, ladies!" He gave them a wide grin and tossed his boater hat onto the hat stand. "What's Bodkin up to downstairs?" he asked as he sat at Churchill's desk.

"He's having a refit," replied Churchill.

"Do you mean him or his shop?" Mr Cavendish laughed loudly at his own joke.

"Since you mention it, I think the baker could do with a refit as well, couldn't he?" said Churchill. "Then again, couldn't we all?" She laughed.

"Oh no, you're too hard on yourself, Mrs Churchill," said Mr Cavendish. "You're perfect just the way you are."

"Tea, Mr Cavendish?" interrupted Pemberley.

"Thank you, that would be marvellous. Now where were we?"

"You were flattering me, Mr Cavendish," replied Churchill.

"Merely stating the truth, Mrs Churchill."

"I expect you say that to all the private detectives."

"'Tis treason to say such a thing! I only have one private detective."

"Oh goody. That's what I like to hear. I expect you'd

like an update on our progress?"

"Absolutely. Go on, I'm all ears."

"Don't you find that expression rather strange? I don't like to imagine anyone being all ears."

"Rather macabre, isn't it?"

Pemberley brought in the tea and Churchill told Mr Cavendish about the break-in at Mr Trollope's office.

"You old devil, you," he said with a wink. "And you wriggled out of an arrest! I'm impressed."

Next she told him about the mysterious Pierre and the disguise she had discovered in Mr Bodkin's bakery.

Mr Cavendish sipped his tea thoughtfully. "It's interesting, isn't it, that every line of investigation leads back to that baker fellow."

"And there's something else, too," said Churchill.

"What's that, then?"

"Pemberley and I happened to follow Bodkin yesterday, and where do you suppose he went?"

"Enlighten me, Mrs Churchill."

"To Mr Verney, your godmother's solicitor!"

"Did he indeed? What was the baker's business with him?"

"We don't know. He went in and closed the door behind him."

"As you would expect," replied Mr Cavendish.

"I think it's suspicious."

"It's exceedingly suspicious. Perhaps he was seeking legal advice."

"He must be, mustn't he, if he's consulting a solicitor," replied Churchill.

"He's seeking legal advice because he knows that the finger of blame is pointed at him! And what's more, he's seeking legal advice because he's guilty! If he has nothing to hide, why is he seeing a solicitor?"

"I'm inclined to agree with you, Mr Cavendish."

"Mappin should have arrested him while he had the opportunity. But instead that cursed baker is walking around like a free man, having his bakery refitted and taking legal advice so he can plan his next evasive move!"

"I couldn't agree more."

"The disguise was found right inside his bakery! Where is it now?"

"I suspect he's disposed of it."

Mr Cavendish sighed and cradled his head. "I can't believe he's getting away with this," he said sadly. "I don't suppose there's much else we can do, Mrs Churchill. He's destroyed key evidence and employed the services of a lawyer who'll run rings around Inspector Mappin. I wish my poor godmother had never set eyes on him, I truly do!"

"There, there, Mr Cavendish, all is not lost." Churchill felt deep sympathy for the man sitting before her and once again fought the urge to clutch him to her bosom. "We'll find a way to ensnare that baker, won't we Miss Pemberley?" She glanced desperately at her secretary for reassurance.

"Of course we will," replied Pemberley. "Where there's a will there's a way."

"I like that sort of talk!" said Churchill. "We never give up on our cases, Mr Cavendish. We fight to the bitter end, and we'll make sure Mr Bodkin faces justice!"

"I think he's too clever," replied Mr Cavendish.

"Not for me, he isn't!" said Churchill. "For forty years I watched my husband from the wings as he carried out his inspectorial duties for the Metropolitan Police. There isn't much I didn't learn from him during the course of those forty years, and now is my opportunity to put all that knowledge to the test. We will catch your godmother's murderer, Mr Cavendish. Don't you fret."

Chapter 38

"IT WOULD BE a breach of client confidentiality to discuss any matter pertaining to Mr Bodkin," said Mr Verney. Sitting in a winged and buttoned leather chair behind an oversized mahogany desk, the short, dusty-looking solicitor regarded them in turn through his thick spectacle lenses.

Churchill and Pemberley sat opposite him on small, uncomfortable chairs which emphasised the inferiority of anyone who had the misfortune of sitting on them.

"Has he asked you to be his defence lawyer?" Churchill asked.

"I am unable to give an answer one way or the other."

"But that's not possible, is it?" said Pemberley. "Mr Verney is a civil lawyer rather than a criminal one, isn't he?"

"Are you a civil lawyer or a criminal lawyer, Mr Verney?" asked Churchill.

"Civil mainly, but I've been known to dabble."

"There you go, Miss Pemberley, he dabbles! I knew it. He's currently working up a watertight defence case for Mr Bodkin."

"May I ask what Mr Bodkin has been accused of?" asked the solicitor.

"Nothing yet. But Miss Pemberley and I believe he is guilty of destroying evidence that could link him to a murder."

"Which murder?"

"The murder of Mrs Furzgate."

"I thought her death was an accident?"

"Ah, there you go, Mr Verney. I see you're practising the watertight defence already."

"Not at all; I'm merely stating a fact. The coroner ruled her death to be an accident. No criminal act has been committed."

"No criminal act has *yet been proven*," retorted Churchill. "But we're pretty close to it, aren't we, Miss Pemberley? And Inspector Mappin is very interested in certain aspects of the case."

"Case? There is no case!"

"That's where you are mistaken, Mr Verney. I have been hired by Mrs Furzgate's godson to conduct an investigation into her death. Therefore, there is a case. I have a case file for it and everything."

"And a detailed incident map on the wall," added Pemberley. "You should come and see it, Mr Verney."

"No, don't invite him to look at it, Pembers. He's the defence, remember? We'll give him even more defensive ideas if he sees our incident board."

"But he needs to be presented with the evidence we have so he can prepare his case," said Pemberley.

"Does he? Well, that doesn't seem fair. Can we find out what his defence is so we can get more evidence?"

"Ladies, may I interrupt your conversation for a moment?" asked the solicitor. "There is no defence case being prepared. My client has neither been charged nor arrested for any offence."

"Ah, but he's been questioned by the police," said Churchill.

"Inspector Mappin asked him a few questions, did he?"

"Yes, he did."

Mr Verney glanced at his watch. "My time is precious, ladies."

"And expensive, no doubt," said Churchill. "What's your hourly rate?"

Mr Verney ignored her question. "You mention that you have evidence that my client was involved in the so-called murder of Mrs Furzgate. May I ask what that evidence is?"

"Are we putting ourselves at a disadvantage if we tell you?" said Churchill.

"No, not at all. I ask merely out of interest."

"What about your defence?"

"There is no defence! Now what have you got on Bodkin?"

Churchill told the solicitor about the letter, and about the wig and glasses. An expression of incredulity spread across his face as she spoke.

"It sounds like something out of a pantomime," he commented when she had finished.

"I beg your pardon?"

"Why would Mr Bodkin push his former lover down the stairs while disguised as a French waiter?" he asked.

"You tell me, Mr Verney. He's your client."

"Then send a letter telling you what he had done and leaving the waiter disguise on the floor of his shop?"

"A clumsy attempt to throw us off the scent."

"What do you mean?"

"I mean that his actions are so clumsy they're deliberately designed to make us think he's being framed by someone else."

"It sounds as though he is."

"No one else would be that foolish."

"So Mr Bodkin is guilty by dint of being foolish?"

"Exactly, Mr Verney. A foolish man who thinks he's being clever; there really is nothing worse."

"I can think of a few worse things, but I'll leave it there for now. I really must get on with my work, ladies."

"So you're not going to tell us why Mr Bodkin visited you?"

"Absolutely not! You could sit on those chairs all day waiting for an answer, but none would come."

"There's no danger of that," said Pemberley. "My buttocks have gone completely numb after a mere five minutes."

"Miss Pemberley!" said Churchill in a shocked tone. "Remember your manners! I do apologise, Mr Verney, for the manner in which my secretary referred to her sit-upon."

"Have you quite finished?" asked the lawyer impatiently.

"Yes, I think we have," Churchill replied. "Thank you for your help with nothing at all, Mr Verney."

Churchill and Pemberley had almost reached their office when Churchill stopped and grabbed Pemberley's arm.

"Wait! What's going on there?"

Mr Bodkin was standing outside his bakery chatting animatedly to Mrs Trollope and a lean, hatchet-faced young man in a smart, striped suit. Two workmen were balanced on ladders attaching new shiny letters to the front of the shop.

"Look at that baker loitering there without a care in the world!" fumed Churchill. "Yapping away to Mrs Trollope and some odd-looking man who looks to be a younger version of her husband. Oh! Do you know what I think, Pembers?"

"What?"

"That young man there must be Timothy Trollope!"

"Yes, it is."

"It is? Then why didn't you tell me?!"

"I was about to."

"But what's he doing here? I thought he lived in the Bahamas."

"He does, but I suppose he must visit his parents from time to time."

"I wonder what they could be talking about. Bodkin seems rather chummy with the Trollopes, doesn't he? Let's stroll slowly past, pretending to be in conversation, and see if we can listen in."

The two ladies sauntered toward their office, trying not to look at the trio.

"The Cotswolds are quite delightful in May, Pemberley, I can recommend a lovely hotel in Stow-on-the-Wold."

"Why have you begun talking about the Cotswolds, Mrs Churchill?"

"I'm trying to make conversation, Pembers!" she hissed. "We're pretending to have a nonchalant chat, remember? Then Bodkin and the Trollopes won't think we're listening in."

"But we can't listen in to what they're saying if we're talking, can we?" whispered Pemberley.

"But if we actually listen in they'll be suspicious. We need to look natural."

"I don't understand how we can do both."

"That's the skill of detective work. Oh dear, they've

spotted us. Good morning, Mrs Trollope! And Mr Bodkin! And who is this young man we have the pleasure of meeting?"

"This is my son, Timothy Trollope," replied Mrs Trollope coldly.

"A young man I have heard much about!" said Churchill. "And how nice it is to meet you at last. Are you planning to remain on these shores for long?"

"Just a week, and then I travel to Monaco." The young man's eyes were set too close together, and he struggled to meet her gaze.

"How glamorous, Mr Trollope. Do you have connections there?"

"Never mind about my son's connections," said Mrs Trollope.

Churchill decided to ignore the rude remark, turning her attentions to the baker instead. "Your shop is coming along nicely, Mr Bodkin."

"A refit was long overdue," he replied gruffly. "Though next time you visit I'd like you to check that any suspected rat is actually a rat."

"I hope I shan't find any more rats in your bakery, Mr Bodkin!"

"Now you come to mention it, there have never been, nor will there ever be, any rats in my bakery."

"The wig and spectacles took me quite by surprise. What were they doing on your premises?"

"I have no idea. I suppose it must have been someone's idea of a joke."

"I can't imagine anyone having such a weak sense of humour. I'm wondering if it was a discarded disguise, perhaps."

"It might have been. Or a fancy dress get-up of some sort."

"I'm inclined to think it more likely that it was a disguise."

"Are you? Very good."

"Can I ask what happened to the disguise, Mr Bodkin?"

"I have no idea. Last I saw it Bodger had beaten the thing to a pulp with a cricket bat in response to your hysterical protestations. And smashed up my serving counter to boot."

"I'm afraid you'll find this is *l'ordre du jour* for Mrs Churchill," said Mrs Trollope. "When she's not breaking into someone else's premises she's destroying them."

"Why are you speaking about me as if I weren't here, Mrs Trollope?" asked Churchill.

The lady looked away, as if pretending not to hear.

"Excuse me, Mrs Trollope," ventured Churchill. "Can you hear me?"

"This lady's trying to talk to you, Mummy," said Timothy.

"I know she is, darling. I'm ignoring her in the hope that she'll lose interest and go away."

"I say!" exclaimed Churchill. "She's not a very polite mummy, is she?"

"Oh, I see. This lady's a *personne indésirable* is she, Mama?" said Timothy.

"Oui, c'est vrai," replied Mrs Trollope.

"Why's everybody speaking French all of a sudden?" asked Churchill.

"*I'm* not," said the baker.

"Thank you, Mr Bodkin."

"Perhaps there's some French blood in the Trollope family," suggested Pemberley.

"Yes, perhaps there is, Miss Pemberley, but as Mrs Trollope is refusing to speak to me I don't suppose we shall ever find out. When are you reopening, Mr Bodkin? I miss your currant buns."

"Tomorrow. This is just a quick refit; I don't want to lose out on too much business."

"Business must have been brisk for you to afford a refit in the first place, Mr Bodkin."

"I had a little capital to spend."

"Did you now? Always nice to be in that position, isn't it?"

"I can't complain."

"No, I don't suppose you can. Now, returning to this disguise of yours."

"Of mine? That flea-ridden wig was nothing to do with me, Mrs Churchill."

"Then what was it doing in your bakery, Mr Bodkin?"

"I can only assume it had been dropped there by a customer."

"Is that what your solicitor told you to say?"

"My solicitor hasn't told me to say anything, Mrs Churchill. What are you driving at?"

"I was wondering what your business with Mr Verney was."

"*My* business with Verney is none of *your* business."

"Mrs Churchill, you really must stop sticking your beak into matters that don't concern you," said Mrs Trollope. "You've seen what happened to the last woman who couldn't help but interfere."

Churchill gasped. "Is that a threat, Mrs Trollope?"

"No, but her story should surely serve as a cautionary tale."

Churchill stared at the lady, then at her narrow-eyed son. She felt a shiver travel down her spine.

"Come along, Miss Pemberley," she said. "Time for a cup of something hot and strengthening."

Chapter 39

"JUST ONE GLANCE at Trollope junior and you can tell he's little more than a brigand," said Churchill as she sipped her tea. "All that education and he's no more than a common thief. He's got his father's eyes, hasn't he?"

"And his mother's nose," added Pemberley.

"Definitely his mother's snout."

"I don't know where he gets his chin from, though."

"Perhaps it skipped a generation?" Churchill drained her cup. "What I want to know, Pembers, is what he's doing here."

"He's en route to Monaco. Isn't he?"

"That's what he said, but I'm not sure whether to believe it or not. Does he regularly come back home to Mummy and Daddy?"

"It's the first time I've seen him for two or three years. He wasn't even around for his mother's mayoral campaign."

"He just wired her the money instead, by the sound of things. There's something fishy about all this, I feel sure of it. Hark! Is that someone coming up the stairs?"

There was a timid knock at the door.

"Enter!" Churchill called out.

She was surprised to see Mr Smallbone step into the room, his moustache bristling nervously. She hadn't thought he would be brave enough to talk to her again after the confrontation over his spell in jail.

"Mr Smallbone! To what do we owe this pleasure?"

"I've come to find out 'ow you's copin' with all that noise downstairs."

"That's uncharacteristically thoughtful of you, Mr Smallbone. It has been rather a nuisance at times, but this afternoon has been fairly... Oh no, there we go. More hammering."

"It's loud up 'ere, ain't it?" said Mr Smallbone. "It's bad enough 'aving to listen from 'cross the road."

"I've coped with worse, Mr Smallbone. While you're here, I have something to ask you. A wig and a pair of spectacles were left inside Mr Bodkin's bakery yesterday. I was wondering whether the items belonged to you."

"No, what would I want with them things?"

"Perhaps you like to disguise yourself with them."

"I don't go in for them sorts of things no more."

"You used to disguise yourself, then?"

"I did once 'pon a time. Shortly before me Isle of Bute days." He gave an awkward cough.

"Of course, those Isle of Bute days. And you haven't disguised yourself since then?"

"No. Why'd I wanna do that?"

"I don't know, Mr Smallbone. It was just a thought."

"Ain't you been wonderin' where Bodkin found the money to do up 'is bakery?"

"As a matter of fact I have, Mr Smallbone. You know me too well. I asked the baker himself, and he told he had a little capital set aside."

"He's come into a bitta money," replied Smallbone.

"Has he indeed? Lucky Mr Bodkin."

"D'you wanna know where it's came from?"

"Well, it's not in my nature to pry, but if you're willing to volunteer the information, Mr Smallbone, I'll gladly hear it."

"Come from Mrs Furzgate, it did. She left it to 'im in 'er will."

Churchill was momentarily taken aback. "We are talking about the same Mrs Furzgate, aren't we? The one who fell down the stairs at Piddleton Hotel?"

"Yep. That's the one."

"She left Bodkin all her money?"

"Yeah, they 'ad a love affair. Ain't you remembered?"

"I hadn't forgotten. On the other hand, I can't say I care much for remembering it either. But that was rather generous of Mrs Furzgate, was it not?"

"It can't have been much," said Pemberley. "She was a woman of modest means."

"Just enough to refit a bakery, I suppose," said Churchill.

"Nope," replied Mr Smallbone. "There was loads of it."

"What? Loads of money? But how?" she probed.

Mr Smallbone shrugged. "Dunno. Family money, p'rhaps. But I knows it were a lot 'cause Bodkin's been boastin' about it down the Wagon and Carrot. He bought everyone in there a drink."

"A shame we missed that one, Miss Pemberley, isn't it? Did Bodkin say how much she had left him?"

"Nope. Just said it was loads."

"How unfortunate that he didn't feel the need to be more specific. And it was definitely Mrs Furzgate's money?"

"Yeah. Verney's has been lookin' after it. 'E's her lawyer, an' 'e's proberly taking a cut for his fee an' all."

"I'm sure he has, Mr Smallbone. I've yet to meet a poverty-stricken lawyer. That might explain what Bodkin was doing at Verney's office the other day, Miss Pemberley. He's been helping himself to the loot."

"It's all above board," said Smallbone. "He was named in 'er will."

"Well, thank you for visiting us and explaining this, Mr Smallbone. It does shed light on the matter."

"An' it means he done it, don't it?" said Smallbone.

"Done what?"

"Murdered her! He pushed Furzgate down the stairs so he could get his 'ands on 'er cash!"

"But there would be no need, would there, if he knew he'd be getting the money some day?"

"I reckons 'e got impatient!" replied Smallbone. "'E kept thinkin' about what his nice new bakery'd look like, and afore long the thought of all that money got turned into murderous intent."

"I must admit that's quite a compelling motive, Mr Smallbone. I had no idea you possessed the skill to turn your mind to detective matters."

"I were on the Isle of Bute for ten years, weren't I?"

"You were indeed, Mr Smallbone. There's nothing quite like a stay on the Isle of Bute to acquaint oneself with the way the criminal classes operate."

"They say as it takes one to know one, Mrs Churchill."

"That they do, Mr Smallbone. Thank you for this excellent piece of intelligence. Can you update the incident board with it, Miss Pemberley?"

"I'd be only too happy to."

"And once you've done that we must hoof it over to

Piddleton Hotel to gather a little more evidence. We're nearly there!"

"Come along with us please, hotel manager. I think we've found your Pierre."

Mr Crumble sat behind his desk in the familiar turquoise plaid suit and glared at Mrs Churchill.

"This isn't a convenient time."

"It may not be for you, Mr Crumble, but it certainly is for us. This may be the moment we ensnare the culprit!"

"But I'm in the middle of something."

"We're all in the middle of something, Mr Crumble. Now come along, there's no time like the present. The sooner we get you there the sooner you can return to whatever you're in the middle of."

"I consider this a great imposition!"

"Do I need to remind you that the private little arrangement you have with the *Compton Poppleford Gazette* could very easily become public knowledge?"

"No, you don't."

"Come along, then. Off we trot."

Mr Crumble sighed and got up from his chair.

"Mr Bodkin?" asked Mr Crumble as they stood outside the bakery. "What's the baker got to do with anything?"

A new sign saying *Bokdin's Bakery* hung proudly across the top of the shop.

"Yes, Mr Bodkin the baker. Or should I say Bokdin?" Churchill chuckled. "There he is, shouting at that workman over there. I'm assuming he's the man who put the sign up."

The workman seemed rather relieved at the interruption as the baker turned to Churchill with a face that reminded her of an angry tomato.

"I do hope we're not interrupting anything, Mr Bodkin," she said brightly. "Would you mind calming yourself a little and facing Mr Crumble here? You do know Mr Crumble from the Piddleton Hotel, don't you?"

"Yes, we were at school together. But this is *not* a convenient time!" he fumed.

"It never is, is it?" replied Churchill. "Mr Crumble said much the same thing, so let's get this over and done with. If you two gentlemen could spare a moment of each other's time, perhaps Mr Crumble you could tell us if the baker is, in fact, Pierre."

"Not a chance," said Mr Crumble.

"Who's Pierre?" asked Mr Bodkin.

"I can see that we're somewhat hampered here by the lack of wig and spectacles." Churchill looked around for suitable replacements. "Ah, Miss Pemberley! Perhaps you can lend Mr Bodkin your spectacles."

"But I need them to see with."

"Of course you do, dear, and I'll hand them back in a jiffy. Just pass them to Mr Bodkin, will you please?"

Pemberley did as she was told.

"I'm not wearing ladies' spectacles!" protested Mr Bodkin.

"Just put them on and stop making a fuss." Churchill surveyed his bald pate. "It's rather hard to imagine you with hair, but perhaps the spectacles will do trick. What do you think, Mr Crumble. Does this man bear a resemblance to Pierre now?"

"None whatsoever."

"You'll have to imagine a mass of dark curly hair, of course. Can you imagine that? Does it ring any bells?"

"None at all."

"Are you sure?"

"Positive."

"How can you be so sure?"

"Because Pierre is about two inches shorter and three inches narrower. And at least twenty years younger."

"Fine," retorted Churchill, feeling deeply unsatisfied with the outcome of the exercise.

"Have you quite finished?" asked Mr Bodkin. "Can I get back to shouting at my workmen?"

"Do you speak any French, Mr Bodkin?" she asked.

"No. Now will you please leave me alone?"

"I should think Pierre will have returned to his motherland by now," said Mr Crumble.

"I don't think he has, Mr Crumble. You see, I think your Pierre was wearing a disguise."

"Ah, so that's why you put Miss Pemberley's spectacles on Mr Bodkin? You think Bodkin disguised himself as Pierre?"

"Yes, that's right."

Mr Crumble gave a loud laugh and slapped his thigh. "What, old *Piggers* here?"

"Piggers?"

"That's what they called me at school," Bodkin replied disdainfully.

"Mrs Churchill," said Mr Crumble as he wiped the tears of mirth away from his eyes. "Did you honestly think I wouldn't recognise Piggers in a wig and spectacles?"

Churchill felt distinctly foolish. "I didn't realise how well acquainted you were with Piggers."

"We weren't that well acquainted," stated Bodkin. "Pip here was best friends with Bruiser."

"Let me guess," said Churchill. "Bruiser was the school bully."

"He was indeed," replied Bodkin.

"Why Pip?" she asked.

"Pip, pippin, Cox's orange pippin, apple, apple crumble," explained Mr Crumble without pausing for breath.

"Bruiser used to put a cricket ball in his pillowcase and thwack fellows over the head with it after lights out," said Bodkin.

"Pleasant chap then, eh?" said Churchill.

"I wonder what he's up to these days," mused Bodkin.

"He's a high court judge," replied Crumble.

"What else?" replied Churchill. "Come on, Miss Pemberley, let's leave these chaps to reminisce about their school days while we get back to the important business of solving crimes."

"I need my spectacles back from Piggers," said Pemberley.

"But I can see better with these on," said Bodkin.

"Then get your own," retorted Pemberley, snatching them off his face.

Chapter 40

"OH, help! I'm so embarrassed, Pemberley!" said Churchill once they were back in their office. "I should have assumed Crumble and Bodkin already knew each other. Everyone knows everyone here, don't they?"

"They do, I'm afraid."

"Did you know that Crumble and Bodkin went to school together?"

"Yes, I did."

"Perhaps you could have mentioned it to me."

"They've both changed a lot since then. There was a slight possibility that Crumble wouldn't have recognised him."

Churchill sighed. "Well, we know now that Bodkin was not Pierre. But what about all this money he's come into? He's certainly enjoying spending it. I'd say he was trying to blow it all before anyone cottons on to the fact that he's the one behind Mrs Furzgate's death."

"But how can he be?"

"I don't know, Pembers; really I don't. He was the only one who stood to gain from her death as she left everything in her will to him. Besides, she had threatened to tell his wife about their love affair, so he had a lot to gain by pushing her down those stairs."

"Perhaps he asked Pierre to do it for him."

"He may well have done. He may have asked the person who disguised himself as Pierre to do it. But who is Pierre?"

"A hitman, I imagine."

"I suppose he must be if he was paid to murder someone."

"Why did Smallbone come and tell us about Bodkin's windfall?" asked Pemberley.

"I assume he was just being helpful."

"Smallbone isn't known for being helpful."

"You're right, Pembers. It's the first time I've ever known him to be helpful."

"I wonder if he was trying to influence proceedings."

"Trying to frame Bodkin, you mean?"

"Your initial thought was that he'd planted the disguise in Bodkin's bakery, wasn't it?"

"Yes, true. I did think that. He was in the shop just before I spotted it there."

"So Smallbone could have planted the disguise before coming to inform us about Bodkin's motive for the murder."

"You're right, Pembers. He's either protecting himself or someone else. What's his relationship with the Trollopes like?"

"Quite friendly, I think."

"Isn't it remarkable how that distasteful pair manage to be on good terms with so many people? How do they do that? I've often found the most popular people are the most unpleasant." Churchill's verbal musings were interrupted by the rumble of an engine from the street below.

. . .

"My sprightly private eye!" enthused Mr Cavendish as he bounced into the room. "And her jaunty accomplice!" he added, giving Pemberley a wink.

"Good afternoon, Mr Cavendish. You're in better spirits than when we last saw you."

"Nothing keeps me down for long, Mrs Churchill," he replied, tossing his boater onto the hat stand and taking a seat.

"Indeed not. You're like a frisky young puppy."

He grinned widely. "What a delightful comparison, Mrs Churchill. I like that very much."

"I hope he's house trained," Pemberley cut in. "Tea, Mr Cavendish?"

"Absolutely. Thank you."

"Did you have a nickname at school, Mr Cavendish?" asked Churchill.

"Not one that I'm willing to share."

"Oh, go on."

"No."

"Please."

"No."

"Is it rude?"

"No, just embarrassing."

"Oh, come on, Mr Cavendish. What's an embarrassing nickname between friends?"

"My lips are sealed."

"Nonsense! I don't believe for one minute that you've ever sealed those lips of yours."

"You know me too well, Mrs Churchill."

"So what was it?"

"Oh, okay then. If you must drag the information out of me… It was Mary."

"Mary?"

"I know. Terrible, isn't it?" He grinned.

"And the logic behind it?"

"Cavendish Square, square leg, leg of lamb, Mary had a little lamb, Mary. There you go, you see."

"That's rather convoluted. There must have been some long, dull nights in your dorm to cook that one up."

"Oh, there were, Mrs Churchill. However, I must ask how the investigation is going. Surely you're closing in on him by now."

"Him?"

"Bodkin."

"Oh yes, him. Thank you for the tea, Miss Pemberley. Yes, well we have uncovered some rather damning news."

"What's that, then?"

"The source of the funds he has used to fund the refit of his bakery."

"Ah."

"It seems your godmother wasn't as hard up as she liked people to think. She left a tidy sum to Bodkin in her will."

"And the chap's happily spending every penny of it by the sound of it." Mr Cavendish sighed heavily and gazed down at the floor.

"Did you know about the money?"

"I only found out about it from Verney a day or two ago. I had no idea about it, of course. Hers was a meagre existence. But when I enquired about the contents of her will, I uncovered the same unhappy news. Every penny has gone to Bodkin."

"You had no doubt hoped she would leave a little something for you, Mr Cavendish?"

"I did indeed when I learned about the money! Until a few days ago I hadn't expected a thing, but when Verney told me about her nest egg my hopes did lift a little; only to be immediately dashed when he told me who would be netting the lot. What did Bodkin do to deserve that?" His eyes grew wide and damp. "The only family she had left was a nephew who swanned off to India many years ago. I don't even know if the chap's still alive. And then there was me, but it seems she overlooked her godson and left it all to that bald-headed baker with the caterpillar eyebrows. Do you know what I think, Mrs Churchill? I think he wasn't even in love with her. She was just a little bit on the side to him. A little iced fancy, and nothing more."

Churchill struggled to picture Mrs Furzgate as an iced fancy.

"Perhaps your godmother thought you were already catered for, Mr Cavendish?"

"I can't deny that the old flesh and blood provide me with a superficial stipend, but this isn't about money, is it? It's about affection! Until recently I had been labouring under the misapprehension that my godmother had held a modicum of fondness for me. I was sorely mistaken."

"You must be extremely disappointed."

"I am, if truth be told. And it's a double disappointment given that the money has gone to the least deserving man in Compton Poppleford!"

"Oh, Mr Cavendish, I don't know what to say."

"Inspector Mappin needs to arrest the man. Bodkin must have known she had money, and that he'd been named in her will. To think he even sent you a note confessing his guilt! And then the French waiter disguise was found in his shop! All the evidence is there, Mrs Churchill, yet that hapless inspector refuses to do his job. He's probably asleep at his desk again as we have this conversation."

"I'm sure he is, Mr Cavendish. He really is useless. My

dear husband would have wiped the floor with him. I'll tell you what I'll do. I'll write up my final report on this case and present it to him. If he fails to act on that we'll take it up with his superiors. Does that sound like a suitable plan to you?"

"It sounds like an excellent plan."

"There is only one matter outstanding, and that's the identity of the elusive French waiter, Pierre, who Bodkin may have paid to administer the final shove to your unsuspecting godmother. But I have an idea, Mr Cavendish. Just leave it with me."

"Thank you, Mrs Churchill. I admire your relentless nature. You never give up on a case, do you?"

"Absolutely not! *Give up* isn't even in my vocabulary."

"It must be," interjected Pemberley. "You just said it."

"Said what?"

"Give up."

"What?"

"You said the words *give up* aren't in your vocabulary, but you just said them."

"Which words?"

Pemberley groaned and rested her head in her hands.

"See, Mr Cavendish? Not even in my vocabulary."

"What's your idea about Pierre?" asked Pemberley once Mr Cavendish had left the room.

"Well, a thought darkened my mind when I first set eyes on that young Timothy Trollope. Remember how he used several French expressions?"

"It's him!" Pemberley leapt up from her chair.

"It's merely an idea at the moment. But with a wig and spectacles on I bet he'd make a suitable Pierre, don't you think?"

"Yes, yes, yes! It's him! It's Timothy Trollope!"

"We need to gather a little more evidence first, Pembers. A little digging around into his past won't do us any harm. Can you get Harrow School on the telephone? Tell the headmaster I'd like to speak to him about one of his former pupils."

Chapter 41

"HOW MANY HOUSES have you narrowed it down to now?" Mr Greenstone asked Churchill as they stood beside the hydrangea and tried not to watch Zeppelin cleaning between his legs.

"Well, there's still this street and the neighbouring one, but the row of houses on the other side of the duck pond has been ruled out."

Mr Greenstone sighed. "Progress seems rather slow."

"To be honest with you, Mr Greenstone, the cat has a tendency to stay put whenever I come to observe him. If I had a shilling for every time I've stood here watching him lick his—"

"I'd say you already have. I paid you ten pounds, didn't I?"

"You did, Mr Greenstone. That almost covers it, I should think."

"Perhaps I should have said this sooner, but you may be better off trying to follow him in the evenings. That's when I think he's mainly being fed by someone else."

"Evenings. Righty-ho. Perhaps we should have established that at the outset. No wonder this case has taken so long."

"Well there's that, and then I think you've been rather distracted by the Furzgate case."

"To be honest with you a second time, Mr Greenstone, I have been. But let me assure you that the Furzgate case is almost solved."

"Is it?"

"Oh, yes. There are only a few pieces of the puzzle to fit into place now."

"You've found the time to do a jigsaw as well?"

"I was speaking figuratively, Mr Greenstone. A case is much like a jigsaw puzzle, don't you see?"

"Not particularly."

"Never mind."

"What if there's a piece missing?" he asked.

"There's invariably a piece missing, but at the very end it all comes together rather nicely."

"Oh, that's encouraging news. What about Zeppelin's jigsaw puzzle?"

"I have every confidence that it will become a tidy and complete picture in due course."

"I see."

"Now where's that mischievous cat gone?" asked Churchill, aware that the space beneath the hydrangea suddenly appeared empty.

"This is what he does, you see," said Mr Greenstone. "One moment he's there, then he sees an opportunity and he's off."

"That's cats for you. I'd better go and find him. I do hope he hasn't squeezed himself under the garden gate at number thirty-five again. The last time I poked my bean in there I got a hosepipe turned on me for my trouble."

"Oh dear, really?"

"They did apologise. Thought I was someone they'd been having a bit of bother with."

"There's always so much bother these days, don't you find?"

"There is, Mr Greenstone, there really is. Allow me to go and look for your cat now. Every moment spent yapping allows him to get further and further away from me."

Churchill stepped over the low hedge and marched down Muckleford Lane. She turned the corner to find a short, smartly dressed man bending down to stroke the cat.

"Mr Verney!" she declared. "It's not you who's been feeding him, is it?"

"Good afternoon, Mrs Churchill. No, I don't carry edibles for cats about my person as a general rule."

"Oh, good. Does he ever visit your home?"

"This one? Oh yes! He's a greedy beggar, but the wife shoos him away with a blast from the shotgun."

"That's a rather extreme strategy, Mr Verney. She might kill him!"

"Oh no, there's no danger of that. She loves cats as a rule, just not this one. She only fires blanks at him."

"I see. Well, I'm trying to find out who's feeding him, as his owner is most upset about it. Mr Greenstone would no doubt be even more disturbed if he knew your wife regularly brandished a shotgun in his vicinity."

"Perhaps we could agree not to inform him?" said Mr Verney with a smirk, which Churchill realised was probably the closest his face ever came to a smile.

"I won't mention it for now, Mr Verney, but I must encourage you to dissuade your wife from frightening him with a gun again."

"I'll have a talk with her, but old habits die hard where Mrs Verney is concerned. Actually, Mrs Churchill, it's rather fortuitous that I've bumped into you. There is something I should inform you about regarding Mrs Furzgate's case."

"Are you about to breach client confidentiality for me, Mr Verney?"

"No, I don't think so. I merely wanted to inform you of a visitor I've been receiving in recent weeks. Quite a regular visitor, in fact."

Chapter 42

"PEMBERLEY, I wonder if you could arrange for Bodkin, Crumble, Smallbone, Mappin and all three Trollopes to gather in the same place? Oh, and I suppose we should probably invite Cavendish too."

"Are you planning a dinner party, Mrs Churchill?"

"It does sound like the perfect guest list, doesn't it? But this is rather more exciting, in actual fact. The time has come to announce the key suspect in the Furzgate case."

Pemberley clapped her hands together in excitement. "Oh, goody! I always liked it when Atkins got to this part."

"I'm sure you did, Pembers, and now Churchy has got to this part herself. Where would be a good venue, do you think?"

"Piddleton Hotel?"

"Where it all began! Of course, Pembers, that's perfect."

"Do you need all of them there, Mrs Churchill?"

"Absolutely!"

"But what if some of them refuse to turn up? You

heard what Timothy Trollope said about you. He called you *personne indésirable*."

"Timothy Trollope needs to be put over someone's knee and spanked with a slipper," replied Churchill. "If anyone expresses any reluctance about attending, tell them that the murderer's identity is about to be unveiled."

"Why does that sound so familiar?"

"I don't know, Pembers. Does it?"

"It also sounds rather intriguing. Will you let interested bystanders attend?"

"Why not? The more the merrier, I say. And tell Inspector Mappin to bring his handcuffs, as an arrest will need to be made."

"Oh, marvellous!" Pemberley clapped her hands again. "So who is it?"

"Who is what?"

"The murderer?"

"You'll have to wait for the announcement at Piddleton Hotel, Pembers."

Her secretary's face fell. "I don't get to find out before then?"

"No, Pembers. Enjoy the suspense."

"But I want to know now. After all, I did help, didn't I? I've helped you every step of the way. I've been your trusty assistant. Your right-hand woman. Your second-in-command. Your auxiliary. Your Girl Friday, if you will. Your sidekick. Your henchwoman. Your dogsbody. Call me your poodle, if that's what you prefer. Without me you couldn't have done it. I deserve to know!" Pemberley's eyes filled up with tears.

"I couldn't have done it without you, Pemberley? What nonsense. Of course I could!"

"I feel left out," wailed Pemberley. "I was always left out of things at school, but I hoped when I reached adulthood those days would be behind me. But nothing's changed. I still get left out, even at the age of—"

"A lady never reveals her age, Pemberley!" Churchill interrupted.

She watched the tears roll down her secretary's face and felt a strong pang of sympathy. "Oh dear, I wish you would stop that crying nonsense. I'm no good with public displays of emotion." She cleared her throat. "All right, Pemberley, you win. On reflection, I have decided that you're quite right. I couldn't have done it without you."

The sobbing secretary sniffed, dabbing at her eyes with her balled-up handkerchief.

"That's it. Dry your eyes, calm yourself down and I'll tell you who the culprit is. But if you breathe a word to anyone—"

"I won't, I swear it!"

"Good. Now, from one lady who was always left out of things to another, let me share my findings with you."

Chapter 43

"I NEVER DID care for the decor in this place," said Mrs Trollope disparagingly as she settled into an armchair in the morning room of Piddleton Hotel. The wallpaper was canary yellow, and the velveteen chairs were a brown and olive check.

Churchill refused to show any sign of agreement with Mrs Trollope's sentiment. Instead, she paced the floor, riffling through some papers as though they were important documents.

Mr Trollope sank down into a chair next to his wife, while Timothy Trollope stood at one of the windows overlooking the grounds, his hands fidgeting about in his trouser pockets.

Churchill had been surprised to see that the Trollopes were the first to turn up. Other than offering a breezy "Good morning" she hadn't made any effort to converse with them. Her moment would come.

Pemberley perched herself on a carved oak chair close to the door. She wore a smart red cardigan and had her notebook and pen at the ready. She had told Churchill she would take minutes of the proceedings so they could be added to the case file before it was passed to the police.

Mr Bodkin was next to arrive, followed shortly after by Mr Smallbone.

"Will this take long, Mrs Churchill?" asked Bodkin. "I've left Bodger in charge and I don't like to leave him in a position of responsibility for too long."

"Least you got someone to leave in charge," Mr Smallbone retorted. "I've had to shut up shop completely. I 'ope I ain't missing out on no payin' customers."

"I shouldn't think there's any danger of that, Mr Smallbone," said Mrs Trollope.

"Tomorrow is print day," said Mr Trollope. "I should be in the office proofing all the copy. This appointment is a blessed nuisance. Remind me why we're here again?"

"Apparently, Mrs Churchill is about to tell us who murdered Mrs Furzgate," his wife said sceptically, lighting a cigarette.

"I thought it was an accident," he replied.

"The suggestion is that it wasn't, but it'll be interesting to see how she plans to explain it."

"Good morning, Inspector Mappin," said Churchill as he entered the room. "Handcuffs at the ready?"

"They are, although I almost didn't bring them as I couldn't find the key. It's been so long since I last used them. Are you sure I'll be needing them?"

"Yes, Inspector, because I'm about to tell you who the murderer is."

"What, one of this lot?" he asked, eyeing the meagre assembly.

"All will be explained in due course."

"I hope so," he replied, plonking himself down in the armchair next to Mr Smallbone. "Oh, hello!" he exclaimed. "My knees are almost higher than my chin. Have the springs gone in this one?"

"Is everyone here?" asked Mr Crumble chirpily as he poked his head around the door.

"Almost," replied Churchill.

"Do we all have coffee?" he asked.

"No, nobody has coffee."

"Oh."

"I say, Pip, have the springs gone in this armchair?" asked Inspector Mappin.

"No, it's just low-slung. I'll ask Griselda to bring some coffee."

"Don't worry about the coffee for now, Mr Crumble," said Churchill. "We need to press on. Come and take a seat."

Churchill cleared her throat and felt her heart begin to race. This was the first case she had ever solved. Everyone in the village of Compton Poppleford would judge her on it. This was the case that would either make or break her fledgling detective agency. Her legs felt uncharacteristically wobbly as she stood to address the room.

Chapter 44

"AS YOU ALL KNOW, I was asked by Mr Cavendish, who will be joining us very shortly, to investigate what he believed to be the murder of his godmother. Mrs Thora Furzgate sadly passed away after a fall down the staircase inside this very hotel. The coroner ruled her death an accident, but Mr Cavendish rightly believed otherwise."

"Sorry I'm late!" said Mr Cavendish in a loud whisper as he breezed into the room. He perched on the arm of Inspector Mappin's chair and gave Churchill a wide grin.

"Good morning, Mr Cavendish. You haven't missed much; I've only just started."

"Let's hear the rest of it, then," Bodkin piped up.

She glared at the baker and continued. "From the outset I was intrigued by the report of a buttered teacake at the scene of the crime. Members of the hotel staff confirmed to me that there had, in fact, been a teacake at the top of the stairs, and it was widely believed that Mrs Furzgate had slipped on it. So how did the teacake get there?

"The answer lay with a mysterious French gentleman

named Pierre, whose presence at the crime scene was suppressed in the reporting of the incident. This was due to an agreement made between the editor of the *Compton Poppleford Gazette*, Mr Trollope, and the manager of Piddleton Hotel, Mr Crumble. Mr Crumble insisted on this arrangement as he feared that adverse publicity could have arisen from the revelation that a member of his staff had somehow caused the accident.

"He has since confirmed to me that a young gentleman named Pierre worked here briefly, and had what he describes as an altercation with Mrs Furzgate. I believe, and I don't think Mr Crumble would disagree with me here, that Pierre purposefully placed the teacake at the top of the staircase and most likely gave Mrs Furzgate a bit of a shove to ensure that she slipped on it."

"Where's Pierre now?" asked Smallbone.

"We'll get to him. First of all, I'd like to explain what Mrs Furzgate was doing at this establishment in the first place. At the time of her fall the Women's Compton Poppleford Bridge Club was having a get-together here, as it does every month. Mrs Furzgate was keen to join the bridge club and had made one of her many attempts to gain acceptance on that fateful day.

"However, she would never have been successful in her endeavours, as months earlier she had organised the Compton Poppleford Village People Against Corruption march. She had done so in response to claims that Mrs Trollope's mayoral campaign had been funded by ill-gotten gains."

"Objection!" Mr Trollope called out. "There is no evidence to support that accusation!"

"I'm not putting you on trial, Mr Trollope," replied Churchill. "I'm merely explaining why Mrs Furzgate decided to organise her march."

"Objection to the use of the word *ill-gotten!*" Mrs Trollope chipped in.

Churchill sighed. "Can I get on with it, please? Now, because Mrs Furzgate had organised this protest march, there was never any chance of her being admitted to the bridge club. Am I correct, Mrs Trollope?"

The lady nodded in reply.

"It could be argued that Mrs Trollope had a motive for wanting Mrs Furzgate to be pushed down the stairs. The woman had single-handedly ruined Mrs Trollope's bid to become mayor!"

"Objection!" shouted Mr Trollope.

"And Mr Smallbone also had a motive," continued Churchill.

"Objection!" shouted Smallbone.

"Can everyone please stop shouting that word out?" demanded Churchill. "It merely has the effect of slowing proceedings down. Mr Smallbone had been accused by Mrs Furzgate of selling fake antiques."

"Well, I must say I agree with her on that one," said Mrs Trollope.

"You take that back!" shouted Mr Smallbone, leaping to his feet.

"Please sit down, Mr Smallbone," said Churchill. "There's still a lot for us to get through. Now, Mrs Furzgate had bought a telescopy thing from Mr Smallbone—"

"A nineteenth-century telescope with a two-and-three-quarter-inch objective lens and an equatorial mount, it were," Mr Smallbone interjected.

"What on earth is an equatorial mount?" asked Mr Trollope.

"It's when the mount is fitted with a polar axis that can be lined up to point at the north celestial pole," Pemberley clarified. "In layman's terms, it means the telescope can follow the stars as they move across the sky."

"Thank you for the explanation, Miss Pemberley," said Churchill impatiently. "Mrs Furzgate demanded a partial refund for the item, and also called Mr Smallbone a whole host of names."

"She called me a crook, an' a thief an' a miscreant an' a reprobate an' a wastrel."

"Which you were understandably upset about, Mr Smallbone. It might even have led to you arranging to have her pushed down the staircase to exact your revenge."

"I ain't never stooped to summat like that!"

"But you are a convicted murderer, are you not, Mr Smallbone?"

A collective gasp rose from everyone in the room. All eyes were suddenly fixed on the shopkeeper.

"You said as you'd never mention it!" he cried out.

"But you've served your time, haven't you, Mr Smallbone?"

"I 'ave. An' 'e 'ad it comin'!"

"Well that settles it, then," said Mrs Trollope. "Smallbone is surely the only person in the room who is capable of murder."

"It's him!" announced Bodkin, pointing at the bric-a-brac shop's owner.

"Actually, it isn't," said Churchill.

"So why'd you go tellin' everyone me darkest secret if I ain't the murderer?" asked Smallbone.

"I must press on. Mr Bodkin, you had a love affair with the late Mrs Furzgate, did you not?"

"Well, it was an affair. I wouldn't really say it was love, though."

"She threatened to tell your wife about it, I believe."

"Yes, she did."

"But despite being jilted by you she still left you a large sum of money in her will, am I right?"

"Furzgate had money?" asked Mrs Trollope with an astounded expression. "But she lived in that little hovel!"

"Yes, it came as a surprise to me too, Mrs Trollope."

"She left it to *him*?" asked Mrs Trollope, pointing at Bodkin.

"Yes, she did," said Mr Cavendish bitterly.

"You poor young man," said Mrs Trollope to Cavendish. "You were the closest thing to family she had, and she left everything to the baker."

"Please don't remind me!" wailed Cavendish.

"She was in love with me," replied Bodkin. "She told me I made her feel like a real woman."

"Did she indeed?" said Churchill, experiencing a slightly unpleasant taste in her mouth. "Throughout most of my investigation, Mr Bodkin, you have been the prime suspect in the case. I received a note purporting to have been written by you in which you seemingly confessed to having committed Mrs Furzgate's murder. And a disguise believed to have been worn by the mysterious French waiter, Pierre, was found in your shop."

"Why would I send letters and leave disguises lying around if I was guilty?" asked Bodkin.

"As a bluff," said Inspector Mappin. "Or a double bluff. Did we decide which in the end?"

Churchill ignored the question and pressed on. "Mr Bodkin, you were worried that Mrs Furzgate was planning to tell your wife about the affair. You also knew that she had decided to leave you a large sum of money in her will. Therefore, you had two reasons to orchestrate her untimely despatch."

"Yes, I had two reasons, but I didn't do it!"

"We know that you couldn't have disguised yourself as

Pierre because your old schoolfriend Mr Crumble would have recognised you."

"Pierre was about two inches shorter and three inches narrower than Piggers. And about twenty years younger," said Mr Crumble.

"Thank you for that, Mr Crumble," said Churchill.

"And about three stones lighter. I forgot to mention that at the time."

Bodkin glared at him.

"So who is this Pierre?" asked Churchill, pausing for dramatic effect.

"He's gotta be younger an' shorter an' narrower an' lighter than what Bodkin is," said Mr Smallbone.

"Indeed he does," said Churchill. "I must say that I was rather interested to meet young Timothy Trollope, having heard so much about him."

Chapter 45

"YOU LEAVE my son out of this!" bellowed Mrs Trollope. She tried to stand, but she succeeded only in wiggling her spindly legs about as she tried to get out of the low-slung chair.

"Don't worry about getting up, Mrs Trollope, I heard you," said Churchill. She watched the young man, who had turned away from the window and was glaring at her with his narrow, mean eyes.

"An acquaintance of mine told me quite a bit about Timothy Trollope's past," said Churchill. "And much of it is most unsavoury."

"Objection!" roared Mr Trollope.

"We've already put a stop to that!" snapped Churchill. "This is the last bit, so just let me get on with it. Now, is it a coincidence that Mrs Furzgate, an enemy of his mother's, is pushed down the stairs of this hotel by a young man disguised as a French waiter at the very same time young Trollope is making a rare visit home to see his ma and pa?"

"Yes, it is," hissed Timothy Trollope.

"Upon seeing the young man, I decided to make some

enquiries at his old school, Harrow, and the resulting conversation shone some interesting light on my investigation."

"Who did you speak to?" demanded Timothy Trollope. "Mr Finkworth, or Old Fizzy as we called him? Or was it Hunkdown, the chap we called Stinkpants? He never liked me."

"You're quite adept at French, aren't you, Mr Trollope?"

"What's that got to do with anything?"

"It comes in rather useful when impersonating a French waiter. Mr Crumble, does Timothy Trollope fit the description of Pierre?"

The hotel owner stared at the young man for a while, then bit his lip.

"I hate to break the news to you, Mrs Churchill, but I'm afraid he doesn't. I know you've gone to a lot of trouble putting your case together and everything, but looking at the man I honestly don't think he could be Pierre. His chin recedes a little too much. It's too weak."

"Oh dear, Mrs Churchill," said Mrs Trollope with a sly smile. "You've been barking up the wrong tree! How do you feel now?"

"I feel extremely well, thank you, Mrs Trollope," replied Churchill, doing her best to remain unflustered. "Only I haven't been barking up the wrong tree at all, have I, Mr Cavendish?"

"I hope not, but it's taking rather a long time to get to the point, Mrs Churchill."

"I'd say the point has now been reached, has it not, Mr Cavendish?"

"Has it?"

"Yes, Mr Cavendish. Or would you prefer to go by the name of Pierre?"

"Pierre? Oh no, no. I've never called myself that name." His face coloured. "Who would want to call himself Pierre?"

"Wait a minute…" Mr Crumble stared at the young man. "Yes… With a dark curly wig and some glasses…" He squinted slightly. "Yes, Mrs Churchill, yes. That's the man!"

He pointed a fat finger at Mr Cavendish, who leapt off the arm of the chair and made a bolt for the door. But Pemberley was too quick for him. She turned the key in the lock and quickly dropped it down the front of her blouse.

"Give me the key, woman!" he snarled.

"Handcuffs, Inspector Mappin!" Churchill called out.

The inspector got to his feet and gave her a dazed look. "Him? But why him? And how?"

Mr Cavendish tried to grab the front of Pemberley's blouse, but the secretary responded with such a sharp slap to the face that Churchill winced. Cavendish recoiled, clasping his hand to his cheek.

"Please restrain him, Inspector, and I shall explain all," said Churchill.

"Come here, young man," said Inspector Mappin, trying to grab Cavendish's arms.

"Get off me!' protested Cavendish. "I've done nothing wrong."

"Perhaps I can be of some assistance," said Bodkin, locking a thick forearm around the young man's neck.

"Get off me, you thief!" cried Cavendish in a strangulated voice.

"I'm not a thief."

"You stole my godmother's money!"

"She left it to me, and you must learn to accept it."

"I never will! I never will accept it, you big, fat—"

"That's quite enough from you, Cavendish," said

Inspector Mappin. "Now quieten down while Mrs Churchill explains how on earth she has come to name you as the culprit."

He locked the handcuffs around Mr Cavendish's wrists and the baker finally let go of him.

"I don't understand," said Mrs Trollope. "How could the man who asked you to identify the murderer turn out to be the murderer himself?"

"Baffling, isn't it?" said Churchill. "Allow me to explain. Mr Cavendish has known for many years that his godmother had a stash of money hidden away."

"How do you know that?" asked Cavendish. His hair had flopped all over his face, which was scarlet with a mix of shame and rage.

"Because you admitted it to her solicitor, Mr Verney. When your godmother died you wasted no time at all in demanding to see her will. During these visits you made it clear that you knew she had money and expected to be the recipient of it. It was a terrible surprise, was it not, Mr Cavendish, to discover that Mr Bodkin was to receive every last penny?"

"She made a mistake!"

"But if Mr Cavendish murdered Mrs Furzgate, why would he ask you to investigate?" asked Mr Trollope. "The coroner had already stated that her death was an accident, so surely he'd already got away with it."

"He had, but he hadn't inherited the money, had he? The matter wasn't as straightforward as he'd originally hoped. He'd carried out the murder but still hadn't got what he wanted. So instead he arranged for his godmother's death to be investigated as a murder so that he could frame Mr Bodkin. He wanted to take his revenge on the baker at the same time."

"So Cavendish sent the letter that was supposedly from me?" asked Bodkin.

"I'm certain he did."

"And he hid the French waiter's disguise in my bakery?"

"He must have done. I suppose he hoped that by planting the evidence Mr Bodkin would be implicated."

"And I was!" said Bodkin.

"He wanted to see you arrested," added Churchill. "And no doubt he hoped that once you'd been found guilty of his godmother's murder her estate would instead be passed on to the closest thing she had to family. In other words, to himself."

"But what did he want with Furzgate's money?" asked Bodkin. "The man's not exactly hard up."

"That has something to do with the man at the window over there," said Churchill, pointing at Timothy Trollope. "When I telephoned Harrow I discovered that Timothy Trollope and Mr Cavendish had been good friends back then. Timothy was two school years above Cavendish, but they got on well.

"It's no secret that Timothy Trollope likes to raise funds for intriguing investment schemes, the legality of which it is not my job to speculate upon. However, I suspect that Timothy had cooked up another money-making scheme and had encouraged his old school friend to chip in. No doubt the promise of a significant return on his investment was promised. Am I right, Mr Cavendish?"

"He told me I could triple my money within a year!"

"Only it wasn't your money, was it? It belonged to your godmother. And then it passed to Mr Bodkin instead of you. Did you know about all this, young Mr Trollope?"

"He told me he would have the funds as soon as he came into his inheritance," replied Timothy. "But I had no idea he planned to do his godmother in to get it. That's below the belt. I admit to having committed some misdemeanours in my time, but to murder your own godmother to get at your inheritance? That's a step too far."

"I didn't *murder* her!" protested Cavendish. "She *slipped*!"

"She slipped on the buttered teacake you threw across her path," said Churchill, "and then you gave her a little nudge just to ensure the job was properly done."

"The attempt to frame Mr Bodkin was rather clumsy," said Inspector Mappin. "A child could have done a better job with that letter."

"Mr Cavendish *is* a child," replied Mrs Churchill. "And he thought I was a portly, gullible old lady from London who didn't have a clue about life in a Dorset village. He was partly right of, course, but – more importantly – he was also partly wrong."

"He underestimated you, Mrs Churchill," said Pemberley with a smile.

"People often do, Miss Pemberley. They tend to underestimate both of us, don't they?"

"Well, it all sounds like a wonderful tall tale, but not a single word of it is true!" Mr Cavendish cried out.

"I should never have employed the man," said Mr Crumble sadly. "And I feel so foolish. To think that Pierre was merely Cavendish in disguise!"

"Don't be too hard on yourself, Mr Crumble," said Churchill. "Mr Cavendish can be quite convincing."

"He's a bit of a charmer," said Pemberley. "You almost fell for his charms, didn't you, Mrs Churchill?"

"No, I did not, Miss Pemberley," replied Churchill, although she could feel her face reddening. "I was merely playing along. It's called rapport."

"I can't say that I agree with any of your methods, Mrs

Churchill," said Mr Trollope. "They are dreadful methods, in fact. Appalling. But I do applaud you on the outcome of your sleuthing."

"Thank you, Mr Trollope. Coming from you I know that is praise indeed."

"Not a bad job," conceded Mrs Trollope.

"I take that to be even higher praise, Mrs Trollope. Thank you. Now then, Miss Pemberley, can you please hand Inspector Mappin the case file? It contains everything you need for the prosecution, Inspector. I'm sure a search of Cavendish's home will yield further evidence. He's not a particularly sophisticated criminal; he's bound to have left something incriminating lying about."

"Come on then, lad, let's be having you," said Inspector Mappin. "Will you be joining us down at the station, Mrs Churchill?"

"No, thank you. I'll leave everything in your capable hands, Inspector. All this mental exertion has left me in need of a lie down. And then I must conclude another case. I've still got a mystery cat feeder to find."

Chapter 46

AS CHURCHILL WATCHED the sunset from beside the hydrangea in Mr Greenstone's garden that evening she reflected on her disappointment at the fact Mr Cavendish had turned out to be a murderer. She had been quite fond of the young man until Mr Verney told her about his quest to secure his godmother's money.

Despite encountering a few unpleasant characters in Compton Poppleford she had found herself beginning to like the village with its pretty little lanes and timber-beamed houses. She enjoyed the peace and quiet of the place, which was at its best on pleasant summer evenings such as this. The scent of honeysuckle hung in the air, and she wondered what her late husband would have made of her sleuthing. She felt sure Chief Inspector Churchill was looking down on her from somewhere and feeling quite proud.

Zeppelin got up from his usual resting place, stretched out his legs and hopped over the slate wall.

"Where are you taking me now, wandering cat?" she

asked. She stepped over the wall and followed him along the lane.

"Perhaps you're finally about to reveal who's been feeding you?" she suggested.

The cat turned right into Froxfield Row.

"Now this is new," commented Churchill. "I don't remember you leading me this way before."

A row of small houses with brightly coloured window boxes lined the lane. Zeppelin stopped by the steps of one with a pea-green door. Churchill noticed the door was slightly ajar.

In two quick jumps Zeppelin was up the steps and pushing at the door with his paw. It creaked open just wide enough for the cat to slip inside.

"Ah-ha!" said Churchill under her breath. "Gotcha!"

"Tilly!" came a voice from beyond the door. "You've come to visit your Auntie Doris! How do you fancy kippers tonight?"

The voice sounded oddly familiar.

Churchill climbed the steps and slowly pushed open the door.

"Pemberley?" she said.

There in the hallway, with Zeppelin rubbing up against her legs, stood Churchill's trusty assistant.

"Mrs Churchill!" she exclaimed. "What brings you here?"

"Zeppelin," replied Churchill, pointing at the cat.

"This isn't Zeppelin, it's Tilly. Isn't she lovely?"

"She is a *he*, Pemberley. And he most certainly *is* Zeppelin. Where did the name Tilly come from?"

"I came up with it. I think it suits her much better."

"*He*. She's a he. If you doubt me, take a look at his—"

"No, I'd rather not. He looks so much like a girl cat."

"Are you the one who's been feeding him?"

"It's rather difficult to become accustomed to considering her a him. But yes, I've been giving the poor cat his supper each evening."

"Did you never suspect that it was Zeppelin?"

"Of course not. I thought it was a female cat, didn't I?"

"Did you not give any consideration to Zeppelin's owner?"

"Mr Greenstone? No, because I didn't think for a moment that it was Zeppelin. And I assumed the owner wasn't feeding this poor cat properly as he was always begging me for food."

"Look at the size of him. Does he look starved to you?"

"But he always seemed so sad."

"That's cats for you, Pemberley. They're manipulative creatures."

"Oh dear, poor cat." Pemberley gazed down at Zeppelin. "I really had no idea."

"Why poor cat? He's had extra meals for several weeks now. Several months, even. I don't know how we're going to explain this little mix-up to Mr Greenstone." Churchill rubbed her brow.

"Would it be all right if I gave Zeppelin his kippers now, do you think? He's so used to having kippers at this time and look at his little face. He's all hopeful."

"Go on, then," said Churchill, "but this has to stop. Perhaps you could get a cat of your own."

"Oh, I don't know about that; it would be too much responsibility. I much prefer feeding other people's. Would you like a cup of something while Tilly – sorry, Zeppelin – has a bite to eat?"

"Why not, Pembers? Thank you."

"So another case is solved, Mrs Churchill!"

"Indeed it is. I wonder what Compton Poppleford will throw at us next."

The End

Thank you

≈

Thank you for reading *Tragedy at Piddleton Hotel*, I really hope you enjoyed it!

Would you like to know when I release new books? Here are some ways to stay updated:

- Join my mailing list and receive the short story *A Troublesome Case*: emilyorgan.com/a-troublesome-case
- Like my Facebook page: facebook.com/emilyorganwriter
- View my other books here: emilyorgan.com

And if you have a moment, I would be very grateful if you would leave a quick review of *Tragedy at Piddleton Hotel* online. Honest reviews of my books help other readers discover them too!

Get a free short mystery

∾

Want more of Churchill & Pemberley? Get a copy of my free short mystery *A Troublesome Case* and sit down to enjoy a thirty minute read.

Churchill and Pemberley are on the train home from a shopping trip when they're caught up with a theft from a suitcase. Inspector Mappin accuses them of stealing the valuables, but in an unusual twist of fate the elderly sleuths are forced to come to his aid!

Visit my website to claim your FREE copy:
    emilyorgan.com/a-troublesome-case

Murder in Cold Mud

A Churchill & Pemberley Mystery Book 2

The Compton Poppleford Horticultural Society Annual Show is just around the corner but there's a problem: someone is murdering the competitors.

Stories of vegetable rivalry abound as the local constabulary, Inspector Mappin, investigates. When the death toll increases, Mappin drafts in assistance but refuses to allow detective duo Churchill and Pemberley to help. The two ladies decide to solve the case themselves, however their efforts are hampered by the inspector's accusations of meddling.

Can Churchill and Pemberley battle the odds to find the culprit before another gardener dies? Compton Poppleford's long-buried secrets are unearthed as Churchill and Pemberley close in on the killer in their midst.

The Penny Green Series

≋

Also by Emily Organ. A series of mysteries set in Victorian London featuring the intrepid Fleet Street reporter, Penny Green.

Books in the Penny Green Series:
Limelight
The Rookery
The Maid's Secret
The Inventor
Curse of the Poppy
The Bermondsey Poisoner
An Unwelcome Guest
Death at the Workhouse
The Gang of St Bride's

Find out more here: emilyorgan.com

Made in the USA
Las Vegas, NV
24 December 2020